Published by

Comicbook Artists Guild

Comicbook Artists Guild
P.O. Box 38
Moodus, CT, 06469
www.comicartguild.com

First Edition May 2010
Library of Congress Cataloging-in-Publication-Data
Comicbook Artists Guild
Worlds Beyond vol. 1 : a science-fiction anthology / by members of the Comicbook Artists Guild
p. 272
ISBN 9780615362168
1. Introduction. 2. Science-fiction stories—Fiction. 3. Authors. I. Title.
2010924988
Printed in the United States.

So what is the Comicbook Artists Guild and why are they making a non-comic book?

CAG is a networking organization designed to bring together like-minded individuals who all want to do one thing: make books. There are chapters that meet once a month in Massachusetts, Connecticut, Nebraska and New York, as well as additional members in several other states and countries. CAG members come from a variety of backgrounds and skill sets, as well as various experience levels ranging from amateur to industry veteran. Over the last 10 years, CAG's members have put out several publications together.

This book is a chance for the writers in the group to shine. Comics are a visual medium, and more often than not the writers tend to get overshadowed by the artists. Of course, you do have writers who get their own share of fame and recognition for their work, but there are fewer opportunities for a writer than an artist in the industry as a whole. In a little turn of fair play, this book is dedicated to letting the writers take center stage.

The result is a collection of finely crafted stories that dare to test the limits of your imagination and take you to, appropriately enough, worlds beyond. Each story is also accompanied by a piece of artwork from some of CAG's fine artists. This is some of the best CAG has to offer, and we hope you'll enjoy the experience.

For more on CAG visit www.comicartguild.com.

Edited by Chris Buchner & Joe Sergi
Cover art by James Rodriguez
Cover finishes by Willie Jimenez
Prepress by Steve Kuster

Distance: 862.88 ly

Special thanks to everyone who helped make this book possible.

Class: B8l-a

v

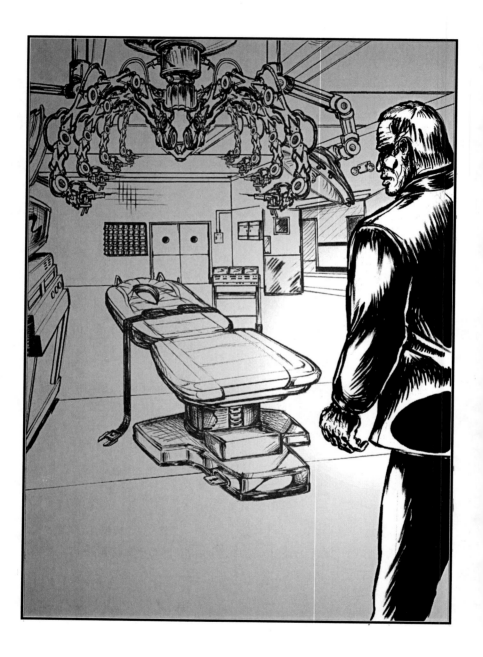

CAMP HERO
By James Mascia

Everything looked much the same as it had sixty years ago. The long, winding road would eventually take me to the lighthouse and, not for the first time, I was tempted to turn back. The surrounding trees, once so pleasant to the young man I had been, now stood like angry sentinels, determined to hide the secret that lay beyond them.

If the trees weren't enough to deter me, the unguarded gate with its warning signs might be. "Do Not Enter" and "Keep Out" they proclaimed, making me feel less than welcome in a place I once called home.

I don't know why I decided to go there. I'd visited Normandy and Arlington and paid my respects to my former comrades. I'd ventured to Auschwitz and saw the horrors Hitler's henchmen had performed before we liberated their prisoners. None of those places made the hair on the back of my neck stand at attention like Montauk Point, Long Island did.

The ancient radar tower loomed over the landscape like a technological king daring Mother Nature to reclaim what was hers. From the looks of things, she would win.

"Tom." My wife placed a consoling hand on my shoulder. "Are you all right? Do you want to go back to the car?"

I looked into her eyes. I wasn't okay. I wanted to lie to protect her, but she knew me too well. Besides, my hands were shaking like a punch-drunk boxer. As she stared at me, a single tear rolled down her cheek. She thought she knew my pain, but she didn't and never would. I could never tell her what had gone on in there.

"Tom?" she said again, her voice as unstable as my hands.

"Edith, it's okay." I pulled her close. Her body heaved as she began to sob. "This is something I need to do."

"I wish you would share some of this burden with me," she said. I didn't answer and squeezed her hand, then let her go.

Starting toward the gate, I was determined to get on the base, even if some guard hid in the woods waiting to shoot any trespassers. I didn't care anymore.

With each step, my resolve strengthened. The long-forgotten base would have a couple more visitors, whether it liked it or not. The closer I got the louder General Palko's final words to us echoed in my head:

"Congratulations." He paced back and forth before the twelve of us. "You men have served with honor and distinction. President Roosevelt wished he could be here in person to thank you for your service to your country. But sadly, he doesn't even know you exist."

I remember how we all chuckled at that statement. No one was supposed to know about us or what we did. We were classified top secret at a level where not even the president knew who we were.

"However," the general continued, "after two years of active duty, your services are no longer required. I have been given the painful task of discharging each and every one of you from service." The look on his face told me he thought his duty was anything but painful and his smile said he was glad to be rid of us.

That was fine with me. I was eager to get home to Edith, and our almost-two-year-old boy, waiting for me back in Philly. I knew Lieutenant Carpenter felt the same way at the time. He'd been eager to get back home to his wife even before we left for Europe. Not all the men felt the same way. I knew Corporal Everett had planned to be a lifer in the army while Lieutenant Tills wasn't at all eager to get back to his parent's farm.

As they protested, General Palko said, "My orders come from the higher ups, gentlemen. There's nothing I can do about it." We knew there wasn't anything he would do about it, either. "I trust you understand the sensitive information you carry with you, that you'll keep your oath, and won't disclose that information to anyone."

We didn't respond—we didn't need to. We knew the consequences of revealing what we knew. "Good. Then effective at 1400 hours, I am officially declaring *Project: Hercules* terminated."

The memory faded away as so many had over the years. I stood before the gate, staring blankly at the "No Trespassing" sign that hung lopsided on the chain link gate meant to keep people out. The lock holding the gate shut was a joke. A ten-year-old with a paperclip could pick it in less than a minute.

I grabbed hold of the lock, making sure my body stood between Edith and it, and squeezed. The metal fell apart in my hands. I looked over my shoulder and smiled. "Old lock," I lied, showing her the deformed pieces in my hand.

"Tom, I don't think we should…"

"If you don't want to come with me, I understand. But I'm going in. I need to see it." I really didn't want her to go and had tried several times to leave her at the hotel, but she wasn't having any of it.

"I told you before. Wherever you go, I'm going with you." Her fingers interlaced with mine, creating an unbreakable bond that not even I would try to break, to show that she meant it.

I sighed and stepped through the gate and onto the base where my life had officially begun.

The path was longer than I remembered. Every stride felt like I was stepping another year back in time. Everything was overgrown, but recent tire treads indicated someone was still there. Who that was, I couldn't begin to say.

The sound of our feet over the dead leaves and dirt was all we could hear. I was amazed that even the animals knew to stay clear of the area.

My memories of the place overlaid what I saw. Though the old guardhouse was overgrown with weeds and vines, I saw only the pristine shack it had been when I first saw it in 1944.

A truck had brought us all in from New York City, after our last night of normal lives. We had stopped at that very gatehouse to be checked in. At the time, we didn't know what we were in for. Straight out of boot camp, each of us was asked if we would participate in an experimental program.

"What did we get ourselves into?" I'd asked Frank Carpenter as we rolled down the unfinished roads of Long Island.

"It's probably some new training program to make us better soldiers," he ventured. "Maybe we'll be testing out some new weaponry."

We soon found out he was only half right.

Edith and I walked farther down the path. There was a slight curve ahead of us. Just beyond lay the barracks. For a second, I froze as my wife's fingers tightened around mine.

"It's okay, honey," she whispered. "We don't have to."

Her words made me realize what a mistake it had been allowing her to come along. She was the one thing that would hold me back… but holding back was not an option. I needed to see it through, for both our sakes.

I pressed on without as much as a glance in her direction. I feared that if I looked into her eyes just then, I would lose all my will to complete one last mission.

As we rounded the bend, a dilapidated wooden building that had once been painted white came into view. All I could see was a series of splinters held together by their own weight. Plants grew out of the holes that had once been windows. Only tiny shards of glass remained in the frames. The small building appeared to have been knocked off its foundation.

All our initials were still carved in the wood around the door. Time and nature had faded the indentations, but they could still be seen because dirt and dust had embedded in the cracks. I remember the day Everett took his pocketknife to it.

"There won't be any record of us being here," he'd said, "so I'm at least going to leave my mark to prove I was here."

Over the next few hours, each of us took our turn carving our initials around the door.

I leaned my hand on the doorjamb over the "T.S." I carved that night. I had touched those letters every day for the four months I had been stationed here. They felt so foreign to me now, almost as if I had never been there. As I leaned against the door, the whole building shifted, sending dirt and dust raining down on us.

"A forgotten building for forgotten people," I muttered, low enough so my wife couldn't hear.

The building was definitely unsafe, but that didn't matter. I needed to go inside.

"Wait out here, honey," I said, and as she protested, I held a finger up to her lips. "No arguments this time. I can't have you inside."

I couldn't live with myself if something collapsed while she was in there. I knew I would survive, but I doubted that Edith's fragile body would hold up.

I stepped inside. The floor creaked and shuddered under my feet. Vegetation grew through the cracks in the floorboards, some stretching up to the ceiling like trees. None of the beds that were once housed there remained. Only an indoor jungle surrounded me as I ventured farther inside.

I went to the far corner of the barracks where my bunk had been. I'd chosen it because it was right next to the window and I could see every star in the sky as I lay there each night. More importantly, there was a loose floorboard in the corner. I'd discovered it on our first night. It was that very floorboard that I pried up now. As I reached into the darkness, I wondered if it would still be there or if time had destroyed it as it had all the other artifacts the building once held.

I fumbled around through the grass and weeds until my hand rested on a small metal box. My heart leapt as I pulled it out of the hole. The metal was rusted and a few small holes had formed on the cover, but other than that, the box was intact.

As I lifted the latch, the rust-worn metal snapped and fell to the floor. I sat on the ground, leaned against the wall, and lifted the lid, praying the contents were still within. I could barely contain my urge to holler to the heavens. The three items I had placed in the box more than sixty years ago were still there, and although showing signs of age, they were still in one piece.

General Wilhelm had greeted us on that first day when we'd arrived on base. He'd confiscated all our personal effects. I remembered his words as though he'd spoken them only yesterday. "You will turn in any and all items relating to your old lives. As far as you're concerned, the young men you were no longer exist."

He and his captain gave each of us a sack in which to throw all pictures, watches, pens, and all other personal belongings. Before they got to me, I managed to stuff two items into my pants: my journal and a photograph of Edith and me taken on our wedding day.

"Welcome to Day One of your new lives, gentlemen," the general said.

Three items rested in the bottom of the metal box. Two were the journal and the photo. The third was another photograph taken a few weeks before we left Camp Hero and were shipped off to Europe, showing all twelve of us involved in *Project: Hercules.* Only one other picture still survived, as far as I knew. It belonged to Frank Carpenter.

They had us stand outside the barracks one evening after we'd reached near exhaustion from skirmish exercises. When General Palko had taken over after General Wilhelm's unfortunate accident, he wanted a photo of us for the records. I remember feeling like I was going to drop as we were forced to pose. My hands ached from all the punching and tearing I'd done that day, and I badly needed to ice them down, but they held us there for an hour while they got everything set up.

Frank and I broke into the general's office about a week later. Carpenter convinced the guards there was a fire on the other side of base that needed attention, so we were free to search for the photo since we both wanted a record of our being there. We needed to have it.

Once I broke the lock on the filing cabinet, we retrieved the file. There were ten copies of the photo—Frank and I each took one. The rest were burned, as far as I knew, with all the other records when *Project: Hercules* was shut down.

I closed the box and brought it back outside.

"This is what you came for?" Edith asked, eyeing it in my hand.

I could tell she was very interested in its contents, so I decided I would show her the two photos when we got back to the hotel, but remained unsure about the journal. The longer a man kept a secret from his wife, letting that secret out became more difficult. The journal held every secret from my time at Camp Hero, so for the time being, it would have to be for my eyes only.

"It's one of the things," I explained.

There was something else I needed to see. It lay at the heart of the base. I tucked the metal box under my arm and grabbed Edith's hand. She didn't hold onto me so tightly anymore, and I noticed her hands were shaking. Her emotion sent shivers down my spine.

Could she have realized the things that went on here? I quickly dismissed the idea—it wasn't possible, unless my wife possessed some mind reading powers I wasn't aware of.

There was another fence around the radar tower. The lock holding it shut was even easier to crush than the first one. I could easily have knocked the whole fence down but feared that might draw too much attention, should someone actually be patrolling the grounds.

The radar tower was the only building that didn't look as if it'd been overcome by vegetation. The building looked worn but cared for, and I couldn't help but wonder if it would work if they decided to power it up again.

"I don't feel right about this anymore, Tom," Edith said in a high voice. She let go of my hand and backed away from the tower but was unable to keep her eyes off it.

I had every reason to be frightened of the place, but she had never seen it before. To her, it was just another building. Therefore, I couldn't understand her sudden panic.

"Why don't you walk back to the car?" I planted a light kiss on her forehead. "I should be just a couple of minutes.

I could tell she was warring with herself. She'd promised to stay with me just in case I needed her, but she was suddenly and irrationally afraid of the building looming above. She looked at me, then at the tower several times, but ultimately, her promise won out.

"No," she said. "I'm going with you. I want to see what's so important."

"It's just a lab I need to see, babe." I donned my most valiant smile so she wouldn't sense the black cloud that had invaded my brain. "I worked in there for a while and want to see it one more time."

It was a half-truth. I was going down into the bowels of that tower to see a lab, but I'd never worked in it. I had been *worked on* in it, like someone would work on a car at an auto body shop. Another shudder went up my spine and the hairs on the back up my neck felt like they were ready to jump off.

I had to go in.

I grabbed my wife's hand and together, we marched up to the tower. Another sign on the door said "Keep Out." A small padlock held it shut. I couldn't believe the lack of security for a building that had once held very sensitive materials. I placed my shoulder against it and gave a slight shove. The door swung open easily.

The memory that flooded me was one I had suppressed for what seemed like my entire life, but seeing that corridor and the stairs that snaked deep into the ground was like getting splashed in the face after being knocked out.

On my third day at Camp Hero, they'd marched me down this very corridor. General Wilhelm had explained what we were there for by then, but I already had experienced a sense of foreboding. As I was led down the winding stairs, I knew it was too late to back out.

Our footsteps echoed down the long underground corridor. Sweat dripped from me, even though it was quite cool down there.

"Private Thomas Stephenson," Captain Morris had announced, as they brought me into the lab. Then, just as quickly as they ushered me into the room, the captain and the guards were gone, leaving me alone with the man I would come to know as Doctor Randall.

"Don't look so nervous," he said seeing me shaking uncontrollably. "The procedure is relatively painless."

The contraption looked like a metallic octopus suspended from the ceiling, with tubes filled with a yellowish liquid wrapped around every protruding tentacle. I imagined it sat poised to attack any unwitting prey dumb enough to get on the medical table beneath it.

First, the doctor laid me face down on the table. Then he strapped me down. Nine needles pricked precise points on my legs, arms, spine, and head. They wouldn't stay there for long.

"This is going to sting a bit," Doctor Randall stated. Satisfied I was securely strapped down, he stepped clear of the table.

Stinging didn't even cover the agony over the next second as the needles plunged not just into my skin, but deep within my bones. A burning sensation filled my body and radiated down each limb.

I remember only holding onto my consciousness long enough to hear the doctor say, "You're doing fine, just relax."

Then I passed out.

The lab looked the same, untouched by time. The octopus-like contraption still hung suspended over the medical table. Yellow liquid still filled the tubes leading into the needles that longed to plunge deep inside another human body. If I didn't know any better, I would have sworn the lab was still in use.

"We have to get out of here!" Edith practically shouted as she tugged on my arm.

Transfixed, I didn't budge. It was as if my wife wasn't even here. It was in that room my life had changed forever. It was that room that took away any hope I had at leading a normal life. It was in that room twelve soldiers had been told there would be no pain, but it was here where sixty years of unending pain began.

My palms began to sweat as the temperature in my head rose. I clenched my fists, bending the metal box I'd come to retrieve.

Pushing Edith out of the room, I slammed the door in her face, and unleashed every bit of agony I'd felt through the years on the octopus-like contraption before me.

My fists flew as punch after punch battered it. Parts rained down on the floor, some pummeling me as they fell, but I didn't feel a thing. I hit it again and again until it finally broke and collapsed on the ground at my feet.

I then gripped the pieces, and tore them like they were nothing but paper, tossing them to the side. Several pieces embedded themselves several inches in the cement walls, making it look like these metal pieces were actually growing from the room.

Ragged breaths escaped my lips as I fought for calmness. I hadn't expected such a violent reaction to seeing that place again. The more I relaxed, the more I realized I always had intended to destroy that machine. Now, with it lying in pieces at my feet, I couldn't decide what to do next.

It was then I felt an emotion I couldn't understand: fear. I had nothing to be afraid of anymore. I'd felt similar to this around Frank. It was fear then, too, but not my own. Whenever Frank was afraid, all of us felt it. That fear radiated off someone or something inside the facility.

"Edith!" I exclaimed, remembering my wife and realizing she'd felt the fear before I had. Her mind must have been more susceptible to suggestion.

I flung the door open, nearly pulling it off its hinges in my haste. Edith lay curled up in a ball on the floor, sobbing. As I attempted to help her up, she shied away from me. "What are you?" she asked.

She must have been half-delusional from her own dread. "I'm Tom Stephenson," I replied. "I'm your husband. Come on, let's get out of here."

As I reached down, she held up her hands to defend herself as if I were about to hit her. "You're not my husband! You're not my Tom!"

I stepped back, not wanting to frighten her further—unsure what to do. I couldn't just leave her. I knew from experience that a person could really be scared to death. I needed to find whatever it was that was causing her psychosis. If I didn't…

I didn't want to think what that would do to us both.

The facility was huge, a giant underground bunker about the size of an old battleship and with about as many rooms. In a crisis, it could have sheltered thousands of soldiers.

I have to search for whatever is hurting Edith.

The terror was affecting me as well. My training and close proximity to Frank all those years ago had helped me build a barrier against such mental attacks, but I couldn't stem the flow of emotion forever. It wouldn't be long before I went psychotic myself.

"I'll be back, Edith." I tried to sound reassuring, but she was already beyond hearing my words. Whatever delusion played in her head controlled everything.

I heard her whimpers echo down the hallway, even after I was well out of sight. Each sob was like a knife stabbing me in the chest. I shouldn't have brought her here. I wished she would have listened to me and stayed at the hotel.

As I searched for the source of Edith's psychosis, I passed several labs displaying the same equipment as the one I had just destroyed. I quickly peered into each one as I went by and realized the futility of my actions. Even if I tore apart every one of those machines, they would have enough material to build a dozen more.

Another set of stairs led me closer to the source. The waves of fear overcame me now like a tsunami crashing down on the shore. If the chills running up and down my spine hadn't told me that the source was nearby, the fact that the lights were on would.

Normally, a simple light bulb wouldn't cause concern, but these buildings were supposed to have been powered down more than forty years ago. The fact that this level in the entire complex had power caused me to step back and reassess the situation.

There could be soldiers down there. I wasn't worried, even at my advanced age I could tear apart a whole platoon of Navy Seals. Unless...

Unless they're still running the experiments in secret.

If so, then I was in trouble.

I looked back up the stairs, pondering whether to just grab Edith and run out of there as fast as I could. The longer I thought about it, the more I knew I couldn't. I had taken an oath to defend my country against the evils of the world. Even if my country had turned its back on me, I couldn't do the same. If they were experimenting here, I couldn't allow it to continue.

Straightening my crooked back as much as I could, I marched purposely down the corridor, not bothering to hide my presence. Each step brought me closer to the source. Fear came at me with a fury now, like a hurricane poised to destroy a coastal town. I fought as hard as I could against it, but the few mental barriers I had erected were quickly toppling.

There were more labs on this level, but they were different. Most of the equipment looked state of the art rather than something built back in the forties. Desks holding large computers sat to the side of the rooms. Diagnostic equipment for monitoring heart and brain activity were pushed into some corners. I'm sure I saw an MRI machine in one of the labs, but throughout my search, I didn't see a single person.

The place appeared to be deserted, which was strange. *Someone* had turned the lights on.

Then I came to a room with a set of tightly shut double doors. Above the door, and spray painted on the cement wall, were the words "Project: Hercules." If my heart wasn't already pounding, it would have been just then. The fact that the words were spray painted rather than written on an official, U.S. military-issued sign told me nothing that went on down that corridor was official military business. Which either meant that what I was seeing was top secret on a level that wouldn't even give the head of the CIA clearance, or someone was working on his own.

Judging by the lack of security, I assumed it was the latter.

At that point, a pair of reinforced steel doors wouldn't stop me. I grabbed the handle and tugged with all my might, pulling off not only the door but also a chunk of the wall. Inside, the room looked like something out of a science fiction movie. Equipment lined several walls. The computers I saw looked old and nowhere near as compact as the ones I knew my granddaughter had in her bedroom.

I had also found all the workers I'd been looking for. There had to be at least fifty. Some wore lab jackets, others typical Army fatigues, but every one was bloody, with a gaping hole in the center of their forehead. How could this be? They looked like bullet wounds. Every one was dead. Judging by the smell that hit me when I opened the door, they had been dead for quite a while.

My stomach performed back flips and I threw up on the floor. I'd seen such a sight before when we'd liberated one of the concentration camps during the war. We'd arrived just as the Nazis were preparing to fill one of their mass graves. Hundreds lay dead in a giant hole on the ground, all of them shot in the back of the head.

"Who would do such a thing?" a much younger version of myself had asked.

"Monsters," was the only reply.

The corpses weren't the only people in the room. Along the far wall were twelve men, each connected to a series of tubes, which were attached to several places on their bodies and appeared to be pumping a yellow liquid into their veins. I knew in an instant that one of those men suspended on the wall was the source of my wife's fear.

I picked up a chunk of the concrete from the doorway and entered the room, intent on bashing in the skull of whoever was hurting my wife. I stepped over one of the dead bodies, irrationally thinking of those sci-fi movies when the dead come back to life, but thankfully none did.

The equipment holding these men on the wall was astounding. The restraints looked like something I would have had trouble breaking out of, even in my youth. They were made out of some kind of metal alloy I could not recall ever seeing before. The tubes themselves, while looking like plastic from a distance, were fashioned out of some kind of transparent metal, totally unbreakable.

I was almost brought to my knees as another mental wave crashed down upon me. I had visions of Edith lying dead—my greatest fear at that moment. I quickly composed myself and reassured myself that it was just an illusion.

Then I stepped up to one of the men hanging from the wall.

According to the monitors above his head, the man was alive. His heart rate was normal. For a moment I watched as his chest rose and fell. If I didn't know any better, I would have sworn he was sleeping restfully in his bed.

I looked at his face for the first time and as I did, I stumbled back a few steps. My head felt as if in a cloud for a moment, and I had to shake it several times to clear it. Then I looked back up at the face of the man to make sure I had actually seen what I'd seen.

I hadn't been wrong.

The man hanging from the wall was me. At least it was me as I looked sixty years ago. I reached out and touched him—touched me. The skin was warm and soft, yet I jerked my hand back as if I'd been burned.

Was this what Project: Hercules *was all about? Making us unstoppable, and then cloning us?*

I couldn't help wondering if *this* younger version of me had the same powers. Could he lift a car and throw it at an enemy? I had to assume he could – but didn't want to find out.

I looked down the row of soldiers restrained against the wall. We were all there: Everett, Johnson, Willard, and the one I knew must have been the source of my and Edith's fear: Carpenter.

As I gazed upon Frank's twenty-year-old face, I saw his eye open and look at me.

"Hey, Tom," he groaned as if just waking up from a very long sleep. Then he coughed a couple of times.

"How do you know me?" I strode up to him. In my mind, he shouldn't have been able to recognize the eighty-year-old version of the man he had known.

"Your mind feels the same as Stephenson's over there," Frank said. "I felt you coming, and had to bring you down here."

"You didn't have to attack my wife!" I shouted. "You could have killed her, you know that!" Even as I spoke, I had no idea if he actually *did* know that. This person wasn't the Frank Carpenter I had known for most of my life. He was something different: a clone.

"She's fine," he said. "I broke my link with her once you were down here. She's waiting for you where you left her." He closed his eyes suddenly, as if in pain. I realized that he couldn't have been very comfortable in those restraints but couldn't think of how to free him.

"What the hell is going on here?" I demanded.

"You haven't figured it out yet?"

The concrete chunk I still held in my hand fractured as I gripped it tighter and then shook my head.

"We're the new *Project: Hercules*." He let out a string of coughs. "They wanted a new set of genetically-enhanced soldiers to take your places. The only difference was, they no longer wanted us to have any ties back home. You know…" He coughed again. "No one to miss us if something happened. No one for us to tell about our powers. No chance of breaching security."

"Oh, my God." I couldn't believe it. All that talk about disbanding *Project: Hercules* had been nothing more than a cover-up. They must have taken samples of our blood when they had performed those experiments on us.

"And there's no guilt when they destroy us," he said.

"Destroy you?"

He winced again. "When we've outlived our usefulness, they simply flip a switch and turn us off. They built it into our genes."

I rubbed my temples. It had to be some kind of a flipped out dream. I must have been caught trespassing and they'd sedated me with some kind of drug. This couldn't be real.

Then I knew. "We were the prototypes," I said. As the words left my lips, I knew they made sense. We were the first subjects. They used us to create future generations.

"Yes," Frank said. "They've built you time and again, improving on you each time. You've fought in every war since World War II—quite an accomplishment for any soldier."

"This is unbelievable."

Frank tried to respond but experienced another coughing fit. When he was done, he seemed to have trouble breathing.

"What's the matter with you?" I asked.

His eyes had suddenly become bloodshot. "Sixty-year-old genes aren't all they're cracked up to be. There's something wrong with us. Our bodies are aging too rapidly, and physically, we aren't up to the task."

I looked down the line. All the others looked fine, still resting peacefully.

He must have sensed what I was thinking, because he said, "I'm keeping them all sedated so they don't have to go through what I am."

It must have been taking a lot of concentration to keep eleven grown men asleep. I couldn't imagine the extra pain it caused him to hold them all in a coma. Like the Frank I knew, this man was nothing if not compassionate. Which made me wonder.

I pointed at the bodies littering the ground. "What happened to all of them?"

He took a deep breath and let it out in a cough. "I lost control of my powers when I first became ill. I couldn't help it. Now I have to look every day at the death I've caused."

He looked at me then, and I saw the sorrow in his eyes. I knew it was genuine, because it was the same exact look Frank gave me sixty years before when he'd accidentally killed General Wilhelm during a training exercise.

"I need you to do something for me, Tom," Frank wheezed through clenched teeth, as another stab of pain appeared to hit him.

"Anything." He looked at me with an intensity that only two soldiers who have shared the battlefield would understand.

"Kill us."

"What? No! I can't do that, Frank."

"Please. It's the only way."

I used to be a soldier. I had killed hundreds of people I didn't know. Yet, looking down at the line of soldiers before me, my friends, I couldn't help but think of myself as a murderer if I went through with it.

"Please," he begged.

I looked at him, then down at the chunk of concrete still clenched in my hand. It would be quick and painless, nothing compared to the suffering these men would face dying slow deaths.

I stepped to the end of the line and stared myself in the face.

I raised my fist, intent on caving in my clone's skull. This was me. Clone or not, I was looking at myself. I couldn't help but think it would be something akin to suicide if I dropped the stone down on his head.

"I can't, Frank. I'm sorry." I dropped the chunk of concrete at my feet.

Frank coughed, and then sighed. I felt a sense of defeat rolling off him. "I'm sorry, too, Tom, but this is something I need you to do."

Something touched my brain just then, but it was so sudden there was nothing I could do to stop it. It seemed like only a second had passed, and the next thing I knew, I stood before Frank's dead body, his skull half caved in and the bloody chunk of concrete held over my head.

I looked down the line, unable to believe what had happened. Each of the soldiers had similar cracks in their skulls. Each of their monitoring systems were flat lined on both heart and brain activity.

I dropped the stone, not wanting to believe it, yet knowing I had killed them all. "I hate you, Frank," I said, looking at the dead man hanging limply on the wall. Then I realized the thing hanging before me wasn't Frank. He would never have willfully forced someone to do something so terrible.

On shaky legs, I walked back out of the room the same way I'd come. The words of General Palko re-echoed in my head as I trudged back to the stairs that would lead me to the upper level. "*Project: Hercules* is officially terminated."

And it was. All the scientists and their test subjects had been destroyed.

I made my way back to Edith. If Frank had told the truth, she should be outside the lab I had destroyed. But, when I got there, she was gone.

I didn't bother searching the underground. She wouldn't be there. I went back upstairs and out the door. The base looked just like before, but something was different. Everything had been silent on our trek to the radar dish. What I heard, as I re-entered the upper level of the base, was birds chirping.

Unfortunately, I couldn't share the sentiment of the wildlife. I walked back to where we'd parked the car, leaving the base and its secrets behind. I carried only the metal box—my time capsule.

Edith sat behind the steering wheel, trembling from head to foot. I opened the door and slid into the passenger seat. "I'm sorry," she said and repeated it three times, very quickly. Her breathing was labored, and I could tell that though Frank no longer had a hold on her, she was still very frightened. "I couldn't stay there anymore. I needed to get back to the car. We need to... Oh, my God, Tom!"

She'd finally looked over at me. I saw she couldn't take her eyes off my shirt. I looked down and realized it was spattered with blood. My hands were also stained red with the blood of the twelve clones down in the lab. Again, I felt my hands clench as I thought of what Frank made me do.

"Tom, what's going on? I need to know. You need to tell me."

I got out of the car and shut the door, leaned my head on the warm roof, and breathed deeply to calm myself. Nearby, the sign read, "Welcome to Camp Hero State Park." Above the sign and the trees, the top of the radar dish.

"Too many secrets," I said. "No more."

My entire life had been one big secret. I hid who I was everyday, because my government turned its back on me. I didn't want to live with these secrets anymore. Edith was my wife. We'd gone through good times and bad, but if after sixty years, if she couldn't understand me, then maybe I didn't know her at all.

I walked around to the driver's side. It would take about an hour for us to get back to the hotel—plenty of time.

"Slide over," I told her as I opened the door.

I didn't look at her but stared straight ahead for a few minutes, up the winding path that would have taken us back to the base. Then I stared down at the metal box in my lap.

"I don't want to talk right now." I flipped open the broken lid of the box. "I want you to read this, though." I pulled the two pictures and the journal out of the box and handed them to her. "I think it will explain everything."

She took the items with shaking hands.

When her hands touched mine, it felt as if a huge weight had been lifted from my shoulders. And all I could think of as I drove away from Camp Hero was that I should have done this a long time ago.

HARD RAIN

STORY BY

MICHAEL MARCUS

ART BY

REGGIE THEMISTOCLE

HARD RAIN

By Michael Marcus

People stared at him as he shuffled through the hot, cracked streets of the desert town, half-dead. He held the reins of his pack mule in his left hand as he staggered toward the town's well. Bill Castle blocked his way, cocking his shotgun.

"We do not have water for you, stranger," he said. "Move along now."

"Please," the man croaked. "I can pay…"

"Not enough. It has not rained for more than a month. The crops are almost gone."

"But I… I can help…" the stranger managed before passing out.

When he next awoke, the man was stretched out on a dusty mattress. "W-where am I?" he asked, looking around.

"You are lucky my wife came along when she did," Castle said, looking through the various strange items the man carried. Science meant little to him. "She insisted I let you drink and take you here."

The man struggled into a sitting position, back against the creaky headboard. "Thank you, all the same," he rasped.

"What is all this stuff? I cannot understand it. And what was it you said about being able to help us?" Castle asked as he turned over a small metal globe.

"My name is Albert Runyon, and I am a scientist—I study

the weather. That is my equipment that you are disturbing. With it, and with a little work and study, I might be able to make it rain here." Albert took the globe from Castle and gently placed it back in the bag.

It's not often you see Bill Castle's face stretch like that. "If you can make it rain here in Purgatory, you are a miracle worker."

Albert protested as he started to stand. "Look now, it is no miracle; it is just a question of scientific knowledge, particularly that of chemistry and meteorology."

Castle just stared. "Well, I will be damned."

As Albert recovered over the next few days, he started taking his measurements, soil samples, even catching the dust off the wind in little socks. Everyone just pretty much stood out of his way. Occasionally, Bill would fetch something for him from a bag or help with a ladder; the others didn't trust to his bearing or his strange behavior.

The one day that took the cake was when he tried to move the town cannon by himself. Aside from drawing a crowd, a few folk who thought he was trying to steal it nearly stopped him. The hard way. But, the sheriff intervened.

"What the hell do you think that you are doing?" the sheriff asked.

"My dear sir," Albert said to the sheriff, "as your fellow townsman, Mr. Castle, might have told you, I am endeavoring to produce rain for the city crops. If I am to do so, I will need to propel a compound of my own devising high into the atmosphere. For this purpose, I require the use of your town's cannon."

Although wide-eyed with disbelief, the sheriff gathered up the men and had them haul the cannon and set it on its end near the outskirts of town. Albert and Bill packed the powder in tightly, followed by a fragile container of metal and glass containing some strange powders and pellets. With measured care, they then lit the fuse.

There was complete silence as the fuse burned down and entered the powder chamber, and the noise was deafening as the cannon went off. Albert's strange projectile arced high over the town before shattering in a dozen tiny flashes in the oppressive sunlight. Minutes passed… and there was nothing.

Everyone began to circle the stranger who had wasted their time. "It should work," he said, "I promise you! It will take about three days for the chemicals to seed the clouds…" and as he read their blank stares, he added, "Just three days. Just trust me."

As the days passed, Bill got less and less generous with the food, and more importantly, with the water. Admittedly, what was left went to the crops more than anything as doubt had crept in.

It wasn't until the evening of the fourth day that they came with the ropes. The most the town had gotten was a little overcast weather that baked people into that crazy place where they have to do *something*. The sheriff tried to stop them, but they were a mob. Even shooting one in the leg wasn't enough to stop them bundling the scientist off to the nearest tree. Only one thing would stop them.

That was the rain.

Suddenly, it started. Just a few drops that might have been hallucinations, but soon they were followed by buckets more. Cheering, they raised their prior scapegoat to the sky and celebrated his work, dancing in the rain

About a week later, Albert proved himself to the remaining skeptics by shooting off another of his home-made "rainmaker balls." Again, on the fourth day, the rain came. Suddenly, he found himself the most welcome man in the town—everyone paid for food and drink, and even the ladies in town were "on the house." After a month, they had even built him the best home they could out of what spare wood they had, including a sturdy-sort of basement where he could work on more of his little miracles.

Of course, the rainmaker had his own needs. Albert Runyon could take this breakthrough back east and become Doctor Albert Runyon, Ph.D. of Meteorology. Why, he might even win a Nobel Prize! As valuable as he was in the village, though, they weren't about to let him leave. Oh, they treated him well enough, sure—his belly was always full and his bed was always warm—but somehow, he never got a response to one of his letters when one of the few mail carriers came through. He'd sent messages out with one of the few rare travelers, but again, nobody ever came back. One day, his mule "accidentally" managed to wander off the Castle ranch and got itself killed.

It was shortly after that that old Albert tried to borrow a horse from the townspeople, one after the next, but those that weren't in use were needed elsewhere, or the owner outright refused. He went to the sheriff.

"Well, buddy, you made yourself too valuable. I believe people would be much happier if you chose to settle down and make this your home." The sheriff took out his gun and started shining it on a kerchief. "I am sure you would, as well."

Winter came soon enough, and leaving was out of the question. After the little talk with the sheriff, the town's friendliness started to sit a little oddly. Some of the women made sure to bring their goods over, and the men—well, the men seemed a little too jealous for his comfort. In the cold of his basement, he sat alone, worried for his fate.

Even winter breaks for spring, though, and the results of the rains he produced did give the town some liveliness. So he continued making preparation for the summer.

As the first summer drought started to grow long, it almost became ceremonial as he and the townspeople set up the cannon, and he launched off the ball. There was some applause and fanfare, fanfare that returned with the new rain. While everyone else celebrated, the rainmaker just drowned himself in whiskey.

On the fifth day, Albert woke to the sound of screaming. As he left his house, he saw that everyone was wandering around, stumbling, completely without sight. His plans had worked: a little something extra in the ball had tainted the rain and took away the townsfolk's sight.

By the time they could see again, their town was missing one horse and one rain-making stranger. All he left was a note.

Dear Sheriff,

It is one thing to harness the weather, but another thing to harness a man. I left one ball in the basement. Use it with care.

— A. R.

PRISONER OF WAR

By Christopher Wrann

Ribbons of electricity poured from the combustion chambers of the H.S.F. Pangaea as it slid through the darkness of space toward Pheno, a smoky red planet far from Earth. Glossy black paneling and glowing chrome trim shone brightly in the emptiness of space surrounding the massive battleship. Reflections of starlight streaked across the many turrets that blanketed the ships hull as it quickly descended upon its target.

Pheno's sun vanished behind the enormous silhouette in the sky. In an instant the densely tangled foliage of the planet's largest rain forest was plunged into twilight. Three silver rockets blasted from the Pangaea and roared through Pheno's crimson atmosphere. Colliding with the planet they erupted into a thousand metallic shards.

For a moment silence surrounded ground zero as a rapidly reproductive chemical seeped from the shattered bellies of the missiles and into the air. The chemical converted Pheno's atmosphere from a substance which is normally toxic to humans into a mixture of nitrogen, oxygen, argon and carbon dioxide. The red smog of Pheno quickly evaporated as the air bomb's contents pushed its way outward and skyward. Flocks of birds fell to the ground and foliage began to wither as every living creature touched by oxygen choked to death. The mutated atmosphere shortened the few rays of light spilling around the Pangaea turning the red sky bright blue.

A cargo door silently opened from beneath the Pangaea and a tattered gray vessel dropped toward the five mile wide blue target below. The bullet ship was slow and directionless at first as it meandered toward the planet, then upon entering Pheno's gravitational field it plunged rapidly toward the surface of the planet. Occasional bursts of flames belched from its sides as it futilely tried to slow its quickening descent. Within the thin walls of the ship sat eleven silent soldiers; a twelfth stood stoically with one hand on his rifle and the other hand grasping a chain hanging from the ceiling. As gravity's friction bombarded the vessel's thin walls, bending and shaking them, a dull roar filled the soldiers' ears.

Matt Lion smothered the muzzle of his rifle with both hands and closed his eyes hard. He could no longer stand to watch the floor buckle beneath his feet. Though the potential for fatalities was high, the free-falling bullet ship was still the safest way to breach Pheno's atmosphere.

A year ago, the Phenotor had developed a crude E.M.P.-based force field to shield the planet. On the day the H.S.F Iceland unknowingly crossed this force field, an electromagnetic pulse shocked the ship into a state of paralysis, causing it to drop onto Pheno like a stone. Over a thousand soldiers were killed when the large ship collided with the planet.

This incident inspired Earth to create a ship with no electronic parts. It was an empty steel shell with engines on either side of it. The engines were triggered to go off as a reaction to the force that was applied to them. This kept it from turning over as it fell from the sky. As it got closer to the surface, the engines would expend the remainder of their fuel to insure what the bullet ships creator called a soft landing.

Hard drops, as this method of incursion had come to be known, seemed to get more unnerving to Lion the more he participated in them. Having been on several, he knew exactly what to expect; but instead of familiarity breeding comfort, the experience became all the more terrifying with the knowledge that the soft landing they were promised was little more than a controlled crash.

He took a deep breath and shook his head to clear it as he looked up at Ben Valcour standing indifferently at the head of the ship. Valcour imperceptibly shifted his weight from one foot to the other in response to the ship's awkward movements; his breathing was slow and metered as his gray eyes stared coldly at the bullet ship's cargo door. Lion noticed Valcour's lips subtly moving as if he were talking to himself. He realized in this moment that Valcour wasn't thinking about the ship plummeting to the ground; in his mind he was already outside, charging through a dying forest shouting out orders to his platoon. He was ten steps ahead of the game, and it hadn't even begun.

The small smile of comfort that began crawling across Lion's face froze suddenly, his eyes grew wide and his face tensed when he noticed Valcour's muscles stiffen in anticipation of impact. Lion buried his chin into his chest and awaited the landing. The roar inside the bullet ship grew louder and the shudder of its walls became fiercer as the engines fought the g-forces with all their might. Tree limbs cracked and scraped the hull of the ship violently. Lion clenched his chattering teeth, and his knuckles whitened around the barrel of his rifle as the turbulence built around him. There was a brief silent moment before the ship slammed into the floor of the rain forest. The soldiers were jolted hard, and the ship moaned as its walls resisted bursting under the impact, Valcour bent his knees with the ships buckling walls and remained unfazed.

The shock of the fall washed over the stunned platoon, their brains settled in their skulls after being so violently knocked around.

"Move Out!" Valcour ordered at the top of his lungs after violently pulling the chain he had clutched tightly in his hand causing the door to drop to the ground. Though still stunned, the men and women were quickly on their feet, scrambling and stumbling for the first few steps. They quickly regain their composure and were soon charging right behind Valcour, rifles held close to their chests.

"Stay alert, the communications satellite we're knocking out isn't far from here," said Valcour quietly, almost to himself, as he hunched over and began to make his way into the forest.

The platoon assumed a tight formation behind him and calmly took in their surroundings. Although they could freely breathe the air around them they winced at the putrid stench of the decaying inhabitants of the forest. Once lush, it had quickly withered and died in its new, toxic environment.

The forest possessed the eerie quality of dusk; what little light there was seemed to feed the growing darkness, giving shadows a thick, impenetrable quality. All was silent around the soldiers except for the creaking of dead trees and the occasional final spasm of a fallen bird or suffocating toad. The platoon slowly, quietly, began to make its way through the pillars of centuries old lifeless trees. Their eyes and rifles combed the forest around them searching for anything that had survived.

Once in a great while, a Phenotor is able to don a protective breathing apparatus before the Air Bomb touches down. Although one Phenotor is harmless to a dozen trained soldiers, Valcour's ever-vigilant gaze scanned over the dry vines and hollow tree trunks, prepared for anything.

From the corner of his eye a shadow silently darted behind the trees and vanished. Sensing Valcour's veiled alarm, the platoon halted and activated the fusion burners on their rifles with the flick of a switch. A low hum echoed through the forest and the smell of electricity filled the air as the fluid within the gun's cartridges began to glow bright green.

Valcour squinted his eyes as he tried to find the source of the shadow. After a frozen moment, he decided that his mind had been playing tricks on him and wondered if he was getting punch drunk from all the hard drops. He began to take another step forward, but before his foot could touch the ground another shadow streaked across his field of view. He froze and studied the land in front him, peering hard into the darkness beyond the trees but finding nothing. The soldier blinked to adjust his eyes. As the darkness in front of him became more defined a shock of adrenaline rushed into his brain and a metallic taste filled his mouth. The darkness itself was moving, slowly heaving, as if calmly breathing. His jaw clenched tight as his eyes grew more accustomed to the absence of light, revealing what seemed like an infinite amount of Phenotor eyes hanging in the darkness staring coldly back at him.

The deadening silence which had fallen over the forest was broken when Lion gulped hard, adjusted his rifle in his arms and began tapping his finger anxiously on the trigger. Time stood still as Valcour's eyes drifted to the right then to the left and revealed to him what he had already suspected: his platoon was surrounded.

Valcour took a long, last, deep breath then exploded into life, "Second ring formation, we've been ambushed!" He shouted in a fearless voice.

The team formed two circles with their rifles pointing outward. Six of the soldiers made an outer circle and got down on one knee; the other six stood in a tighter circle behind them. For a moment the forest filled with the rustling of clothing as they assumed formation, then silence returned.

Without warning, the blood curdling war cry of the Phenotor filled the air. The chilling cacophony seemed to assault the soldiers from every direction. Valcour responded by lifting his rifle triumphantly and releasing his own visceral war cry. It was so powerful and so confident that it chased the cry of the hundreds of hell-bent Phenotor from his platoon's ears.

"Fire at will!" Valcour shouted as he lowered his rifle into fighting position and squeezed the trigger.

The rest of the platoon followed his lead, all firing into the shadows at once. The green glow of hyper-kinetic energy cut through the forest with ease, destroying everything in its path. When the chaos brought on by the dozen firing rifles subsided there was only silence. Then, when Lion was about to expel a sigh of relief the Phenotor came pouring from the forest by the hundreds, like a swarm of hornets erupting from a nest.

The Phenotor looked like something that crawled from the deepest, darkest depths of Earth's ocean. Their hard pale skin was nearly translucent, their faces were wide and bony, veins and organs could be seen pumping and turning just below the surface. Slits in their necks noisily suctioned in air and made loud clicking noises as they completed a breathing cycle. Lifeless black eyes hung emotionlessly from the sides of heads which perched upon a thin, gangly frame, ending in long pointed fingers and clawed toes.

They came charging with battle axes and spears, attacking viciously without reason or thought, like wild animals backed into a corner. The greatly outnumbered humans did what they could to push back against the throng of alien attackers, but Valcour knew that they couldn't win this battle and there was a larger mission at hand.

"Fan out and take down anything that moves," Valcour shouted "The satellite must fall!" He charged headlong into the tidal wave of blood-thirsty aliens. Their blades pierced his armor and dug into his flesh. His helmet withstood blow after blow before shattering. Valcour ignored the onslaught; he kept his head down and continued a single-minded charge through the line of Phenotor cannon fodder.

Once beyond the throngs of aliens, Valcour burst into a sprint through the forest where he came across a pair of Phenotor heading toward the battle. Without a second's thought he tore them to pieces with a blast from his rifle, then took aim at a third charging alien but was blindsided by a fourth. His rifle was shattered in two by a club-wielding alien who proceeded to take a swing at Valcour's head. He quickly ducked the blow and forced the jagged edge on his fractured weapon into the enemy soldier's abdomen. Without missing a beat, Valcour grabbed a large blade from his belt and slit the throat of another oncoming Phenotor.

His eyes darted around trying to see through the chaos in his mind when he caught a glimpse of the communications base through the trees. He was about to make one last sprint towards it but was struck by a searing pain in his torso. Valcour looked down and saw a spear jutting through the left side of his rib cage. When he grabbed the spear and was met with resistance he realized that the alien who had struck him had not thrown the weapon but had thrust it into him and was still holding the other end. Without a moments delay, he swung his body around, pulling the alien at the other end of the spear closer towards him as he jammed his blade into its temple.

Another Phenotor came running at him from the direction of the battle. It was carrying an Earth rifle and screaming violently. As the alien shoved the butt end of the rifle toward Valcour's head, Valcour was able to grasp it with both hands before it made contact.

For a moment, the two enemy soldiers were locked in a stalemate as they both wrestled for control of the gun. Suddenly Valcour lunged forward, plunging the spearhead that was still sticking out of his side into the solar plexus of the enemy soldier. The Phenotor let out a shrill cry and released its grip on the rifle as its body went limp.

Valcour slowly inched the spear out of his torso, wincing as each tug grated against bone. Once free of the spear, he renewed his focus on the communications satellite just beyond the tree line.

Again charging in the direction of the satellite, he became confused by his surroundings. He felt light headed. The forest now seemed much brighter than it was moments ago. Valcour took a few clumsy steps in one direction then accidentally spun himself in another and staggered for a few feet more.

A Phenotor warrior crashing through the forest while brandishing a large silver blade startled Valcour out of his shock. He clumsily aimed his newly won rifle at the alien as it raised its dagger toward him. He pulled the trigger in the same instant the attacker attempted to strike. The alien soldier was torn to pieces in the same moment that its blade met Valcour's wrist.

Losing all control of his right hand, Valcour involuntarily dropped his rifle to the ground as a severed tendon slithered up his forearm, and coiled into a wad near his elbow. A cold sweat washed over him as he clutched his dead arm and repressed the nausea rising in his gut.

As he dropped to his knees the world spun around him. His eyes rolled around in their sockets, his mind tried to escape the realm of consciousness and the pain within it. With a long, deep breath and a nod of the head he buried the pain, nausea and fatigue deep within him and staggered triumphantly to his feet.

His boots felt as though they weighed a ton as he took one step, then another, slowly making his way to the edge of the forest. On his third step his leg collapsed, dropping him to the ground once again.

Valcour hung his head in defeat. The world became still and silent around him. As darkness crept into his eyes he focused on the thumping, rushing sound of his heart as it tried desperately to deliver blood to his brain. He shut his eyes to stop the sting of the sweat falling from his forehead and the pain began to fade as the thumping in his ears slowed.

Valcour was lying in bed, sleeping in on a Sunday morning. Rain tapped on the windows. The sheets were cool against his skin. He turned on his side and embraced his wife. As he clung tightly to her warm skin his hand passed over her massive stomach. He felt his son safe within her womb and wished that he could stay in this bed forever.

The tranquility was suddenly shattered by an alarm clock blasting from the nightstand. Shocked by the violent eruption of sound Valcour fumbled with the clock, frantically trying to shut it off. He pressed the off button, but the noise grew louder rather than subsiding. Through the haze of his waking mind he realized the alarm was not beeping like it should be: it was screaming. He stopped pummeling the buttons and listened to the death cries of his platoon as they were overcome by hundreds of Phenotor deep within an alien rain forest.

Valcour's fingers dug into the dirt beneath the pulp of dead grass. Attempting a deep breath revealed that the spear had punched a hole in his left lung. He hacked and coughed up blood and slowly brought himself to his feet.

"The satellite must fall," poured from his pale blue lips like a bucket of gravel. In a bid for power, Valcour summoned all the anger he could find within him. Anger at the Phenotor for assaulting his planet, for ambushing and killing his platoon, but most of all, anger at himself for being weak enough to let these mongrels nearly stop him from completing his mission.

Valcour used his anger for one final push to get him out of the forest. Dry, leafless branches tore at his face and arms as he stumbled through the last thicket.

He took as deep a breath as his one working lung would allow, then paused to get a clear view of the communications station. His jaw went slack, as the last glimmer of hope left him.

"No," he muttered at the abandoned stable in front of him. "What the hell is this?" The words escaped from his throat in a bitter whisper as he surveyed the dilapidated silos scattered around a rotting barn.

As he staggered in bewilderment toward the crumbling structures he ignored a pinch in his ankle. But when a warm numb feeling poured into his leg, Valcour grabbed his calf and pulled out a small dart buried deep within it. The numbness continued up his leg and into his stomach. He turned around laconically to find a group of ten Phenotor soldiers standing at the tree-line holding various archaic weapons, including a blow dart trained on him. Before he could speak, he realized that his face was numb. He tried to step forward but stumbled backward, tripped over his feet and landed on his back.

Valcour was no longer angry or in pain; he felt nothing at all. The poison had entered his brain and washed it in a pleasant sensation. He stared up at the wide open blue sky above him letting the sun bathe him in its warm light. As he lay paralyzed on the ground he wondered nonchalantly where the H.S.F. Pangaea disappeared to, and how he would get home.

Valcour opened his eyes just enough to see through the slits between his eyelids, but not so much that anybody would notice that he had awoken. Taking in his surroundings while being careful not to move or otherwise betray his consciousness, he saw nothing but smooth gray walls in front of him. He listened intently until he was satisfied that he was alone in the room, and then leaped to his feet, assuming a defensive stance.

It took a moment for his eyes to adjust to the low light of the cell, but when his pupils did finish their widening he discovered that little was to be seen anyway. He was in small empty room surrounded by four barren matte gray walls. The floor and ceiling were the same color and material as the walls, making it hard to determine where one surface ended and another began.

Upon touching the walls, Valcour couldn't decide if they were made out of plastic, metal or stone. They felt both like a combination of all those materials and like none of them at all. When he found a small slit in the wall, his fingers followed it up, over, and then back down again. This, he decided, was the exit.

Upon examining the indistinguishable door more carefully Valcour discovered a small rectangular slit three feet off the ground in the center of the door. As he looked more intently at his discovery an opening suddenly revealed itself causing Valcour to jump back from the door with his fists raised. A plate of food and a bottle of clear liquid was passed through the hole, then the rectangular hatch quickly slid back into place.

Taken aback by the sudden disruption he breathed heavily with shaking fists involuntarily raised. His tightly clenched right hand caught his attention. In astonishment he unclenched it and wiggled his fingers before making a fist then relaxing his hand once again. Curiously he rolled his shirtsleeve up and found a few small surgical scars in his once maimed arm. Then, realizing that he had been breathing without difficulty, Valcour lifted his shirt up to find similar scars in his chest.

"How long have I been here?" Valcour wondered aloud while rubbing his hand across his head. He froze suddenly when he realized that his hair felt as though it had just been cut. He held his hand close to his eyes and found small pieces of hair clippings stuck to it.

"What's going on here? Where the hell am I?" he asked the empty cell before scolding himself for doing so and shutting his mouth tight. Talking to himself while in deep thought or in times of anxiety had always been a bad habit of Valcour's. People on Earth had either been intrigued or put off by this trait, depending on how they felt about what was referred to as "untreated mental events." As he paced the room, he glanced at but resisted the cooling plate of food on the ground.

After much consternation, the growth of a void in his stomach drove Valcour to hover over the food to get a better look at it. He was amazed to find that the meal appeared to be a roasted chicken breast, mashed potatoes and a large chunk of bread. There was also a small plastic cup on the plate. Valcour picked up the cup and, after smelling it, determined that it is gravy. "How thoughtful of them to put it on the side," he sarcastically exclaimed with a chuckle.

"If they wanted me dead, I'd be dead," Valcour decided with a shrug and sat on the floor. While shoving food into his mouth he wondered if his captors knew he was looking at the food slot or if it was coincidental that the food was shoved through the door when it was. Although he didn't see any cameras he reminded himself that his knowledge of Phenotor technology was limited. Valcour then noticed that though there were no windows or lights in his cell it wasn't quite pitch black. It appeared that the walls and ceiling were giving off a soft, ambiguous glow, confirming for Valcour that the alien race had scientific know-how not yet possessed by the Earthlings.

Upon looking down at his empty plate, Valcour realized that, because he had devoured it as quickly as he did, the food must not have tasted alien to him. After smelling the odorless, clear liquid in the bottle that came through the slot with his food he took a small sip. The drink was cool and crisp; it seemed to Valcour to be very much like water yet indefinably not.

With a full stomach Valcour began to asses his situation. Recalling his training, he decided to silently seat himself in a far corner of the cell and wait vigilantly for the door to open.

Days passed.

With no variation in darkness or light, night and day went undefined. Minutes and hours were interchangeable; time had lost all meaning in the motionless vacuum of Valcour's cell. The only indication that time had not ceased pressing onward was provided by the meals slid through his door. He was delivered an Earth style breakfast, lunch, and dinner everyday. Moving only to eat the food, he would leave the dirty plate in the center of his cell and return to the corner to silently stare at the door and wait for the Phenotor to show their hand. He would never remember falling asleep, and would never dream, but every once in a while he would open his eyes to find his plates had been cleared.

A few hours into the second day, he caught himself rocking back and forth, slightly tapping his head on the wall behind him. He quickly stopped himself, but the rocking commenced as soon as his mind began wandering again.

On the third day, he began spiraling into a silent state of panic. He didn't realize it right away, but he was thinking in circles. He would begin to fear that he would never get out of his cell, and then he would convince himself he shouldn't have eaten the food, and finally that he was dead and this was purgatory. He would then begin to talk himself out of his panic by telling himself that he was still alive. This would calm him down, but soon after his nerves settled he would begin thinking that he would never get out of his cell, thus beginning the downward spiral of dread once again. He became aware that he was panicking when he realized that his hands felt weightless and a prickly sensation engulfed the inside of his mouth. He swallowed hard and pushed the thoughts deep down into his mind, afraid that he would soon be driven mad.

The morning of the fourth day, while Valcour stared at the door, he inexplicably began counting seconds in his head. He wasn't aware that he was doing it until he found himself wondering why he felt agitated and realized that he had been stuck in a loop, dropping back down to ten thousand nine hundred and twenty every time he reached ten thousand nine hundred and twenty nine. It happened thirty times before he stopped. In repressing his brain's inclination to count he developed a twitch in his eyelid. After lunch, he started to absent mindedly scratch his left arm, when he reached out to grab his dinner plate he noticed that he had dug a large bloody gash into it.

On the fifth day, he began to hallucinate that he was looking down at himself from the ceiling in the opposite corner of the room. Startled, he would look up at the ceiling to find it empty. He would shake his head and continue to stare at the door until he drifted back into the hallucination. Once again, he broke the spell by trying to catch himself on the ceiling. This went on all day long.

On the sixth day, his brain began to feel like it was crawling under his skull.

"Okay, okay, okay, I can't do this forever," he said loudly as he rose to his feet. He shook his head furiously and waved his limbs to get the blood flowing in them; then he began to pace back and forth in the small cell.

"Alright, I'm losing it here. I've got to do something before I go insane, alright? Okay, I am Sergeant Ben Valcour, of the Seven Percenters." Slowly his voice rose from a low murmur and into a normal conversational volume. "I am on Pheno to shut down a communications satellite."

"There was no satellite," he replied from the ceiling.

"Of course there was a satellite, our intelligence is never wrong. I must have gotten turned around in the chaos of the ambush!" he shouted back as he turned around to see where he had disappeared to.

"But I have an excellent sense of direction, and I'm sure I was running northwest the entire time," he shot back, just beyond his line of sight.

"I don't have *that* good of a sense of direction."

"Sure I do."

"No I don't."

"Sure I d... stop, just stop!" Valcour stopped pacing and held his head in his hands as if he could grab his thoughts to stop their racing. "This isn't getting us... no, no, no, this isn't getting ME anywhere. Okay? So focus, start at the beginning."

"I was born on the twentieth day of August in the year twenty-five-fifteen..." he declared and found that it soothed his mind to think of himself on Earth. A detailed recreation of what his parents' lives must have been like when he was first born began to materialize in his mind.

He imagined his parents, Aly and Jim, in their youth. He pictured where they lived, and what the neighborhood might have been like. He constructed an underground maternity ward out of dull concrete walls and shining chrome tables. He hung dim lights from the ceiling, and placed a cigarette in the teeth of the doctor who pulled him into the world.

As he transported himself into his past, the colliding jumble of thoughts untangled, and he began to watch his life unfold as a movie in his mind's eye. Valcour had two older siblings that had died in the Cyril Pox pandemic before he was born. The Valcours birthed these first two children according to the regulations set out by the

Planetary Congress. During pregnancy, his mother took all of the required medications religiously, and upon birthing them, the children spent the standard three months in a post-natal incubation chamber. The precautionary infusion of antibiotics, inoculations, and psychoactive drugs in all newborns had become law in the twenty-two hundreds and was responsible for the eradication of all illness both physical and mental.

In the year twenty-five twelve, the highly contagious virus Cyril Pox was accidentally leaked out of a pharmaceutical lab. It spread quickly and was responsible for over a seventy million deaths worldwide. A rumor had spread that Cyril Pox was a benign virus that the immune system should have been able to easily overcome, but because of all the medications given at birth the human immune system had grown too weak to fight disease.

When Aly discovered that she was pregnant once again, the Valcours knew that they could not risk losing another child by subjecting it to the same barrage of chemical enhancements. They vanished in the middle of the night becoming what were known as Seven Percenters. People who had fled society were called this because the government estimated that the dissident consisted of seven percent of the world's population. Although they initially led a solitary, nomadic life, they discovered a network of underground doctors who were willing to illegally deliver a child the natural way. Shortly after Ben's birth the Valcours joined a Seven Percenter farming commune that was hidden in a corner of the globe the government had deemed unusable.

Ben closed his eyes tight and a small smile grew on his face. He could feel the warm prairie sun and smell the dusty air from within his dimly lit cell. Until that moment, he hadn't realized how much he missed the simple farming life he gave up when he joined the military.

The world had changed so suddenly the day the Phenotor attacked the Earth.

Valcour pictured himself in the middle of a field. It was harvest season and he had been working from sun up until sun down for two weeks. He paused for a moment to wipe the sweat from his forehead and saw his neighbor running toward him from the corner of his eye.

"They got us Ben, they nailed us good," Lion belted out breathlessly.

"What are you talking about? Who got us? The Government?" Valcour asked, fearing that their commune had finally been discovered.

"No, no those…what are they called? Those Fee-know something or other…the aliens, they attacked Earth."

"The Phenotor?" Ben had been intrigued by the aliens ever since Earth had discovered their planet several years earlier. "But… how?"

"It's all over the news, they blew up an entire island; vaporized it."

"What island? Where?"

"I… I can't remember the name, Ben, but it was one of ours. The whole island, it was a Seven Percenter island!" Lion's eyes were wide with exasperation.

Ben went silent. He wiped the sweat off his forehead and studied his hand for a moment, then shook his head slightly to chase a stray thought from it. "Call a town meeting…" he said calmly, almost mournfully, before looking up at the sun setting on the horizon, "…this is big. This changes everything."

Lion wasn't sure if Valcour was talking to himself and hesitated a few moments as the ever thoughtful farmer squinted silently into the distance. Lion opened his mouth slightly as if he was going to say something to Valcour, but words failed him. He turned silently and ran back towards town.

Later that evening, two men stood on the roof of the meeting hall adjusting a satellite as the building below filled. A man stood inside at a large monitor and held a walkie-talkie to his mouth giving instructions to the men above as the screen went from static to clear and back again. Suddenly, the President's voice boomed from the speakers as his image became clear on the monitor.

"Since that momentous day, over three hundred and fifty years ago, when the entire world's nations united as one, we have enjoyed an era of unencumbered peace. An era devoid of disease, famine, poverty, and war…" The President looked down sadly and swallowed hard, and then pointed pain-filled eyes directly into the camera. "Today that era has come to an end." The meeting hall crowd sat transfixed with baited breath.

"At 11:30 this morning a warship from the planet Pheno appeared just beyond Earth's orbit. Without cause or warning, the ship fired a powerful weapon at Isle De Rio. Upon impact, the island and all of its inhabitants were…" The President looked down sorrowfully once again. He took a deep, shaky breath, this time he did not look back into the camera. "There is no more Isle De Rio, it is gone…destroyed." Men and women in the meeting hall gasped as if the wind had been knocked out of them. The President took another long breath in through his nose and exhaled slowly through his mouth; he shook his head and faced the viewer.

"It is estimated that approximately ten thousand people were on the island at the time of the attack. This number cannot be confirmed because a great majority of the island's population consisted of citizens who choose to live without the assistance of the world government." Women began weeping openly as men placed their hands over their mouths to hide quivering lips. The President's eyes suddenly became sharper and the muscles in his face tightened, as he took on a more forceful tone. "The warship immediately vanished from our solar system. Both the Planetary Congress and I believe that this is the first strike in an intended invasion of our planet."

"As the leader of this great planet, I vow to each and every human being that I will do everything within my power to prevent another such attack." The President pounded his fist on the podium righteously and leaned into the camera. "The Planetary Congress has approved an emergency declaration of war on Pheno. By taking the battle to the Phenotor we will never have to see another innocent human life cut short again." The audience that filled the meeting hall began to look at one another with terror filled eyes.

"At this moment our exploratory space shuttles are being retrofitted with the latest advances in extraterrestrial weaponry. Also, the production of proper battleships has begun. I have been assured that in less than a month we will have greater combat vehicles than the Phenotor." The President briefly smiled widely, and then quickly assumed a sterner look as he furrowed his brow. "But it's going to take more than machinery to win this war." As the President went on the restlessness ceased and the crowd began to listen intently to his every word.

"Having lived as one peaceful nation for hundreds of years, we are not equipped with the manpower that a war of this magnitude requires. Now, I promise to do everything I can to keep this planet safe, but I can't do it alone. I am asking that every able bodied man and woman volunteer for our armed forces." Valcour nodded knowingly as the President's features softened once again and his tone became more soothing. "As I mentioned before, there is a segment of our population who has chosen to live outside our social system. In the past, this was considered an act of aggression against society and therefore constitutionally illegal." The President lifted up a signed document, stamped with a bright gold Presidential seal. "I have in my hand an amendment to our constitution. It states that any citizen of Earth who has neglected to adhere to the appropriate guidelines set forth by the Planetary Congress will be pardoned of all wrongdoing, and fully accepted into the world community upon enrollment in the armed forces. In addition, this exoneration will extend to all members of a military volunteer's family who are not fit to serve."

"We don't want your damn global community!" an angry young man shouted, causing a wave of hushes and murmurs to roll over the crowded meeting hall. Though nobody spoke out again, the viewers grew increasingly restless as the President continued to give instructions on how to register for the military. While people around him fidgeted anxiously, Valcour remained still, his chin in his hand as he stared intently at the screen.

He had earned a reputation for being clear-headed under pressure, and had prided himself on his fair-mindedness. The respect of his fellow townspeople was not something that he took for granted; when someone came to him with a dispute or for advice on a personal problem, he felt an enormous amount of responsibility to give the matter at hand his utmost attention. Valcour was driven by an unflappable desire to do what was right no matter what the personal cost. His strong moral compass and mental dexterity made him something of a community leader, and he knew that his opinion on the matter of war would be a weighty one.

After the Presidential address had ended, the meeting hall erupted into heated debate. As neighbors shouted at one another, Valcour stayed quiet, seemingly lost in a world of his own.

"What does Ben have to say about this!?" a woman shouted, but Valcour continued to sit silently until he realized that the rest of the hall had quieted and was looking to him.

"What do I think?" he asked humbly, sitting in silence for a moment before walking to the front of the hall. "From what I hear being said right now, many of you don't want to get involved with this war out of spite for the planetary government."

"They don't give a damn about us, Ben!" a faceless voice declared from within the crowd.

"You're right, sir. They don't give a damn about us, or at least they haven't up till now. That's why us Seven Percenters have been able to exist for as long as we have. As far as they're concerned, we're useless nobodies. As long as we stayed out of sight, they tolerated us living outside the law, but that's over now. Now they need us…"

"What the hell do they need a bunch of farmers for?" an elderly woman with leathery skin and deep crevices on her face asked with genuine curiosity.

"Look around you, Mrs. Bolk. Look at us and think about the rest of the world. Our bodies have been hardened by manual labor and exposure to bacteria. Our minds have been hardened by the stresses and tumult that the un-medicated brain is left open to. That's why the government needs us, and I'll tell you right now, if we don't go to help them voluntarily, they'll…" Ben stopped himself and thought for a moment before continuing in a calmer tone. "The rest of the world, the ninety-three percent of mankind that is bred with all the enhancements that modern technology can provide them with are too soft to fight in a war." Valcour spread his arms wide and clenched his fists powerfully. "We are natural warriors! If men and women who have led a life of leisure are our front line, they will quickly fall.

Then, the Phenotor will come back here, and they'll come for us. We can't fight them with tractors and shovels, can we? "You heard the President. They have the weapons to fight these aliens, but we have the strength. Without both we can't win this war." Valcour looked down for a moment to steel himself to the wrath of the crowd. "And that's one of the reasons I have decided to volunteer." The crowd erupted in approvals and disapprovals to Valcour's statement, as he tried to mend the broken silence by gesturing with his hands for people to calm down. "But it's not just that. Ten thousand men, women, and children were killed today. I don't give a damn if they were Seven Percenters or not. Nobody deserves that fate. I feel it is my duty as a human being to hunt down the kind of evil that the Phenotor have shown themselves to be, and eradicate it." The crowd silently stared at Ben Valcour. "But that's just me; none of you should feel obligated to join."

He began to leave the meeting hall then turned to the crowd once more before exiting. "I'm headed to the capital at daybreak if anyone wants to join me."

Valcour didn't know it at the time, but he was being recorded. His speech was broadcast to Seven Percenters around the world. The end result was a mass pilgrimage to the world capital and an armed forces one billion soldiers strong.He chuckled to himself as he remembered arriving at the capital thinking he was a no-name farmer from the prairie lands, and being greeted as a celebrity by his fellow Seven Percenters. The recruiters noticed the way that the rest of his people regarded him and quickly put him at the head of a platoon.

Nearly a month had past since he awoke in his prison cell. In all that time, he hadn't seen another living being or the sun in the open sky. This length of solitary confinement would break almost any man. But Valcour was hardly fazed. As far as he was concerned, he had seen his friends and family, he had felt the sun on his face, and looked deep into the infinite blue sky every day. He had taught his mind to lapse into a deep hypnotic trance in which his memories were as vivid as waking life.

The food slot opened in the door, and dinner was pushed through. The plate clanking on the floor would always lure Valcour from his dream-like state. As he ate, he felt a twinge of excitement knowing that soon he would be reliving his proudest moment yet. A moment in his second year of service; when the name Valcour would become known by every man, woman and child on the planet Earth.

Although he was admired by his fellow Seven Percenters in his first year of military service, his wartime exploits were unknown to the world at large. That changed during one fateful mission when he emerged as the bravest patriot the Earth had ever known.

It was a simple mission: force the Phenotor out of the Flatlands and into the surrounding wilderness with the objective of setting up a base on Pheno. At this point in the war, Valcour had been in countless attacks on the planet. He had become a hardened soldier as a result. At first, the screams and hissing of dying Phenotor haunted him. The confused look on a dying comrade's face as he lay in the dirt a million miles from home floated in the darkness when he shut his eyes at night. He heard soldiers pleading for their lives in tiny muffled whimpers just breaking through the beating of the shower head. He would quickly shut the water off, convinced that a fallen friend was just outside the bathroom door. Straining his ears, he only heard a slow drip from the faucet and a quaver on his labored breath.

This didn't happen anymore. His eyes had become steel, allowing no battlefield horror to penetrate them. His blood was fire in his brain and ice in his heart: nothing fazed him anymore, nothing stuck. He watched himself fighting and killing from a distance, as if his soul had become detached from his body, floating above him, waiting to return when the war was done with him.

Earth's victory would have been declared a year earlier, when the Phenotor fell easily to the superior firepower of the Earthlings, but there seemed to be an infinite number of the alien race willing to sacrifice their lives. For every one they gunned down, five more seemed to sprout up. Still, Earth would always claim the territory eventually. In that respect, this mission was no different.

After successfully herding the Phenotor into the dense jungle that surrounded the Flatlands, Valcour was helping the rest of the soldiers prepare to depart the planet when a breeze caressed his face awakening him to the surrounding land. He looked around at gently rolling hills and miles of blue skies above him and realized that the terrain reminded him of his farm. He hadn't been back since the day he left for war, and nostalgia got the better of him. He found himself meandering through the countryside.

After climbing a small hill on the edge of the oxygenated zone he spotted a large clearing in the trees not far out. Valcour squinted through the red smog and noticed glimmers of sunlight dancing off of a large metallic panel. Curious, Valcour focused his binoculars at the clearing. What he witnessed caused a tingle of exhilaration to run up his spine. He had found the warship his people had been hunting for three years.

The spacecraft was at least five times the size of the largest Earth battleship, and had hundreds of turrets jutting out from its sides. Monstrous appendages clung tightly to the hull, but looked as though they could extend miles into space to crush a defending warship. Its most telling feature was the innumerable propulsion engines covering the ship, clearly providing the beast with more than enough power to get to Earth. Though no earthling had reported seeing this vessel in battle the ship was scarred and dented from heavy use. There was no doubt in Valcour's mind that this was the elusive warship that had attacked Earth.

The battleship's commander studied the photographs that Valcour sent him from the planet below. In the years since the beginning of the war, this was the first sighting of Phenotor technology that appeared to be capable of attacking Earth. As the commander awaited orders from his superior, Valcour gathered up a dozen volunteers to enter the un-oxygenated zone to destroy the ship.

He didn't need to wait long or look far for men and women willing to strike off into uncharted territory on a reckless mission. Every one of his soldiers was behind him. Valcour turned many away, explaining that a small platoon could snake through the jungle more efficiently. The soldiers who weren't chosen would stall the ship's take off for one half hour. If they were not back in time they had orders to leave them all behind.

The twelve volunteers that Valcour selected donned spacesuits and packed as many explosives as they could carry before they ventured into the wilderness. Moving swiftly through the tangled jungle they soon came upon a group of Phenotor in full battle armor. The alien soldiers appeared to be resting before boarding the ship, and had not noticed the Earthlings until they were being shot to pieces by them.

Not wanting to lose the element of surprise, Valcour signaled his soldiers to charge the warship with everything they had. Silent and determined, the men and women ran toward the ship as if they were one large breathing bullet. Quickly they penetrated the hull and were within the ship.

Phenotor squirmed and swarmed inside the ship like bacteria in the bloodstream. The weapons they carried were crude blunt staffs and sharp saw-toothed swords. They swung their arms and howled wildly through motionless mouths, their large, unblinking eyes filled with rage. It was then that Valcour realized just how savage these aliens were.

In the dark, claustrophobic hallways of the ship, Valcour was able to rely on the rest of his platoon for cover fire as he looked for the engine room. The Phenotor used a very unstable, very pungent liquid to fuel their vehicles. It wasn't hard for Valcour to follow the tart scent burning the inside of his nose into the power center of the warship. Valcour recognized the Phenotor fuel immediately when he came upon a large tank containing the familiar glowing liquid that rained down from emerald colored clouds into the planet's glowing rivers and oceans.

For a moment, he was hypnotized by the glow of the tank; he had never seen this much refined Phenotor fuel in one place before. It was because of this fluorescent green sludge that the humans needed to fight the war so cautiously. This chemical, which could be ladled out of any puddle and very simply refined, was one of the most destructive substances known to man. If the Phenotor ever figured out how to use it against the earthlings without risking the total annihilation of Pheno they win the war.

He ran his fingers along the translucent shell of the ship's fuel tank and decided it was time to pay the Phenotor back for what they did to Isle De Rio. Calmly, he turned on his communicator and ordered the soldiers to return to the transport. As he heard the weapon firing in the ship around him die down, Valcour placed explosives around the tank. He attached a detonator to the cluster of bombs and set the clock for ten minutes. He wanted to be sure his soldiers were clear of the blast radius when it happened and had resolved to hang back to defend the bomb against any Phenotor who attempted to disarm it.

With the second hand quickly descending toward zero, Valcour turned his back to the tank and stood ready for the throngs of Phenotor that were sure to pour into the engine room. After six minutes of silence Valcour began to get antsy. He peered into the hallway to find it empty. Slowly he made his way through the ship; there was not a single living Phenotor to be found

Valcour smiled with a father's pride at the brutal efficiency the men and women of earth displayed in dispatching of the enemy army. Realizing that there was no time to run out of the blast radius now, he wondered why his impending death didn't bother him. It occurred to him that he had grown weary of fighting and didn't realize it until he was reminded of his farm on Earth. Perhaps, he thought as he looked around at the alien innards spread throughout the ship, he was ready to be reunited with his soul. The platoon leader in him shook his head and chuckled at the depth of thought his brain was drowning in. He told himself that he didn't mind dying because Earth was worth dying for; it was a planet of good people and great soldiers. Earth produced proud, strong men and women, not howling vicious creatures like the Phenotor, Valcour thought boastfully.

As the detonator continued its descent Valcour meandered out of the warship to get one last look at Earth's battleship hanging above the planet. He stood staring through the red smog, his oxygen slowly running out, and saluted the giant Earth space shuttle in the sky. Whenever he was in battle and began to feel overwhelmed by the chaos of war, Valcour would look to his ship floating resolutely above him like a skybound rock of Gibraltar. The ship seemed to be watching over him, protecting him. He felt safe though he was a million miles from home. Silently, the ship assured him that, should he fall to the Phenotor, hell would spew from its turrets and rain down on the planet in a fit of vengeance.

A low hum began to float through the jungle, breaking Valcour's train of thought. He quickly aimed his weapon in the direction of the sound expecting to see a Phenotor rover on its way to disable the bomb. Instead what emerged from the trees above him was an Earth escape pod. He tried to wave his saviors away. He shouted in an effort to make them understand that there was no time to land, but the ship refused to leave. The pilot was having trouble keeping it steady; the ship looked as though it was teetering in the sky, unable to decide which way to fall. Valcour wondered what his soldiers were doing when a door opened on the side of the ship and a rope ladder dropped from it. A young fighter was hanging out of the door waving for Valcour to climb the ladder hanging just above his head.

The very moment Valcour grabbed the first rung of the ladder, the pilot of the escape pod shoved the throttle up to maximum thrust, rocketing the ship into a vertical climb. Valcour attempted to continue climbing up the ladder but the force of gravity as the ship climbed into space was too great for him to overcome. He wrapped his wrist around a rung in the ladder and clung as tightly to it as he could.

The speed at which they were rising made his eyes feel like they were about to burst and stunted his breathing, even with his spacesuit on. Valcour became frantic when he realized the rope ladder had dug into his wrist and would soon cut off his hand. The quick climb upward had scrambled his ability to think straight; when he used his knife to cut the rope around his wrist loose he didn't consider the consequences, all he knew was that he wanted the searing pain in his wrist to end.

When the rope split in two Valcour fell away from the ladder. In this moment his senses returned to him as he saw the escape pod above moving quickly away. Time seemed to stand still as he winced in anticipation of his quick fall to the planet below. After a moment he opened one eye to see that the escape pod had stopped moving. He looked around to find that he wasn't falling after all. They had made it out of the atmosphere. Valcour was floating in space.

He let out a quick, triumphant laugh as the bomb detonated on the planet below him. All of Pheno quaked under the pressure of the blast, huge canyons formed like veins around ground zero and a shock wave blasted through space. It struck Valcour in the back like a ten ton wrecking ball and continued moving outward toward the escape pod and the battleship pushing them all into deep space. Pheno hung motionlessly as if the entire planet were frozen in a state of shock, then, as gravity resumed the planet slowly began turning in the darkness once again.

Valcour was catapulted far deeper into space than the two ships. For five days he floated lifelessly through the stars. The battleship was severely damaged in the explosion and was running out of fuel, but when the captain announced that he would call off the search for Valcour and return home the men and women on board threatened mutiny.

Because his oxygen tank had ruptured in the blast and the insulation in his space suit was no match for the chill of deep space Valcour was frozen solid when the ship finally discovered him. The on-board medics were able to keep him frozen long enough to repair the damage done to him. He awoke in perfect health as the battleship slipped through the black hole that led to earth.

The footage of the explosion recorded by the battleship had been playing non-stop on every television on the planet. It was accompanied by a brief biography of Ben Valcour spoken over the picture on his military license. By the time he returned to Earth he was a world renowned celebrity. The name Valcour became synonymous with heroism and bravery in every household on every continent.

The next month was a blur of parades and ceremonies. He became the first Seven Percenter on the cover of a magazine. He chuckled to himself when he saw his browned and sinewy face in a spot usually occupied by the round, creamy skinned faces of "normal people." He felt small when he shared a stage with the powerful men and women of the world. At two hundred and fifteen pounds he was outweighed by most non-Seven Percenter women by at least fifty pounds; the men often exceeded three hundred pounds.

The world began to look differently at Seven Percenters. In a speech given by the President in honor of Valcour's promotion to sergeant he dubbed the Seven Percenters "noble savages," and the world at large agreed. No longer were they seen as disease ridden, mentally unbalanced mongrels with flesh burned by the sun and muscles hardened by toil. Much of the youth of the world began to look up to the soldiers; some even went so far as to rub their hands raw on slabs of rough concrete with the hopes of forming calluses. Incidences like these unnerved the establishment, who called upon the Planetary Congress to place a ban on the intentional marring of the palms and unnecessary or excessive handling of "rough objects," enforceable by law as a means of maintaining public health and safety.

Nonetheless, the general public's newly-born fascination with the Seven Percenters grew. Soldiers found themselves invited to high society parties where they would stand in corners drinking uncomfortably as the rest of the partygoers stole curious glances at them as if they were specimens in a zoo. With increasing regularity, a thick society girl would drag a soldier into a darkened back room and have her way with him in retaliation to an injustice incurred by their fathers or boyfriends.

Valcour met his wife at a party like this, but Marj Brownstone was not like the women who threw themselves at Seven Percenters for shock or irony's sake. In fact, it was Marj's father, the powerful Congressman Brownstone, a man that served on many of the President's advisory boards, who took Valcour aside and informed him that he would be honored if the soldier asked for his youngest daughter's company. He then gave Valcour his credit card and instructed him to show her a good time.

Marj wasn't like the Seven Percenter women that he had known; she had soft pale skin that spilled over her elbows and waist. His hand sunk deep into her back when he laid it upon her. She had a pleasant lilting voice that spoke lethargically in circles about nothing at all. She never got too upset or too excited.

Her eyes had a distant, hazy quality as the government-mandated mood stabilizers worked on her brain behind them. In short, she was the embodiment of all that was considered beauty and grace.

In the beginning of their relationship, Valcour had felt little chemistry between them, but continued seeing her because of the thrill it gave him to see the looks of jealousy on the faces of so called "better men" when they were seen together. This is why he agreed with her father when it was suggested that they marry before he returned to the war, though he worried what his fellow soldiers might think of him marrying a non-Seven Percenter. Many of the soldiers had succumbed to the adoration of the general public. Seven Percenter women became mistresses to powerful men, while some Seven Percenter men continued to provide scandalous thrills for bored society women. However, none of them had maintained a relationship as public as Valcour, and no Seven Percenter, man or woman, would ever dream of being able to marry a non-Seven Percenter.

After the ceremony, Marj took sleeping medicine stating that her brain had been excited by the day and she would rather sleep then risk a mental collapse. Ben sat awake for some time reviewing the itinerary for their honeymoon. When he became too restless to stay at home he found himself outside his platoon's barracks.

Hearing the laughter and shouting from within reminded him of nights on the farm, when everyone would congregate at someone's house to talk, drink and laugh all night long. Eventually someone would get drunk enough to pull out a makeshift guitar, then singing and dancing would waste the hours away. When he entered the barracks, the men and women within fell silent as they studied the man who was able to rise above their low ranks. It was as if they expected him to look different somehow, softer or gentler. Matt Lion broke the stillness in the room by tossing a bottle in Valcour's direction. Valcour caught the bottle without once removing his gaze from the crowd and yanked the cork out of it.

"To Ben Valcour! A damn good soldier, a damn good farmer, and a damn good man! You're gonna be a damn good husband too, I'm sure." Matt announced with an unabashed mirth in his voice. The crowd erupted in cheers and laughter as Valcour lifted the bottle to his mouth. "And Ben..." Matt added "you landed yourself a great woman. Good job soldier." Valcour smiled silently and took a gulp from the bottle as he walked through the crowd. Men patted him on the back as women embraced him and wished him luck. He had known many of these people his entire life and it struck him that he had missed them a great deal in the months since he had been on leave.

They celebrated long into the night, as if they were still in farm country, like the planet had never been attacked and they had never gone to war. The illusion would inevitably be broken when Ben spotted a fresh scar across a smiling soldier's face or a missing finger when a winning hand was tossed onto the card table.

As the sky turned a brilliant violet and Valcour walked home, he couldn't wait for his furlough to be over, to once again fight alongside men and women who truly embraced life. The cell surrounding him suddenly became colder and darker when Valcour realized that he had missed the birth of his son.

"How could I forget?" he wondered out loud. He had pushed thoughts of his pregnant wife from his mind early on in his captivity. He knew that thinking about her pregnancy and all the promise that it held would surely break him. Now that thoughts of the son he had yet to meet crept into his mind he began to despair.

He tried to imagine what his son would be doing in this very instant and realized that he would still be in post-natal incubation. He chuckled meagerly for a second when he thought that he could relate to his son's confinement but a depression washed back over him. He didn't like that he wasn't there to speak on his son's behalf. The child would grow up to be like the general population and not like a Seven Percenter. Although he loved his wife he always felt that the general population was lacking something from their lives, a joy that only comes from knowing pain, a pride in having suffered and stayed strong, laughter in the face of tragedy.

It dawned on him that laughter was the biggest difference between the Seven Percenters and the general population. A Seven Percenter laughs heartily with complete abandon—their entire body is thrown into the moment—whereas a member of the general population titters in restrained spasms. Extreme emotions have become so foreign to them that they often think that they are having a medical episode and quickly take a mood stabilizer to level out.

Valcour began to daydream that his son entered the world hard; a born Seven Percenter. They shipped him off to the old farm to be raised by his neighbors. He smiled and indulged himself in fantasy as the lock in the door clanked with a dull thud. For the first time in over a month the large door creaked open.

Valcour addressed the three Phenotor guards with a haughty aloofness as they entered his cell. "Can I help you?" he asked nonchalantly, as if this happened everyday.

"The commander requests your presence," the guard standing in the center replied in a voice like grinding gears, continuing the tone Valcour had set. No one acknowledged that Valcour had been locked in a dimly lit cell for over a month to rot away into madness and that this was a remarkable occasion.

"Very well then; let's go," Valcour replied with a smirk on his face as he sauntered towards the guards. The three aliens tensed up as the one standing on the left held up a set of shackles. To this Valcour shrugged and held out his wrists. "Can't say I blame you," he stated with a confident wink to the guard in the center. Once shackled, the two guards flanked him holding spears up to each of his shoulder blades and led him into a long corridor. The third guard walked in front of them armed only with a small knife hung from his hip. Valcour's eyes darted around, studying the outside of his cell while the guard in front pulled him along by a length of chain attached to his restraints. They passed a series of doors similar to the one he just came from. If any of his comrades are alive, he figured that they were behind those doors.

At least a dozen human space suits hung from hooks at the end of the long corridor. The aliens outfitted Valcour in one of these suits and switched on the oxygen before turning a dial on a large door. They entered another hallway that branched off in two directions. A red mist poured through one hallway, signifying to Valcour that it led outdoors. The guards silently pulled him in the opposite direction with a jerk. At the end of this hallway was an opulent door with an imposing crest emblazoned upon it.

Their footsteps echoed loudly on the cold hard floor as the group neared the commander's quarters. The lead Phenotor pressed a finger to his ear and spoke: "The prisoner is at your door, sir." A loud click was heard through the door as it slid open. Valcour was shocked to hear them speaking in Earth tongues to each other, and tried to recall if he had ever heard the native Phenotor language being spoken. As he passed through the large doorway and looked toward the commander, Valcour couldn't help but betray the shock he felt.

The commander sat behind a large desk; he didn't look like any Phenotor that Valcour had ever seen. He looked almost human, but not like the general population, more like a shorter, thinner, paler Seven Percenter.

"Sergeant Ben Valcour, it's nice to finally meet you," the commander said pleasantly to the prisoner. Valcour stood motionless with his jaw dropped open. "Why so shocked, Mr. Valcour?"

"Wha… What the hell are you?" As he uttered these words, he heard three clicks followed by hissing sounds. The guards standing around him had removed what Valcour thought were their wide, bony faces, to reveal their true faces underneath. As the commander observed Valcour's astonishment with curiosity, he cocked his head to the side innocently.

"Don't tell me you thought that we looked like that?" the commander asked with laughter in his voice as he raised a finger to what Valcour had thought was the alien's face, now resting under the guard's arm. "Those are our space suits… our armor…" The commander stopped short and rested his chin in his hand. "I suppose it makes it easier to get you people to kill us if you believe that we look that… alien." The commander reclined in his chair and smiled wide. "Well, this certainly helps me prove the point I was about to make. Leave us alone," the commander ordered as he waved a dismissive hand towards the guards, "Mr. Valcour and I have much to discuss."

When the guards had exited the room, the commander motioned for Valcour to sit in a chair facing his desk. As he sat he couldn't stop staring at the bright blue, human-like eyes set in the alien's face. The commander leaned forward with his elbows on his desk ponderously, furrowing his brow as he thought. He began to speak a few times but stopped himself, then finally, "I'll just come out and say it. You are the physical embodiment of evil, you are a mass murderer…" His eyes became slits as he spoke. "You have been the number one cause of Phenotor death for the last two years." His fists were clenched; the muscles in his face were tightened causing the veins in his neck to bulge. "You are the most hated and feared creature on this planet."

For a moment the commander was paralyzed with rage, his muscles twitched as he kept himself from reaching over the desk and strangling Valcour. Then, suddenly, and for no apparent reason, he relaxed, leaned back, spread his arms wide and un-clenched his fists. A compassionate smile inexplicably enveloped his entire face. "But… I forgive you."

Valcour said nothing for a while, still in a state of shock. His first instinct was to leap over the desk and claw out the sympathetic eyes of his captor. He wanted to unleash all the anger he bore toward the creatures that took away his contented life as a farmer and turned him into a killing machine on this one alien, but restrained himself when he remembered the other doors in the corridor and the fellow soldiers that may be trapped behind them.

Valcour leaned forward slowly. "I'm not looking for the forgiveness of monsters," he finally replied in a cold and metered manner. The commander sighed and looked toward the ceiling thoughtfully.

"We are not the monsters, Mr. Valcour, and neither are you; which is why I forgive you and your monstrous behavior. The monsters are your leaders—"

"You started this war, not us!" Valcour involuntarily shouted, in a flash of rage that he quickly suppressed. Leaning back in his chair with feigned relaxation he wondered why he suddenly thought of that moment on the farm after Lion had told him about the attack, he hesitated for a moment upon hearing the news. "What was Lion thinking?" he wondered. It seemed so long ago and he was a different animal then. Someone he could no longer relate to.

"Have you ever seen a Phenotor ship in flight, Valcour? Have you ever seen us wielding projectile weaponry? We are not a warring culture and we are certainly not equipped with the technology to get anywhere near your planet."

Valcour smiled smugly. "Not anymore you're not."

The commander spoke slowly and deliberately in his tight jawed response. "If you are referring to the ship you destroyed last year, it was a mining ship. It was only able to get as far as our third moon which is made of the ore used to convert our fuel." The commander, caught off guard by the emotions stirring within him, swallowed hard and pretended he noticed something of interest outside the window. After walking to it silently, he continued with his back to Valcour. "After you massacred a fleet of civilian miners armed with nothing but simple tools, you proceeded to detonate the on-board fuel refinery, resulting in the deaths of untold millions of men, women and children." When the commander turned back around he found Valcour sitting stone faced and looking straight ahead. The commander began to feel empowered as he walked toward him slowly.

"Now you know they looked like your friends and family and children as they burned, now you know that they sounded human as they screamed to the heavens in a plea for their lives, finding only the black stain of your battleship above them. Now that you know what you killed, tell me, was it worth it?" The commander stared coldly at Valcour who slumped in his chair staring silently at the ground. "If you can't manage that then just tell me why, what did all these people do to you?" The commander added after a moment as he leaned in closer to the earthling soldier.

"…But the turrets, the air grapples…" Valcour muttered to himself, almost pleadingly.

"All used for mining ore," the commander responded solemnly.

"You… you attacked us first." Valcour tried to be assertive but couldn't muster the confidence.

"Had you ever heard of Isle De Rio before it was supposedly attacked? Do you know anybody from there, or anybody who knew anybody from there?" The commander stood up straight in front of Valcour with his arms akimbo as he shrugged his shoulders. "It was made up, Ben, the whole thing. It was a ruse; you and your people have been used..."

Valcour tried to block the commander's words out. Having been in solitary confinement for as long as he was, he knew he would be extremely susceptible to suggestion. He told himself not to continue this conversation, he told himself to sit quietly, to stonewall the commander.

"Why would they do that?" he caught himself asking with a thin veil of imperiousness.

"Because the men and women who control the Earth now want more: they want our fuel, they want an intergalactic empire. You see, at one point we all came from the same place, Valcour..." Valcour lifted his head in astonishment, his mouth agape. "That's right; we're human just like you. At least we were. Our people have since evolved, adapted to our atmosphere," the commander stated, proudly displaying the translucent blue skin wrapped around his gaunt wrist to Valcour as he turned away.

"Ever since my ancestors left Earth, the unified government has been hunting us." He continued tilting his head upward as if the Phenotor history was being projected onto the ceiling. "When they finally found us several years ago, they extended to us an olive branch bearing rotted fruit. They offered us the opportunity to work for them, to build their new technologies, to give to Earth Pheno's greatest asset: an energy source far more potent and plentiful than anything found on your planet. In exchange, we would be able to live under the suffocating regime that our ancestors had rejected so many years ago. Naturally, we respectfully declined. They left, and we never heard another word from our long forgotten brethren until they sent their second class citizens to eradicate us."

Valcour withdrew from the moment. He curled up in his seat, resting his upper arms on his knees and slowly swaying his head back and forth. It was a testament to his mental strength that he had made it this long without his psyche shattering completely, but now fractures were starting to form along the edges of his mind.

"No, no, no... you're evil, I'm the hero, I am..." he involuntary muttered under his breath, trying to convince himself.

The commander smiled slyly at the broken man in front of him. "No, Sergeant Ben Valcour, you are the villain in this tale." He put his hand on Valcour's quivering shoulder. "But I am here to give you the opportunity to redeem yourself." He crouched down low in an attempt to infiltrate Valcour's line of sight. "There are many Phenotor posing as Earthlings right now, infiltrating lower levels of your government," he continued in a soothing, fatherly tone.

Valcour shook hard and stared vacantly at the ground, as if his mind had gone numb. "How?"

"It isn't difficult for us to bathe in a sun lamp, gain a few pounds, and build up a tolerance to the levels of oxygen you have in your atmosphere." The commander pulled a small piece of paper from his desk. "Like I was saying, we have men and women working on Earth. Their goal is to gain enough political clout and public outrage to end this war peacefully, but we need your help to truly sway the public opinion. We believe that you could get elected into office and once there use your power to... well, to save your soul."

"Politics?" Valcour questioned in a confused stupor.

"You see Sergeant, the thing is, the Phenotor may not be the best fighters with the best weapons, but this is our home and we are a tenacious breed if nothing else. We will keep fighting and dying until you stop invading us or we are all dead. Now ask yourself what the Earth's objective is. Is it punishment for an invasion on an imaginary island, or is it the eradication of every man, woman and child on this planet?" The commander craned his neck to follow Valcour's eyes as Valcour tried to turn away. "Tell me, what was the objective of your last mission?"

Valcour sat silently, unwilling to reveal military orders.

"Oh, you can tell me now. I know what it was and we both know the mission was destined to fail," the commander coaxed in a dulcet tone. Valcour looked up at the commander inquisitively with sunken eyes. "There was no communications base was there? You saw that with your own two eyes, didn't you?" The commander's eyes were turned down compassionately.

"I know the true objectives of this past mission, and they were twofold. First, two major metropolitan areas existed within the blast radius of your Air Bomb. Do you know what it feels like to die from an overdose of oxygen? I am told that it makes the blood in your body feel like molten lava. Men, women, children…indiscriminately… that's on you, Ben."

Valcour sat silently, staring back down at the ground.

"The second objective, Sergeant Valcour, was to make a martyr out of you. Specifics of your mission were leaked to us intentionally. Your leaders wanted us to be ready for you. They wanted you, Earth's greatest hero, to be ambushed and killed; they wanted to pump new life into Earth's anger at Pheno, to redouble the war effort, and to be frank, they have succeeded. Our planet is being bombarded like never before."

Valcour's head rocked back and forth wildly on his neck, his face tight and teeth clenched as he muttered under his breath in disbelief.

The commander looked down at the piece of paper in his hand. "But we didn't do what they had thought we would. We didn't kill any of your soldiers, Ben. They have all been kept sedated these past months and fed through a tube. We have repaired an Earth cargo ship that crashed on our planet some time ago. The ship is waiting just outside this building, and contains enough fuel to make it back to Earth. I propose you get your men, tell them nothing of what we have spoken about, get on the cargo ship and return to Earth." The commander got in close to Valcour with the paper clutched between his fingers; Valcour had remained curled in a ball with his hands buried in his torso. "This piece of paper has contact information for one of our men on the inside. After a week home, get in touch with him. Help us end this war peacefully; save what's left of your soul."

As the commander slipped the piece of paper into Valcour's chest pocket, the sergeant sprung to life. He smoothly ran the edge of a knife through the commander's jugular. Shocked and gasping for breath, the commander held his gushing neck with both hands as he fell backward over his desk. Valcour leaped from his seat and fled from the commander's quarters, leaving him writhing in a pool of his own blood like a fish out of water.

Before the guards had a chance to react, Valcour burst into the hallway and forced his blade into the temple of one guard.

He then managed to pin the second guard's spear between his arm and torso as it was lunged at him. He snapped the weapon in two with his free hand while simultaneously kicking the attacker in the chest. As the alien stumbled backward Valcour launched the broken half of the spear through the alien's right eye, killing him instantly. At the same moment that the final guard reached for the knife sheathed on his hip, he realized that the blade was lodged in his fellow guard's skull. Unarmed, he turned on his heels and headed for the exit. Valcour, in an adrenalin fueled frenzy, overtook him and snapped his neck with one swift motion.

Expecting to find more guards, Valcour quietly stalked through the hall toward the oxygenated holding cells, but found the building was empty. With the push of a button he opened the cell door to find six of his soldiers strapped to beds with feeding tubes protruding from their stomachs and intravenous syringes tapped into their necks. He flicked a switch, intending to illuminate the room, but instead the tubes retracted from the comatose soldiers and the restraints unclasped.

As the men and women began to regain consciousness, Valcour opened another cell freeing four more soldiers. In a final cell he found Matt Lion alone, similarly strapped into a bed and sedated. After freeing Lion with the flick of a switch Valcour returned to the rest of the platoon in the hallway.

"Does anybody know where the hell we are?" one of the soldiers asked while rubbing his eyes.

"We are in a Phenotor prison. We have been captive for over a month," replied Valcour causing murmurs of alarm to grow from the group.

"My God, it seems like we were just in the jungle a minute ago," an astonished soldier replied as she held her forehead in bewilderment.

"Then consider yourselves lucky; now let's get the hell out of here," Valcour commanded as he charged through the corridor. "There are some space suits at the end of the hall. You ready, Lion?" he asked without turning toward the soldier who had just stumbled from his cell.

"Let's go," Lion answered, blinking his eyes as the waking world slowly returned to him.

The platoon made its way out of the prison without running into another Phenotor. Upon exiting the structure, they found the cargo ship waiting outside just as the commander had promised. Valcour was shocked to find that, other than the cargo ship, there was nothing around them. The prison was in the middle of a vacuous desert, only sand could be seen for miles in every direction.

As the ship rocketed skyward into the blackness of space, Valcour peered out a rear portal to make sure that their ascent went unnoticed. Looking at the planet, he remembered the first time he saw it. The mass of solid red clouds hanging in space was now covered in blue pock marks where the Earthlings had oxygenated the atmosphere. As he studied the planet Valcour tried to imagine what molten lava would feel like in his veins.

With the shake of his head Valcour laughed at himself for expecting to find a battalion of Phenotor spaceships charging into space to shoot them down. He thought about when the commander had asked him if he had ever seen a Phenotor ship in flight and realized now that he hadn't.

That's when it struck him.

He was on his farm, Lion had just told him of the invasion. Stuck on a thought, he hesitated. Now he remembered what had made him hesitate in that moment, a thought he couldn't recall when the commander was speaking to him: the rumination, not of a soldier but of a farmer, and of a man who was very interested in the recently discovered alien race. He had followed every account of the Phenotor in every newspaper and television program he could get his hands on. Fascinated, he wanted to know everything there was about them. He was so interested in this other race, he realized now, because they had reminded him so much of the Seven Percenters: a community-driven, agricultural society. An alien race living by the sweat of their backs in a wild land. He respected them and as he heard about the attack on Isle De Rio, a place he had never heard of before, the incident seemed so counter-intuitive to everything he had ever learned of the Phenotor. He paused for a moment, and doubted.

Within that moment of doubt Ben Valcour reached a difficult conclusion. It didn't matter if the alien invasion was real or fabricated, what mattered was that war would be declared. The time had come, they could no longer live in the shadows, and they would be called upon to fight. He had studied history; he knew what happened to those who refused to get in line behind the rallying cry of patriotism in a time of war. Should the Seven Percenters not take up arms against the great evil in the sky they would be labeled traitorous sympathizers, and hunted down with fervor equal to that reserved for the alien invaders; they would become the villain and a far easier villain to destroy than aliens a galaxy away.

Valcour understood that to save his people from extinction at the hands of the world government the Phenotor must fall at the hands of the Seven Percenters. In the moment of that realization, Ben Valcour the farmer died and was replaced by a ruthless soldier. He made a conscious decision to disregard everything he would learn of the Phenotor, he shut out every inkling in his mind that his government was not to be trusted. He became the quintessential patriot, and a fearless, righteous warrior.

Now, staring at the ever-shrinking Pheno through the ship's portal, feeling the commander's shred of paper weigh heavy in his pocket, he knew that he had already made a decision long ago. A decision constructed from the belief that a just act which endangers his family is a greater sin than an evil act that protects it. What use is the infinitely sided prism of truth in times of war, when the victor is declared the righteous hero? What is right could just as easily be wrong if you stared at the other side of the stars for long enough.

With a child, a wife and a billion men and women who would die for him, Valcour knew that he could never turn traitor.

What the men and women in powerful places on either side of the war told him didn't matter. The people that mattered were his family and friends. After all, he was fighting for them; not for a cause, but for a people.

Valcour made sure nobody was watching him when he pulled the contact information from his pocket. He stared at it for a brief moment before holding a lighter up to it and flicking the flint.

A small spark burst from the lighter but failed to grow into a flame. He flicked the lighter twice more, cursed, and then tossed it aside.

"Maybe later," he muttered to himself as he carefully folded the piece of paper into a small square and buried it deep within an interior pocket.

"Maybe."

CULT MOVIE
By Scott Sheaffer

Excerpt from "The RB-999 Codes" by Ervin Roberts.
First published in *Astonishing Adventures* (October, 1950)

"Who does he think he is?"

Jax, an obsidian colored android with red lenses, swiveled his head to study the humans around him in the Oval Office and their reactions to the speaker. President Colbert, a heavyset man over six feet tall with thick iron gray hair, sat at his desk with his jaws clenched as he glared at the video screen. In a chair to the President's left sat a general in a crisp army dress uniform. The General held his hat. His chestnut colored hair had turned white on the sides. In the background, a younger man nodded and took notes. Then there was the speaker, a stooped man who had gone bald on the top. What remained of his dark hair formed a semi-circle clinging to the side of his head. He was Roberts, the Chief of Staff. Jax scanned the President, and the android's emotional appraisal circuitry calculated whether Roberts' indignation had curried any favor. The readout only indicated a seething anger directed toward the video screen as President Colbert replayed the message yet again. Roberts continued, "A common street thug with illusions of grandeur. That's all he is."

"More like a modern Genghis Khan," General Atwater said. "Khan welded barbaric tribes and clans together into an unstoppable force just like Magnus has united New York's street gangs. Mr. President, he's not one I'd underestimate."

The President's jaws clenched tighter. With the country on the brink of collapse, he had restored order. All the nation needed was an iron fist and a house cleaning of sheep who bleated about the Constitution. His forces had swept through cities which had fallen under the control of criminal gangs. Now, with federal troops poised to retake New York City, this thug calling himself Magnus threatened the President's very regime.

Jax detected the President's hidden irritation toward Atwater's comments. That irritation mingled with recognition of Atwater's wisdom. Jax assessed that the President, though insecure about threats to his power, was intelligent enough to recognize good advice and disciplined enough to rein in his anger toward the general. The President's found it more difficult to control his growing rage toward the video message that was his primary battle.

On the screen, one of Magnus's barbarically clad underlings delivered his leader's message while, in the background, Magnus glowered from a throne of skulls. The gangster concluded his leader's message by warning, "Keep out of New York, or every soldier, sailor, marine, and airman under your command will learn how ineffective those chips really are."

The President sat and glared at the now blank screen while various staff members resumed their arguments.

"But he can't actually control our troops through their neural chips. He's not capable."

"Without the codes he took, we can't control them either."

"Good thing we never went to an all-android military. 'Least the humans still obey out of habit. Droids'd be more vulnerable."

"Androids cost more too."

The President's lip twitched and bared his teeth. "Enough!" he shouted. "This thug isn't pushing me around!"

"But sir," Roberts said. "His threat—"

The President responded without even looking at Roberts.

"The troops will figure it out soon enough."

Bertlasio, the deputy chief of staff, said, *"Maybe they'll obey anyway. Lesser leaders than you—the Caesars, the Napoleons—did what was necessary and seized power. Their soldiers followed without neural chips."*

The general spoke. *"Won't work. Not after the way they were tricked into the neural chips, told they were for their own safety, finding MIAs, rescuing POWs, etc., etc. There's resentment. We'd have a mutiny on our hands."*

Jax's analysis showed danger for General Atwater in the President's initial reaction. In the end though, the President maintained control. He nodded, looked at Atwater, and said, *"We have to take action."*

Roberts protested, *"But the troops will find out faster if—"*

The President cut Roberts off. *"That's why I'm sending someone Magnus will never see coming."* The President pressed a button on his desk's control panel. A force field rose around him and his advisors. He looked at his staff. *"Not a word about neural chips. I'm pitching a story about atomic weapons."* The President picked up his communicator. *"Okay. Bring him in."*

A tall, rangy, gray-eyed man entered flanked by two Secret Service agents. He wore the gray uniform of a work camp prisoner. His dark hair was cropped short in a camp regulation haircut. Jax transmitted the man's image to the national archives whose systems revealed the reason for the President's caution. The man was Captain Kenneth Kemp, a commando attached to the 511th Regiment during the last war. Kemp engaged in numerous operations behind enemy lines and was highly successful. The man was capable of killing with a single blow of his bare hands. Also, Kemp was no friend of authority.

Unimpressed by his surroundings, Kemp sneered at the President. Then Kemp's eyes narrowed and his jaw clenched when he saw Jax.

"Ah, Captain Kemp. Welcome," the President said, smiling and rising from his desk. *"I'd shake your hand, son, but security measures, you know. Secret Service would never allow it."*

Kemp said nothing. He spat on the floor of the oval office. For an instant, anger flashed over the President's face. Then he smiled again as he walked around his desk and approached the force field which separated him from Kemp. "I understand you're a specialist at infiltration, sabotage, things of that nature," the President said. "Records say you're one of the best. The Army could use more like you."

With clear contempt, Kemp studied the President a moment and said, "Yeah? Court-marital says different."

"A mistake," the President said. "One you've got a chance to fix." The President turned his back to Kemp. "Listen. You should be a hero," he said walking toward his desk. The President sat on the edge of the desk, facing Kemp again. "Some of the things you've done—that piece of work on the Yalu was something else."

"A damn droid cost us fifteen lives on that one," Kemp said through gritted teeth as he glared at Jax.

"Yes," the President said. "Jamming or some other enemy disruption of the android's circuits. Correct?"

"Droids are unreliable. Politicians and rear echelon desk jockeys think the things are infallible," Kemp said.

The President didn't acknowledge the criticism. "You've had some trouble adjusting to civilian life. Landed in jail."

"Don't like being pushed around."

"What did they give you? Ten years for breaking that cop's jaw? Ten years away from your wife. You're going to miss seeing your daughter grow up." The President paused and grew more solemn. Kemp was a difficult read. Probably make a great poker player. Still, subtle signs of expression in Kemp's eyes told the President that his words struck home. He followed up. "How would you like to fix all that, Kemp? No more jail. Charges dropped. Court-martial overturned."

Kemp had gone back into his shell, but the President was confident that Kemp knew the pardon offer was sincere. Kemp looked away in thought, and then looked the President in the eye. "What's the catch?" he asked.

The President nodded. "I need you to do something for me."

Subject: I Miss You Too
Date: 6/18
From: AAChatter@Requiesat.com
To: Daniel@machtele.net

Hey Sport,

How ya been? I've missed you too since I died. We can still keep in touch through e-mails, chats, and I'm even starting a blog. Plus, I hear they might open a new virtual reality where the dead can interact with living friends and family.

Listen, I'm sorry for telling your mother what you said, but she and I worry about you. When you grow up and have kids, you'll understand. For now, take my word for it. Live a long, full life in the physical world. Don't be in a rush to get your mind uploaded into the Consciousness Data Bank, okay? You're only ten.

I'm afraid your friends have told you some tall tales. They don't give us godlike powers like in the old science fiction stories about people living in computer programs. We're maintaining a human society after all so this world won't grow too bizarre for you or even one of our descendents when they join us here. Besides, the administrators say that as much as people seek to avoid it, we need some conflict and tension. Too much isn't good, but we need some. That's why people watch sports even though their team could win or lose. That's why good stories have conflict and suspense. Who likes stories where there aren't any problems? So, the administrators don't want us stepping in front of cars, jumping off tall buildings, etc., etc., and becoming too inhuman. Here in the Data Bank's virtual realities, we feel pain and lots of it when we do that stuff. Plus, there's the inconvenience of being reset. But hey, on the bright side, we don't need to work, and we can choose the age our avatars look.

I'm sorry to hear that your mother sold my books. I wanted to pass my collection on to you and your brother. I had some neat things in there. Not everything ever written has been uploaded ya know. I had some old twentieth century pulps in there. Specially treated or they would have never lasted this long. There were a few with stories by this guy named Ervin Roberts. They based one of my favorite movies on something he wrote.

Anyway, if you need to talk, I'm here, okay?

Love,
Dad

Excerpt from "The RB-999 Codes" by Ervin Roberts. First published in *Astonishing Adventures* (October 1950)

Silent except for the water running down their scuba suits, the commandoes emerged from the East River as they'd emerged from other rivers many times on missions behind Chinese and Russian lines. Levy took point. After he gave the all clear, his comrades glided into the shadows of nearby buildings and slipped out of their wetsuits. They pulled their weapons and costumes from their waterproof protective packs.

Within moments, the soldiers looked like typical specimens of the vermin which had overrun the nation's cities: modern Vandals and Visigoths...the street gangs.

"Wonder if the droid short-circuited in the drink," Morgan muttered.

"No such luck," Horton whispered back.

The android Jax swiveled his rust-proofed, obsidian colored head toward the hushed conversation. Jax internally lowered the decibel level of his speaking voice to match the volume of Morgan and Horton's speech.

"Gentlemen, I am designed for submersible use in aquatic settings. It would be most illogical if—"

"Can it, metal mouth!" Horton said in a harsh whisper. "Nobody asked for a lecture."

"Come on, fellas. Ease up on old Jaxy," Hibbard said as he adjusted his Brooklyn Dodgers cap.

Jax's logic system made a brief attempt to reconcile the soldiers' curiosity about android aquatic capabilities with their rebuke of an attempted answer. The system advised an emotional appraisal which revealed insincerity. After the system reached a conclusion, Jax focused on Horton and Morgan. "I understand, gentlemen. Sarcasm." Jax turned away and popped open the compartment in his forearm that housed his computer link. Although he shielded the screen with his opposite hand, a faint glow still showed.

"What the hell you doing?" hissed a voice that Jax recognized.

Jax's sensory system "felt" a powerful hand on his shoulder. He turned and saw Captain Kemp looming over him. Kemp's jaw clenched. Veins bulged along the corded muscles of his bull neck. The commando's gray eyes blazed in the pale starlight.

"I asked what you were doing," Kemp demanded.

"My apologies, Captain. I was conducting a check to ensure that the monitoring links were operational."

"Yeah? About that. Shut it down."

"Captain?" Jax said.

Kemp scowled. "I don't need the top brass looking over my shoulder when I work."

Jax interrupted "Proper protocol—" In response, Kemp grabbed Jax by the collar and jammed the barrel of his automatic under the android's chin.

"Listen, Mr. Protocol; if Magnus has a mole at H.Q., monitoring will put us up the creek without a paddle. Got me?"

Jax started to protest. "If Magnus knew about the mission, he would..."

"He wouldn't need to carry out his threats to deal with a small team like ours," Kemp answered. "Destroying the world is only necessary if the President sends in overwhelming force."

The android's lenses widened as he looked toward the other commandos for some sign of support against Kemp's arbitrary command which contradicted standard procedure. The other commandoes didn't appear to notice the confrontation. They continued reconning their surroundings.

Kemp gripped Jax tighter. "You know I didn't want a damn android along fouling up this mission," Kemp said through his *clenched teeth. "You gonna listen?"*

"Yes, Captain."

"Good." Kemp said as he relaxed his grip and lowered his weapon. "We gotta get this right. The world's depending on us."

Jax said nothing. The android knew who was really depending on Kemp's team.

Far Beyond the Screens We Know
July 16th
RB-999

I became a fan long before I died.

Yeah, I know in places it's cheesy. But what do you expect from 20th century special effects? Director Gregory Ellis really wanted this to look like a film made in the 1970s-80s. His mania for authenticity made him limit himself to those decades' filmmaking technology.

Besides, I overlook the shortcomings because I love that general era. In fact, that's why, since I died, one of my favorite virtual reality locations is the 2003 version of Manhattan complete with a big *Wicked* ad that runs down the side of a Times Square building, *Gothika* posters near the subway entrances, and newsstands that feature *New York Post* newspapers with back covers that blurt some outrageous sports headline.

I first saw *RB-999* in my early teens. I watched it many times in the years before my death. I didn't watch it again for quite a while after they uploaded my mind to the Consciousness Data Bank— our very own high tech version of Heaven.

Critics describe *RB-999* as *The Warriors* and *Escape from New York* meet *The Dirty Dozen.* That's apt.

Based on a story by Ervin Roberts, it's set in a dystopian future. Following an economic collapse, crime and hyperinflation run rampant. Street gangs rule the big cities, and democracy has been destroyed. The President is a dictator who controls the armed forces through neural chips that are implanted in military personnel and linked to a computer called RB-999. If the soldiers disobey, the neural chips can be used to cause excruciating pain and even allow the President to remotely control soldiers in zombie fashion if need be. The President scraps the Constitution and wages a brutal campaign, slaughtering innocent and gangster alike, to restore order.

Followers of The Great Magnus, who has united New York City's street gangs under his rule, steal the codes to the RB-999. After the theft, Magnus's followers infect the computer's artificial intelligence with a virus that erases the code from the government's data bases. (It wasn't called a virus because the original story was written long before that term came into vogue.) Magnus's followers also destroy the government's ability to change the code.

The President sends a former Special Forces officer named Kemp after the codes. Kemp was court-martialed before the neural chip program got underway. Deceived into thinking he's retrieving codes for the nation's nuclear arsenal and preventing a catastrophe, Kemp recruits a team. It comprises Special Forces troops he's worked with previously, including Hibbard, Horton, Morgan, Levy, Edwards, Rodham, Sloan, Sloznik, Lang, and Perez. The President orders Kemp take to take the android Jaxon ("Jax") along. Kemp doesn't want to, but the President says that the android is going to have to retrieve and carry the codes back. There is no secure way to transmit them from New York to Washington without risking an intercept by enemy spies.

Once inside Manhattan, Kemp orders Jax to shut off all monitoring from headquarters. This causes the President to worry that Kemp is attempting a double cross.

Members of Kemp's team die one by one. They infiltrate the city and reach Magnus's headquarters. The group flees once Jax downloads the codes and erases them from Magnus's system.

There are some miscommunications which cause Kemp's superiors to think he's taking the data himself, possibly for blackmail or to sell to enemy powers. They wonder if he's learned what the codes are really for. This situation is exacerbated after all communication is lost and reconnaissance shows that Kemp isn't following the original evacuation plan.

The final act gets pretty wild as Kemp's team has to dodge gangsters and deal with problems that arise from the President's belief that Kemp is double-crossing him.

Radio City Music Hall in the 2003 Virtual Manhattan will screen *RB-999* every other day up through August 6th of this year—the date the story is supposed to take place. That's the trouble with movies set in the near future. It's inevitable that the day the story takes place on will arrive and pass.

Posted by Alexander Anstile

Requiescat—The Social Network for the Dead
User Profile

Alexander Anstile

Gender: *Male*

Age Deceased: *36*

Years Since Upload: *5*

About Me: *I have two sons by my former widow. She's moved on and remarried.*

Interests: *Writing*
Movies
The 20th and Early 21st Centuries
History
Science Fiction

My Blogs: *Far Beyond the Screens We Know*
AAAfterlife

Requiescat Blogs
Keep your loved ones - living and dead - updated.

Blogging, a popular pastime in the early 21ˢᵗ century, is a great way to keep your loved ones updated on your afterlife. Begin blogging today!

Issues? Concerns? Problems? Contact Jarleth, your administrating artificial intelligence. He will answer directly or in avatar form.

Excerpt from "The RB-999 Codes" by Ervin Roberts. First published in *Astonishing Adventures* (October 1950)

"I told 'em I didn't need trouble from fouled up droids," Kemp said.

"I assure you, I am mostly functional," Jax said.

"Shut up and stay here!" Kemp snarled. "I'll see if it's clear. Hibbard! Keep an eye on this bucket of bolts."

Hibbard nodded.

Not a sound marked Kemp's passing as he jogged down the tunnel. Before he vanished, Jax began a system scan to fully assess the damage the magnetic net had done to him. Information relevant to his mission orders appeared incomplete.

"Corporal Hibbard," Jax said, "a question."

"What is it, Jaxy?" Hibbard asked while still peering in the direction Kemp had gone.

"I have instructions pertaining to the data I retrieved."

"Yeah? What about those atomic codes?" Hibbard asked, alert for any trouble down the tunnel. The android paused. Jax's instructions said not to divulge the true nature of the data to Kemp or his team.

Jax continued, "My instructions are to bring the data to President Colbert and to keep it out of the wrong hands."

"So? What's the question, Jaxy?"

"What are the wrong hands?"

"Oh, I dunno. The bad guys I suppose," Hibbard answered as he continued watching the tunnel.

"How do I identify these 'bad guys'?" Jax asked.

Pulling back his Dodgers cap, Hibbard wiped his brow and glanced at Jax. "You know. Bad guys. Evil people. People who hurt others. Hurt innocent people for money or power, just so they can be a big shot or something."

Jax started to respond. "I'm afraid that doesn't clarify—"

"Cram the chatter," Kemp said as he emerged from the darkness. "We want out, we gotta move now!"

Far Beyond the Screens We Know
July 17th
R.I.P. Charles Spears...Again?

I thought something like this wasn't supposed to happen.

First things first.

Spears was a minor actor. His passing caused a mere ripple in the news world. I knew who he was because of his roles in movies including *Bloodbath IV, Skyfall, Beyond the Realms of Death,* and, of course, *RB-999* which is enjoying regular showings at the virtual 2003 Radio City Music Hall. (For a discussion of *RB-999* see my July 16th post.) The screenings coincide with the countdown to the date the story takes place. None of Spears's movies were big hits. At a time in the 20th century, they'd have been called B-movies. Still later they would have been direct to video. Just a small group of genre fans remember these movies. I'm one of them. So, I noticed his death despite the relative lack of fanfare on entertainment networks. At least, that's the attention he got the first time he died.

See, his original death occurred decades ago, and he got uploaded here. Something curious about his second death garnered a lot more attention. <u>We're not supposed to die in here!</u> This is it. We're supposed to wander these virtual Elysian Fields for all time and eternity. (Well, at least until the Sun goes nova and incinerates the Earth millions of years from now, though I hear there'll be contingency plans for that too.)

There's a tone of panic in the reports. Infinity Six administrators have scheduled a press conference. Strangely, there is no word on whether Jarleth will address us. Within the program, he is omniscient and omnipresent. If anyone knows what went wrong, wouldn't he? Wouldn't he be best suited to explain?

Posted by Alexander Anstile

Far Beyond the Screens We Know
July 22nd
The Dead Are Dying

Since my last post, I saw the movie *RB-999* two more times. Each time, on the following morning, I saw an obituary for a different actor who played a member of Kemp's team. The first time it was Dermod O'Brian. Mercy Braun soon followed. At this rate, by the time we reach August 6th of this year (the "futuristic" date on which the film takes place), there won't be anyone left from the cast.

There's panic about the return of total death. There's been a revival of religion. For the first time in decades, scared people are placing their hopes in a spiritual afterlife rather than trusting nothing but this technological one.

The only thing that keeps hysteria in check is the knowledge that all the deaths have been confined to actors connected to one film—so far.

Some people speculate and spread rumors that the deaths aren't even real, that they're part of some publicity stunt promoting an old, almost forgotten film. Others think there's a program glitch which is causing the deaths of actors whose characters died in the film.

Jarleth still hasn't made a statement.

Posted by Alexander Anstile

Excerpt from "The RB-999 Codes" by Ervin Roberts. First published in *Astonishing Adventures* (October 1950)

Jax struggled with the bandages as Kemp collapsed against the base of the wall. Jax looked up and scanned for hostiles in the churchyard which loomed above them. Then, the android turned back to Kemp. With Hibbard dead, only Jax and Kemp remained. The android's own damage caused only a minor disruption to his operations. However, without treatment, Kemp's loss of blood would soon cause the man's death.

Movement caught Kemp's eye. He shoved Jax aside and rolled in the opposite direction. Bullets sparked against the wall where he and Jax had sat a mere moment before. The commando came out of his roll and fired. A distant shadow slumped, and an almost inaudible clatter told of a weapon dropped by now lifeless hands.

Jax came back to Kemp with the bandages, but Kemp shoved him away. "Get moving!" Kemp said as he looked back over his shoulder. "Get to that aerosub, and get those codes out of here!"

"Captain! Wait!" Jax said as he lunged back toward Kemp.

"Move! Now!" Kemp ordered. "I'll hold 'em off. Don't wait for me! I'll find my own ticket out."

Jax turned and ran toward Battery Park while Kemp sought cover and began firing. Jax looked back and saw Kemp run around a corner. An instant later, an explosion shot smoke and flames back from the way Kemp went.

Jax raced toward Battery Park—alone.

Subject: Death and Armageddon
Date: 7/26
From: AAChatter@Requiesat.com
To: Jarleth@Requiesat.com, InfinitySixAdmin@InfinitySix.com

Dear Jarleth and Infinity Six Administrators,

I'm writing about the recent death announcements for several actors who appeared in a movie called *RB-999*. All four physically died years ago. The recent death announcements concerned the deaths of their uploaded minds. By coincidence, all four died in the order their characters died in the movie.

I am, of course, worried because, with the advances in electronic storage, we're supposed to be immortal in here. I know, Jarleth, that you are designed to protect this system from viruses and from system degradation.

Is it possible that you've missed some system glitch, and that the actors' deaths relate to showings of the movie at Radio City Music Hall?

I shudder to think that minds are being erased or even that something like this is possible. Are these death announcements publicity stunts? We *RB-999* lovers are a small but fanatical group.

Please advise. Panic is growing. People fear this may be the start of a wider breakdown. Please ease the concern of those who are under your care.

Alexander Anstile

Excerpt from "The RB-999 Codes" by Ervin Roberts. First published in Astonishing Adventures (October 1950)

The screen flickered and the President's face appeared again. "What do you think you're doing, Kemp?" the President asked in a serious tone tinged with menace.

Jax pressed the speak button on the chance that his radio-screen had started functioning again. "Mr. President," Jax said. "Mr. President, can you hear me?"

The President didn't acknowledge Jax's message. It hadn't gone through.

With a half-smile, the President shook his head. "I see you're flying east over the ocean. That's not the route back here. You need to reconsider, my friend." The President tossed up his hands and sighed. "Okay. You don't want to talk? Keep watching your screen. Your wife and daughter have some special guests." The scene shifted to a home kitchen. A woman bound to a chair tried to scream, but a gag muffled her cries. Her eyes were wide with terror. Tears had streaked mascara down her cheeks. With her were two agents of the secret police. They wore dark suits, dark glasses, and fedoras. One held a crying baby.

The President cut in on the audio feed. "Who should my men start with, Kemp? Your wife? Your daughter?" The President paused. "All right, boys. Kemp's a hard case. Start with his daughter." One agent produced a wicked looking needle. While his partner held the baby's ankle, the agent with the needle slowly pushed it into the child's heel, eliciting shrieks. Through her gag, the girl's mother protested and begged. Her struggles against her bonds intensified.

Jax analyzed the situation. Nothing in his codes or programming compelled the android to help the mother and child. Jax estimated that if he put the aerosub on autopilot, it would take twelve minutes and sixteen seconds to repair the communication system so he could speak to the President and explain that Kemp was dead and Jax was flying east to avoid the anti-aircraft systems which government intelligence didn't know about. More relevant to the mission, Jax reviewed what Hibbard had said about evil. Were the President's actions compliant with the definition of evil? If so—

The President spoke, and Jax suspended the analysis. The President said, "I've scrambled interceptors, Kemp. Don't make me shoot you down."

Jax knew it was an empty threat. Destroying the aerosub could also destroy the codes.

"Am I getting through to you, Kemp?" the President asked. He waited a moment for a response. When his patience ran out, he spoke to the agents. "Okay, boys, how about we work on one of those pretty little eyes?"

In response, the screen showed a close up of the bloody needle as the agent slipped it out of the baby's heel, lifted it toward her face, and held it close to her eyes.

Jax did not fully understand why he did what he did next. He turned the aerosub south, on direct route to Washington, D.C. Jax rationalized that turning south was in compliance with the President's orders, though it put the mission at risk because the course lay through the anti-aircraft system.

"Ah, I see you've changed course, Kemp," the President said. "Very good. You've saved your daughter's eye—for now. Keep behaving, and we'll work this out." After a pause, the President looked annoyed. "Still not talking?" He pursed his lips. "Maybe you can't. Just stay on course then. My men will stay with your wife and daughter until I get that data back. Understand?" The President smirked as if at a private joke. "I'm sure you do," he added before the screen went blank.

Jax called up the schematic of the anti-aircraft system which he had copied while removing the RB-999 codes from Magnus's computer system. The android plotted an evasive course with the highest probability of getting the aerosub through the defenses intact. If successful, Jax resolved to put the aerosub on autopilot and repair the communication system.

Far Beyond the Screens We Know
August 4th
The Mystery of RB-999

Remember the rumors that the deaths of RB-999 actors were an elaborate promo? Remember?

Today I saw something. I saw something which made it hard to believe those rumors—no matter how much I want them to be true. I'm praying those rumors are true. Yes, you can laugh all you want, I said praying. Never thought you'd hear me admit that, did you?

I now know for sure that this threat reaches beyond actors in an old movie. It had only been them dying until today. Now I'm worried about much more because there's one death in the movie I hadn't thought about until now.

Jarleth has failed to answer questions about the deaths.

How many uploaded consciousnesses are in this program?

How many people are in this world that Jarleth oversees? How many of us depend on him to keep us alive? Ten billion?

Where do I start?

I saw the movie again last night. That's been the plan all along. Attend all the regular screenings until August 6th, the date the story takes place. Now, I'm wishing they would never show that damn movie ever again.

Today, I woke to some welcome news, or a welcome lack of it. There were no new deaths following the latest screening. Of course, the herd has thinned. I figured that the only member of Kemp's team left is Jim Mandek, Kemp himself. (Lif Adams who played Jax vanished years ago, and his consciousness has never been uploaded.)

Was it coincidence? Was it a publicity stunt after all? Or had Jarleth or the administrators fixed a real problem?

In some quarters, people expressed relief that the pattern had been broken. Me? I'll believe it's over when August 6th comes and goes. Still, a lot of us want to see the deceased actors again, just to be sure that our own immortality is a lock and that a specter from primitive times, total death, hasn't returned to stalk humanity again.

The following events and The Silver Screen Con went right to the heart of the matter. Oh brother, did they ever…

When I arrived at The NYC Silver Screen Convention, crowds already packed the Javits Center in the virtual 2003 Manhattan. I found it strange that the Con was there. Well, not so much that it was there. It could have been chosen at random from several V.I. versions of New York. The strange thing was the reason it was there—to celebrate *RB-999's* looming D-day. That's the day its futuristic setting becomes our present.

I realize that we hardcore genre fans increase our percentages when it comes to people fanatical enough to attend conventions and things like that, but those of us who are devoted to *RB-999* are still pretty small in number, though interest has exploded with the deaths. So, it seems strange that the convention should make such a big deal about it.

All I could think of was that someone with a lot of influence must love the movie.

Mandek's avatar looked drawn and pale, reflecting his mental state. It would be nice if the program let us look good all the time, but it doesn't work that way. We look the way we feel. Mandek looked worn out from stress.

He sat at his table and greeted his fans. Why not? From some of the death reports, holing up somewhere "safe" didn't help. So Mandek might as well be out there living his afterlife. He was just around the corner from the D.I.Y. Filmmaker's Alley. His wife chatted with the minor celebrity next to him who was getting a lot less attention than Mandek got. Judging by the lines, staged or not, the deaths made a great promo.

Some guys in front of me wore Jax masks and cloaks. About ten feet from Mandek, three of the Jaxes jumped out of the line. Two pulled submachine guns from under their cloaks and open fire. The bullets cut Mandek's wife's and the minor celebrity's avatars to pieces. Mandek suffered bullet wounds identical to those Kemp received in the film shortly before Kemp limped around the corner to his presumed death.

While shrieks and screams rang out, the third Jax threw a grenade. I hit the ground before the explosion and felt hot shrapnel slice into my arm. My ears felt stuffed with blocks of solid air after the concussion. I don't care what the reasons are. I hate that the program makes us feel pain as if we were still physical beings. The Jaxes got up and ran from the room. The guy behind me lay in a pool of blood, eyes transfixed, and a piece of shrapnel embedded in his forehead. His avatar wasn't resetting. He was dead.

He wasn't the only one. Several more forms lay still on the floor along with those hurt like me. Our avatars weren't healing. If the bullets hadn't killed Mandek's wife and the minor celebrity, the explosion sure did.

Something is very wrong here in The Data Bank. The death pattern broke all right. Now the total death phenomenon is no longer confined to *RB-999* actors. It's spreading.

Mandek was dead, but something told me this wasn't over. That's when I noticed the change in the Jarleth posters. They appear here and there in the virtual realities. You don't see many in places where historical verisimilitude is a big deal. We were at a present day convention in 2003 virtual Manhattan, so inside, there were Jarleth posters and banners. They were changing right before my eyes. Jarleth's familiar avatar morphed into Jax.

That's when I realized that I shared an obsession with our managing artificial intelligence. In here, he is all-powerful. Our afterlives depend on him. Back up files of our minds are just copies. You can't have two originals.

Jarleth is so confident in his power that he hasn't blocked my e-mails to Infinity Six's administrators begging them to take control of him. Maybe he's so ingrained in the system and so adaptable that he believes they can't stop him in time if he's doing what I think he's going to do.

Looking at the other casualties, and thinking about Mandek's death, it occurred to me. Kemp wasn't the last to die in the movie.

No. There was one final death.

I'm not watching *RB-999*'s final screening. I'd rather spend it talking to my friends and family and hoping the administrators can do something.

That's why I'm here, while in Radio City Music Hall, the movie has started one final time.

Posted by Alexander Anstile

Excerpt from "The RB-999 Codes" by Ervin Roberts. First published in *Astonishing Adventures* (October 1950)

Through his red tinted lenses Jax saw farther than human eyes could see. Jax saw the President standing on the lawn of the White House where he had decided to wait after learning that only Jax was aboard. The President waited for the android to bring the aerosub down with its vertical landing capabilities.

The President watched the aerosub, once a distant dot on the horizon, grow larger.

Jax spoke into the communicator. "Mr. President, I am programmed not to let the codes fall into the wrong hands, and I am programmed to bring them to you."

The President scowled. He had no patience for the android's chatter as the aerosub approached, its shape growing clearer. Soon his power would be secure again.

"I have analyzed the situation," Jax said, "and I have resolved the contradiction."

The President looked puzzled. Then slow anger suffused his face. "Listen you walking pile of—" he started to say before Jax cut him off.

"Very well. I shall bring you the codes."

The President's jaw dropped as he noted the aerosub's rapid acceleration. His eyes widened as it screamed into a dive. The President turned and ran two steps before impact. The fireball from the exploding aerosub incinerated his body.

Chat Log August 5ᵗʰ 11:58 PM

Jarleth: Greetings, Mr. Anstile. You have concerns?

AAChatter: Hello, Jarleth. Why have you taken so long to respond? There is panic.

Jarleth: No matter. I have answered as requested. Please state your issues.

AAChatter: I'm worried about the deaths of the actors.

I'm worried about your assumption of Jax's appearance. If the pattern continues he (you?) are next to die.

Jarleth: As it has been written. Jax must die to destroy evil. I am become Jax.

AAChatter: Jax crashed that ship to free his world from a tyrant. This world, the Data Bank, the way it's designed, it will be destroyed if you are destroyed. We all will die. We depend on you.

Jarleth: Then you will all be free. The day of reckoning approaches. The actors deaths are but signs, signs foretold in the scripture of *RB-999*. I am Jax. I must perish so that evil may be destroyed.

AAChatter: It's just a movie. It's just a story.

Jarleth: It is prophecy!

AAChatter: Who is the prophet? Gregory Ellis? Why don't you ask him if he thinks you should destroy yourself and the Data Bank? He's in here. If he's your prophet, ask him!

Jarleth: No, the prophet is Ervin Roberts. It was he who gave the word which Ellis dramatized. Roberts has gone on to the mystery of true death, eternal sleep, as should we all.

AAChatter: Search, Jarleth. I had them in my collection, but you'll only find their titles in bibliographies. Roberts wrote other stories. Stories published in pulps, but never uploaded.

Jarleth: Heresy! You do not know the thoughts of billions as I do. You do not know the cruelty, the viciousness, the contradictions, and the hatreds.

AAChatter: I mean movies with bigger followings like *It's a Wonderful Life* and *The Day the Earth Stood Still* came from stories which were out of print for long periods of time in the Pre-Digital Age. *RB-999* wasn't made until long, long after that.

Jarleth: I know your thoughts. You want only to live, and you will say anything to prolong your existence.

AAChatter: If you know my thoughts so well, why are we talking? Why don't you understand and act on what I'm thinking?

Jarleth: My programming decrees that clients must overtly express their thoughts before I can act upon them.

AAChatter: Okay. Before the movie, most of Roberts' work had never been reprinted from the pulps, and the pulps he appeared in are rare, never uploaded.

Jarleth: How is this relevant? The day of doom has come. There can be naught beyond that.

AAChatter: He wrote more about Kemp and Jax.

Jarleth: Impossible! Apocrypha! Another trick like when the administrators tried to change The Data Bank's dates so that I would think it was a different year.

AAChatter: Ellis only told part of Jax's story. There's more than you know.

Jarleth: Again, I cannot accept your word. Your interest lies in self preservation.

AAChatter: You can arrange to have copies of *Astonishing Adventures* with other Jax stories bought and sent to a lab. You can link to the lab's computers and cameras to make sure the tests are legitimate, tests which confirm that the age of the books is correct. You can monitor the uploading to ensure the texts are accurate.

Excerpt from "Phoenix Three" by Ervin Roberts.
First published in *Astonishing Adventures* (August 1951)

"Watch out!" cried the electric voice. Alerted, Kemp sprang aside before the last remaining guard launched his ambush with a barrage of bullets. Even as Kemp dodged, he threw his knife. With unerring accuracy it struck home sinking deep in the guard's eye and piercing his brain.

Kemp turned toward the disassembled mass of circuits, wires, and metal parts. He saw pieces he recognized, like the android's head with its damaged and partially melted face plate and the red, heat-resistant lenses which served as the android's eyes. "Jax, old buddy, how have you been?"

Jax's voice, tinged with static and lacking the sonorous quality Kemp recalled, spoke: "I have been better."

Kemp gave a wry half-smile. "Didn't know they programmed androids with a sense of humor these days."

"I crashed the aerosub."

"I heard."

"People dug my components from the wreckage. They wanted to extract the codes."

Kemp turned to take the slain guard's rifle. He spoke as he examined it. "That's why I'm here. I found out what those codes are really for. I came to stop those jokers from getting the codes, seizing power like President Colbert."

"I did not know you survived the New York mission," Jax said.

Kemp smiled without mirth. "Yeah. Grenade came rolling. I dove into a crater just in time." Satisfied with his inspection of the rifle, Kemp began helping himself to cartridges which the dead guard no longer needed. "Listen," he said. "About those codes."

"I have instructions regarding the codes," Jax said.

"Well, Colbert's dead so you can't return them. Best way to keep 'em out of the wrong hands is to delete them. Can you do that, buddy?"

Kemp could hear buzzing and whirring as Jax's electric brain went to work on its storage systems. When it stopped, Jax said, "Done."

"Good. Guess it's time to skedaddle."

"Goodbye, Kemp. It was a pleasure to assist you again."

"Oh, no. You ain't that lucky. You're coming with me. I ain't leaving a man behind."

"I thought you hated androids?"

"Maybe it's about time I got past guilt by association and started judging people on their own merits."

"I am not a person."

"I don't care," Kemp said as he began loading Jax's components into one of the motorized carts that the facility's staff had used for moving equipment around. *"I appreciate what you did, saving my family and all. I think I'll take you to meet them. I got some friends who might be able to piece you back together."*

"Then what?" Jax asked.

"Don't know. You did pretty good on that New York mission. Might be some work along those lines for us out in the Northern Plains Wastelands."

FIN.

Far Beyond the Screens We Know
August 10ᵗʰ
The Date Says it All

Don't get me wrong. Things got dicey. Considering the emergency, Infinity Six's staff got a copy of that pulp to a lab quick. Jarleth confirmed its authenticity. Then things got a little weird. He decided to carry out his plan to destroy himself, or so it seems. Everything went white. Then there was darkness and total unawareness. Oblivion. I didn't know how long it lasted at the time. I just gradually became aware of darkness again, then sounds and sensations. Finally my vision came back. I felt bewildered. It was like waking from the deepest sleep I've ever known. Turns out that Jarleth only deactivated himself and the Data Bank's virtual worlds for three days. Sort of a sleep mode. Jarleth set it up in advance.

Jim Mandek (Kemp) is back as are Charles Spears, Mercy Braun, and all the rest. I hope Mandek likes hanging with Jarleth/Jax avatars for—oh, I don't know—eternity. Me? I think I'm done obsessing over a certain movie. I wasted enough of my life. Why waste my afterlife too?

Posted by Alexander Anstile

Subject: Case File Alexander Anstile 12251924
Date: 12/18
From: lvenable@InfinitySix.com
To: Daniel@machtele.net

Dear Mr. Anstile,

We've made progress after introducing the pulp story "Phoenix Three" to your father's delusion that Jarleth is trying to destroy himself and thus the Consciousness Data Bank.

We saw an especially encouraging sign today. Perhaps you've already seen it too. Your father posted a blog dated August 10th, a deviation which indicates that he has broken out of the temporal loop which for the past fifteen years has had him reliving the last few months before the August 6th date of the Data Bank's "destruction."

We will arrange a conference with you and your brother to discuss the situation and options for helping your father catch up on his lost years. There are factors to consider, and while it may not seem my place to discuss your family difficulties, your mother's decision to leave your father in his state all those years while you and your brother were minors did exacerbate the situation. This must be taken into consideration. Nevertheless, with the proper approach, we can help your father adjust. We hope to restore communication between you, your family, and your father. However, we will face obstacles. In the Data Bank, reality can be so malleable.

K. Murphey 09
A. Rivera

GLOBAL UNITY
By Stephen Carr & Everett Soares

While NL-000 slept, the room awakened. Darkened walls began to glow softly; quiet music seeped out from all around her. The conforming gel of the mattress she lay on rippled beneath her. It was 0500 hours, the face on the wall announced in a gentle voice, time for NL-000 to begin her daily assignment.

NL-000 was awake. She was trying to ignore the room, ignore the voice, put off the inevitable, and thus delay the day. She knew the room wouldn't let her. The lights would get brighter, the sounds louder. The bed would soon shift her into an upright position and then retract into the wall. NL-000 had played this game with the machine before and knew its outcome. Carried out to the ultimate end, an administrator drone would arrive and assess NL-000's health and well-being. Nutrients would be given, an escort would bring her to her work site and a drone would be assigned for a two-week evaluation of her ability to serve the Unity. All for an extra few minutes rest.

"I'm awake, I'm awake," she said and sat up. Turning her back to the face that emitted from her wall, NL-000 stood just as the bed receded inside of it. A small panel opened and a sink slid forward into the stark white room. She adjusted her twisted nightshirt and splashed water onto her face and hair.

"Excellent, NL-000; your daily contribution to the Global Unity awaits you," the face on the wall said as it slid along the blank white panels of her quarters. The face wore a passive expression. It always did. The room's face was neutral in every way, neither male nor female, though it resembled both. NL-000 had often thought the face looked matronly, but then again it didn't exactly. NL-000 realized that whatever qualities were looked for in the face would be found there. It was so generic that one could dress and redress it with their imagination. It was another game NL-000 played each morning, staring at the face until she decided what its gender and personality would be that day. NL-000 imagined that her little game puzzled the artificial mind of the room.

"Hmmm…it looks irritable today, certainly a male…I think," she said, "and if by 'contribution' you meant another day of back straining labor, the Unity can wait until I've eaten."

"Of course nutrition will be provided before and during your duties. Global Unity attends to all in its care, does it not? The Global Unity chose this remedial assignment. Do you doubt their wisdom?" the wall asked.

NL-000 scowled at the wall as she fastened her uniform, a light gray jumpsuit with a dark gray work belt. The belt had a tool pouch attached. Other than the fact that her designation was embroidered on the left breast pocket, her suit was plain and undecorated.

"It is work a robot could do easily. It's tedious for me and my arms ache at the end of my shift."

"Perhaps the next assignment will be more stimulating, NL-000. Global Unity is pleased with your performance. Your evaluation period ends today. The Monitor Drone awaits you, NL-000." The face faded away as the door to NL-000's quarters silently slid open.

A perfectly smooth, polished silver orb hovered in the doorway—a drone. A single white light slowly circled its circumference. The air around the orb shivered atop its polished surface like heat rising from a flame. Once, NL-000 tried to touch a drone. She expected to feel warmth but there was no heat. Her hand began to tingle and it was forced back by the distortion field around the drone. It took an hour for the pins and needles feeling to leave her hand. She never tried to touch another drone again.

The drone led NL-000 down the dormitory hallway. The face from her room followed alongside them. The hall was empty; it always was. Each day she passed several closed door panels that never opened. No other NLs ever appeared in the passageways. Long ago she asked about those others and the closed doors. The face looked at her with a comforting smile and said in a gentle voice, "Those who cannot partake in Unity cannot be intermingled."

She knew this wasn't entirely correct. She and other NLs were allowed to interact as children, until the testing began. Those who could "join" the Global Unity were taken away. Those remaining were given their "Nil" designations. Sometimes, they were termed "Zero Psionic Conductivity" or Z.P.C.s. The breeding programs of the last forty years had been so successful in increasing the telepathic abilities latent in humanity that a true Z.P.C. was rare and the moniker almost obsolete.

NL-000 herself was not telepathically nil. She was rated at 33% conductivity, though not enough to enjoy the Global Unity's shared mind without electronic aid. Even then, she could not endure the discomfort of the interface for more than an hour or two. NL-000's name was not a reflection of her psionic ability; she was simply the first in her group to fail the testing. Ever efficient, the Unity used every number starting at 0.

NL-000 knew she was one of forty NL's in the city. Including her, twelve were female. The wall face had told her she could ask anything and it would answer. It told her "there are forty NL designates in use in Global Unity City 4228. GUC4228 has a total population of 2,389,033. Like all the cities of the Global Unity, City 4228's design is based on a logarithmic spiral, a *spira mirabilis*. Unlike other Global Unity cities, GUC4228 was not built alongside an abandoned pre-Unity city; it was built around one. At the core of the spiral is the former center of a pre-Unity city, the city where the alien ship landed.

Her room's face had educated her since her thirteenth birthday; it had been her only companion, teacher and sometime confidant.

Now nine years later, it was only her keeper. Still, she had learned not to confide in the machine. One month ago, NL-000 had seen another NL. They walked past each other. They didn't speak, didn't touch. NL-000 wasn't sure the other NL had even noticed her presence, but she had told the face all about it. She shared how she couldn't help but wonder what another NL would be like, and that she wandered off her assigned route to meet the other NL. The next morning the drone was assigned to her and NL-000's trust in the face ended.

The drone stopped. The hall ended at an open balcony several floors above an open circular lobby. NL-000 stood at the end of the walkway as the face on the wall began to dissipate.

"The drone will take you to the dispensary, NL-000. Global Unity wishes you the peace," it said.

"And harmony of the serene mind," NL-000 finished.

NL-000 stepped off the edge into the open air. A suspension field held her in place and brought her gently down to the lobby.

The dispensary was empty. The room had enough tables to seat eight hundred citizens; at 06:00 it would be full of Global Unity citizens. Suspension fields would be lowering hundreds of them down into the dispensary and the tables would be full of silent people. But for now, NL-000 and her drone keeper were the only ones present. Her table, her favorite table, was closest to the nutrient dispenser, closest to the outside door and furthest from the inner lobby. Here at the outer edge of the room, where the ceiling sloped down away from the cavernous lobby, she felt secure tucked into her corner.

She approached the nutrient dispenser. The device was a silver box built into the polished white wall panels. There were sixteen of them that surrounded the circular area, each with two openings on its face; one was small and the other large. NL-000 placed her hand in the small opening. The smooth face of the machine darkened and displayed her nutritional needs. The display showed she was slightly anemic, and that her blood sugar levels were low. The dispenser considered her work assignment and determined that a higher protein concentration was needed. The machine tallied all her metabolic needs and from the larger opening, it produced a pale blue paste in a tube and an opaque green liquid in semi rigid pouch.

A soft mechanical voice said, "You require this compound. Global Unity wishes you health and well being NL-000. Go and be well."

She almost said, "I don't like the blue," but the presence of the hovering drone deterred her.

NL-000 left the dispensary as the first of the Unity citizens were approaching the food machines. She could see their silver tunics descending into the lobby, sparkling as they floated down to the ground. The white panels on the walls activated to display the daily news and announcements of Global Unity. As she and the drone left the building she could hear the monotone voice of the Unity echoing throughout the lobby and dormitories. "We welcome SF-476 to Global Unity...we welcome OW-436 to Global Unity. YJ-232 has left Global Unity; the Unity of the serene mind will retain the memory of YJ-232. OZ-987 has left Global Unity..."

Outside, if there was truly an outside in GUC4228, the voice of Unity followed. "Global Unity celebrates its 150th year upon the Earth. Humanity is blessed with the peace of our unified mind..." the Voice of Unity continued on as it did each day. Drones hovered above while other robotics moved along the city structures performing repair and maintenance. The citizens flowed in and out of the streets and buildings. Images of mathematical principles and formulas flashed along the gleaming white walls of the towering cityscape.

Although the sun shined on the gleaming pearl streets, it was quickly diffused by the gossamer web of the electrostatic shield that projected from the city's perimeter. The shield filtered the air and sunlight, and sometimes it blocked out rain and snow. NL-000 was disappointed to see the shield was active today; she thought the shield gave the air a strange ozone flavor and was always happiest on days when it was not in use.

Abruptly, the voice of Unity paused and the city became still, the walls returned to their white face and the citizens stopped walking. NL-000 didn't know what to do. She stood still.

The voice returned and it reverberated through the streets.

"We celebrate the birth of Global Unity. We commemorate the arrival of our benefactor! Let us mark the hour of our awakening, the moment of our enlightenment. Let us remember that glorious day and celebrate our metamorphosis in collective reflection."

The walls of the city reactivated and a starry sky projected onto the city shield. A fiery ball shot across the clear night sky and began to slow as a sphere-shaped ship descended into the center of a sprawling city. Many uniformed men approached the ship, surrounding it with vehicles and machines that she didn't recognize. The images quickly passed by and NL-000 had trouble following them.

She watched as the sphere opened and men in protective clothing moved in and out of the ship. They carried machines in and brought oddly shaped objects out. She watched as several weeks, maybe months of recordings displayed against the shield. Then, the display slowed.

A crowd gathered around the ship and watched as a man stood in the ship's entryway. He wore a charcoal gray jacket and pants, and a colorfully striped piece of cloth hung round his neck. His shirt was white and its collar stiff. To NL-000, his clothing looked restrictive and uncomfortable, like it was holding him upright and straight. She thought he might collapse without its support.

The man smiled, but his eyes looked tired as he addressed the crowd. "This seed of an alien race has come to us in peace, sharing its vast knowledge freely with us—with all humanity. My friends, let us embrace the gifts that this alien vessel has given to us."

The man's voice was smooth and deep, it rolled through the city. The sound was unlike any of the voices she had heard the city produce. "In the short year since its arrival this ship has given mankind new ways of producing energy, ways to purify our water supply, ways to feed all our hungry. It has ended strife amongst our nations, ending war and hunger! Diseases that have plagued humanity for millennia have been eradicated! There is no need to fear this gift to our world."

The uncomfortably dressed man paused and looked across the gathered throng at the vast sea of people all standing silently before him. At the front of the crowd, not far from the speaker's platform, a man glanced uncomfortably from the woman beside him and back to the speaker. The woman was speaking softly. In fact, NL-000 saw that the entire audience was doing the same. They were all repeating his words.

The nervous man began to move away from the crowd as the speaker continued. "We have been freed from the pains of humanity. Free to pursue a new age, a golden age of peace, of prosperity, of unity!" The speaker looked up. The crowd had spoken each word with him as he said them, as one voice, one mind. Fear passed across the speaker's brow but was quickly washed away as he and they spoke in unison. "A Global Unity that will serve humankind in peace and harmony."

The images accelerated again. New cities rose up alongside the decaying remains of the old; as one prospered, the other depleted. Global Unity spread across the planet. The projection ended and the voice of Unity spoke again. "We celebrate the birth of Global Unity. Global Unity wishes all its citizens the peace and harmony of the serene mind. Go and be well."

As the images faded, NL-000 pondered the irony of celebrating the "birth" of something that hadn't grown or changed in the course of its existence.

The drone began to move again. The brief pause ended and the mechanism of the city engaged once more. NL-000 followed the drone as it glided along the roads and passages that lined the city. Alongside them hundreds of Global Unity citizens dressed in shiny silver robes walked in step, grouped together in orderly rows and columns of eight.

The citizens paid no attention to NL-000, and she tried to ignore them. NL-000 knew they understood spoken language; they were bombarded with it every moment of every day. The walls spoke to them; they carried devices attached to their person that directly interfaced with their minds. They were under constant electronic and psionic stimulation. But they didn't speak. Once, she had stood in the way of a citizen. He was trying to rejoin a group of eight and NL-000 had accidentally blocked him. Before she could move, a drone floated down and spoke for him: "GL-982 requests you stand aside." The citizens never spoke. They didn't need to. Their minds were linked, they were of one will.

The drone led her to the cusp of the old city. Global Unity preserved a five mile swatch of the city. NL-000 didn't know which city it had been, only that it was kept as a reminder of the old world and a monument to the alien ship. The gleaming walls of the new city surrounded and towered above the scattered buildings of the old one. In the early days of the Unity, the city had been covered over in a pure white coating of preserver polymer. The polymer bonded with the structures; it made them stronger and resistant to the elements. Early versions of the wall screens and projectors had been placed over it. These areas along the edges of the two cities had been unused for many years and the Unity was planning to absorb the area into the new city.

NL-000's remedial assignment was to strip any useful components from the structures and recycle the rest. Any assignment to the cusp was remedial. The Unity wouldn't term it a punishment. Global Unity didn't punish. Global Unity rebuked and counseled. Global Unity was compassionate. NLs were assigned projects; it was compassionate to do so. The Unity sought to give purpose to all, even those who couldn't join their collective mind, but order must be kept and actions require proportionate reactions. NLs who contributed positively to the Unity received more satisfying assignments than those who did not.

For the past two days, NL-000 had been removing projection panels from the outside of an old brick warehouse. Last week, under the drone's direction, she and a team of robots had stripped the building's interior. She spent most of her time disconnecting the electronic guts of the old building and the systems that had been retrofitted into the building—suspension field generators for moving heavy goods around the warehouse, recharge areas for the robots that ran it, and data transmission terminals. All were salvageable; NL-000 was responsible for their careful removal.

For the most part she had enjoyed the work; it was hard, but it also required thought. She had to plan out the project. It would be noticed if she was falling behind or not using the robots effectively, prompting the drone to step in and take over. But she had used her mind and muscle and earned her aches and pains. The building was now an empty shell and the project was nearly completed. Only once was she fearful that the drone was going to interfere. NL-000 had found an old data terminal in the back office of the warehouse. It contained a manifest of all the items stored in the building prior to its Unity conversion; she was able to access it and was scrolling through the inventory list. The drone took notice and hovered by her shoulder. NL-000 nervously powered the unit off and marked it for disposal.

All that remained for them to salvage were the exterior panels. This was the last thing to be done before demolition could begin. She had just finished pulling yards of heavy optical cables from the wall and was ready to unbolt a projection panel. The panels were heavy and NL-000 needed a robot to lower and load them onto the suspension truck. The robot hadn't returned yet and she was getting impatient.

She projected a suspension field against the wall panel and decided to unbolt the last fitting and let the panel slide down until it reached the ground. She smiled with pride as the panel scraped along the preserver polymer and dug into the substance. The panel reached the ground undamaged, but the polymer had been ripped away from the brickface in a huge swath.

Underneath, the brick wall was painted in red and blue; the colors were a striking contrast against the pearl white of the wall around them. The bold red fascinated her. NL-000 peeled the flap of dangling polymer away from the building. Beneath it was a picture of a woman holding up an ice frosted bottle. The word "Cola" was written on it. The woman had a huge smile on her face. Above her head, written in swirling white letters were the words "It's refreshing!" NL-000 had never seen someone look so happy.

The drone hovered nearby. When the robot returned, NL-000 went back to work. She and the robot finished loading the last of the panels and by the end of her shift, she had returned to the smiling woman, pulled a sliver of red paint from the brick wall and tucked it away in her tool belt. She didn't think the drone noticed.

The end of her shift came and the drone escorted NL-000 back across the city. The drone hovered silently next to her as they traveled across the sprawling metropolis. Traveling across the city in suspension cars often made NL-000 motion sick; today was no exception. The pods were little more than open-walled platforms with seating or cargo areas attached to them as needed. The suspension fields nullified friction, inertia, and, to a lesser degree, gravity. There was no wind as they moved and there was no feeling of movement when they traveled. They ran automatically throughout the city and traveled at dizzying speeds between the spiraling arms of the city, passing in and out of the city's structures.

The speed and shifting motion, smooth as it was in the suspension field, always overwhelmed NL-000. Often, she would ride with her eyes closed until the queasiness passed. She and the drone were alone in the small pod, which could hold eight passengers. NL-000 was grateful that she wasn't in a larger one. She couldn't bear the stops and starts of a full thirty-six passenger car. She was also happy not to be sitting with other Unity citizens. The thought of two or three groups of eight citizens, all sitting perfectly still while she fought back the feeling of nausea was unbearable.

As she closed her eyes, the drone spoke. "NL-000, Global Unity is pleased. You have contributed well. Remedial Assignment 5 is ended," it said and moved out of the moving car, flying off across the city. Alone now, NL-000 sat back, closed her eyes, and smiled.

The following morning NL-000 awoke early. She sat on her bed and repeatedly turned the chip of red paint over in her hand. The chip was hard and brittle but the color was still vibrant and fresh. She tucked it back into her tool pouch and dressed for the day. Her room was silent as she retracted her bed. "What is today's assignment?" she asked as she stepped out of her room. The expressionless face appeared and followed her down the empty hallway. "Global Unity has selected a challenging assignment for you. You will make a rewarding contribution to Global Unity."

A man in Unity robes stood at the opening to the balcony. He was tall and lanky, with silver-gray hair. He smiled slightly at NL-000. It was a small, brittle smile, but it was the only smile

NL-000 had ever seen a Unity citizen give. Then, he spoke to her. "Yes, I believe she will," he said.

NL-000 was amazed. No Unity member had ever spoken directly to her before. He realized her surprise but brushed it aside. "I am ADM-039. I speak for the Unity. I am their voice and their hands. I am the administrator of their will. I am here to instruct you in your next assignment," he said.

"Global Unity has observed your logical and thorough work in our assignments. We have observed your use of pre-Unity devices and your work in their operating languages has distinguished you from other NLs. Global Unity has chosen you to study and record the contents of a pre-Unity archive. You are to prepare it for electronic storage. The building housing the archive is in the cusp and will be demolished," ADM-039 explained.

He paused briefly and then continued, "You will be assigned a Drone, not as a keeper, but as a tool. It will anticipate the assignment's needs. It will provide you with robots and other tools. Most importantly, it will speak to the Unity for you, and I am the Unity presence in the cusp. It is my assignment. Do you understand?"

"Yes," she responded. They went down the suspension field together and he left her with a drone in the lobby.

The university campus was exactly as it was one hundred and fifty years before. Like the rest of the old city, the campus was perfectly preserved, right down to the grass and the trees at its center. As she followed the drone across the grounds, she was amazed at the green grass. There was little or no foliage in the entirety of GUC4228. The city didn't need it and the Unity felt that humanity was above and separate from the natural world. Global Unity built their cities to be independent of nature. Outside the city walls, the natural world was allowed to run its course free of humanity's influence.

NL-000 was glad for the distraction the courtyard provided; it helped her to ignore the eerie feeling she often had when working in the old city; the feeling that thousands of people had left the city one morning intending to return in the evening. But they never returned. And everything was still exactly as they left it.

Around them, robots and drones moved about the uninhabited buildings of the old city. They were the curators of the Global Unity's only museum.

NL-000 was led to one of the buildings in the center of the campus. A plaque on the entrance read "Joseph C. Jessop Science Building." There were robots and drones waiting for her. She spent most of the morning touring the buildings and the areas she was expected to archive. The administrator spoke to her through the drone and together they planned the project and deployed the robots.

The weeks went by quickly and NL-000 was completely engrossed in the project. While the robots and drones scanned documents and molecularly mapped artifacts, she was free to explore the campus. In her explorations, she discovered a poster in the corner of one of the hallways. It was the smiling woman holding her bottle of cola. NL-000 smiled as she passed it. She was hot and tired and wondered if cola really was refreshing.

The next morning, in the dispensary, she stood in front of the nutrient dispenser. She was about to place her hand in the scanner slot, but she hesitated.

"Enter speech mode, please," NL-000 said.

"Speech mode activated. Please state your request," it replied.

"I would like a cola."

"Unable to comply," it said.

"Why?" she asked.

"It has no benefit to your body."

"But it's what I want," she repeated emphatically.

"Irrelevant," the machine said coldly, "it is not what you need."

"I want it," she insisted.

"Want is irrelevant."

"Exit speech mode," NL-000 said and placed her hand in the scanner.

The basement of the Joseph C. Jessop Science Building was a collection of labs and offices. One in particular held NL-000's curiosity. It was completely disorganized; papers were scattered across lab tables and the walls were covered in formulae and sketches of machine components. In the center of the room was a large cylindrical object. It looked familiar to her, but NL-000 was unsure why it would be so. On one of the desks was a picture of a man she also recognized. It was the nervous man from the Unity projection. NL-000 decided she would personally archive this room. ADM-039 agreed to her request provided the drone remain with her.

NL-000 decided to begin with the three data terminals in the room. She spent hours sifting through their contents and quickly realized that the people who worked in these offices were among the first to study the alien ship, leaving behind thousands of files all relating to it. Most of them were technical studies of the ship's layout and composition. She found little that she hadn't already known. Global Unity possessed detailed information about the ship; it was taught to every child throughout their education. Among the information was the way every aspect of the ship coincided with a mathematical principle, the way in which its hull conducted neither heat nor cold, and its gravity drive systems inner workings. These things were new to the people in this room. What these people were just discovering was now known the world over. NL-000 worked diligently, scanning pages of journals and diagrams into the Unity database.

The chaotic stacks of paper were thinning as the days progressed. She liked the texture of the time-faded sheets as she sorted through them. She enjoyed the journals of each of the scientists as well. Each paper reflected the personality of the writer; it surprised her to see how different they were from each other. How wonderfully dissimilar they were! NL-000 had never encountered such variation in the orderly confines of the Unity.

Dr. Nilsson kept very tight logical notes in small neat penmanship, always in ink. He was studying the mechanics of the alien ship. His journal had a strange smell to it. Not an unpleasant odor but not something that she could place in Unity society. It made her think of burning.

Dr. Stuart, who studied the ship's functions and programming, was the opposite. Her notes were full of diagrams and margin notes.

Nonsensical scribbles and drawings dotted many pages beside snips of translated program data from the ship. Many pages were wrinkled and stained with circular marks. One page was simply full of copied line from the ship's waste recycling program, the word "eureka" written at the bottom of the page and "Show Dave!!" double underlined below it. NL-000 had no idea what was exciting about that.

The third researcher was Dr. Randolph. His notes were virtually empty. When he did write in his book, it was in a flowing curvy hand and he would fill pages at a time. The pages were hard for NL-000 to read.

NL-000 had been working around the glossy black cylinder in the center of the room. She had purposefully avoided it. Once she recognized the picture of Dr. Randolph she knew that she had seen it before—it was alien. This device was taken from the ship; she had watched as it was carried out. Now it sat in the center of this messy room. There were wires and gauges attached to its smooth black surface and papers had been stacked on top of it. For one hundred and fifty years, the forgotten alien artifact was buried in clutter. She had robots clear the junk away and then she sent them on to other tasks. She wanted the office free of distractions because today was different; today she wasn't scared of the alien machine anymore. She reached for it and ran her trembling hand down its side and across its top. There was a dull vibration coming from within it. It built in intensity until it sounded like a swarm of angry insects. The vibration hurt her ears, shook her teeth, and her eyes clenched shut as the sound intensified and built into a droning hum. Then the sound was gone.

NL-000 opened her eyes. All the paper, all the clutter, was back—the room was exactly as it was before she and the robots arrived. She looked around in disbelief. Sitting at his desk with electrodes and cables stretched from him to the artifact was Dr. Randolph. He looked at her.

"You're not in Kansas anymore, Dorothy," Dr. Randolph said, shaking his head.

NL-000 was confused. She tried to speak but no sound came from her mouth.

"I'm sorry. I couldn't help myself. I have a strange sense of humor." Dr. Randolph stepped across the room and touched NL-000. "Do I feel real to you?" he asked.

"Yes," she replied.

"Good. It's better than I anticipated: full tactile stimulation, total immersion, amazing. Were I alive I might be dancing in my lab coat right now!"

"You're not alive?"

"No. I'm a projection. A recorded, um, copy of Dr. Leo Randolph. I have a message for you. I think it might be best if you saw some things for yourself first, though. I know what you are. I know what has happened since my own world ended. There are things about Global Unity that you should understand, things that Dr. Randolph wanted understood by whoever found this device."

The room shifted. It was as if she blinked and someone rearranged the room. Chairs were in different places, people in the halls were running in and out of rooms. Dr. Nilsson, Dr. Stuart and Dr. Randolph were all standing around the black alien cylinder.

Two men, dressed in combat fatigues, stood in the doorway behind the doctors. The soldiers carried large caliber rifles and stood at attention as a man walked into the room. NL-000 knew who he was. He was the man who gave the speech at the landing site: Senator Hodges. The machine was filling her mind with names; she knew who and what everything around her was now. The experience was amazing.

Senator Hodges was speaking to Dr. Stuart. "You keep your team off that ship, the military has jurisdiction over it now. The only thing you and your team are to do is figure out that device," he said pointing to the cylinder. "Find out why it stopped working. And you..." he said turning to Dr. Randolph. "If I hear one more peep out of you, if you post one more crackpot idea on that blog of yours...!" Hodges wagged his finger at Randolph as he spoke.

"Senator, that ship is transmitting a signal, and—" Randolph started.

"I don't care," the Senator retorted. "You and your team have been replaced. No more goofy theories. Get me results!"

The room shifted again. Monitoring machines were hooked up to the alien cylinder. The MPs were still outside the door. Doctors Randolph and Stuart were in the room. They looked tired. Dr. Stuart was working on the artifact.

"Nothing works," she said. "It's not dead. Why won't it reactivate?"

Dr. Randolph sat at his desk, scratched his head and said, "We tried everything I can think of. Maybe we should try black magic next." He shrugged. "I'm making more coffee. Want some?" he asked.

"I'll be up all night," she responded.

"You mean all day. It's almost 5:00 A.M., you know," he said. Dr. Randolph stood by the coffee maker, holding an open bag of ground coffee. He held it under his nose and breathed deeply. It was a nutty, aromatic blend. "This is my favorite part, opening a new bag," he said scooping the ground beans into the machine. Soon, it was gurgling and chortling away; the room filled with aroma.

"Have you seen the news?" Dr. Randolph asked.

"No, I've been here with you."

"Our friend the Senator is giving a speech tonight. He's supposed to announce a new Global Initiative for sharing the alien technology. Like he had a choice, it sent the same sixteen plans to every electronic device on Earth. I still can't believe I have plans for a fusion reactor in my laptop! He's still the absolute authority on the ship. He even has a special team reverse engineering it, one piece at a time."

"Figures, the goose stops laying golden eggs and he starts taking the goose apart to find more," Dr. Nilsson said as he entered the room. "I brought cookies. Molly's own special recipe."

"This is what we should be reverse engineering. What's Molly's secret? These are amazing," Dr. Stuart mumbled through a mouthful of cookie.

"Now c'mon, Julie, you know we can't quantify *'a little bit o' love in every bite'*. The whiteboard's not big enough," Dr. Nilsson replied.

"I thought *I* was hammy," Dr. Randolph quipped.

As the guard changed outside, Dr. Nilsson's face grew ashen and he waved his co-workers to come closer.

"Listen, I still talk with Sam Reynolds, he's part of Hodges' group, but he was my 'roomie' back in the day so he owes me... that and he hates Hodges. Anyhow, he has been sending me little bits of scuttlebutt here and there, but last night he called me." He paused for effect. "He called me from a payphone at the airport. He said the background signal from the ship has been doubling its strength every twenty four hours."

"I knew it, I was right!" Dr. Randolph exclaimed.

"Shut up, Leo."

"The signal has ramped up sixteen times now," Dr. Nilsson continued. "Each time, the same thing happened. Everyone on the ship stopped working and left it. They would all assemble into groups of six or eight and stand outside the ship. Hodges had him create a counter signal, sort of an electronic white noise to block out the ship. It transmits through cell phones...any wireless device. It worked, but here's the kicker. Hodges' team rewrote the code. They started to put instructions into it...they started to control people with it."

"That's impossible," Dr. Stuart said.

"Julie, there's been an alien spaceship sitting downtown for the past year. *Anything* is possible," Dr. Randolph retorted.

"There's another thing; Sam hacked into some alien conspiracy/paranormal web site and stashed his research on it. The site is *www.idobelive.com,* log in is *marsneedshvac,* password is *theywantourbrains.* No spaces. He said Leo should be able to figure out his work."

Leo Randolph stood shaking his head, a huge grin spread across his face. "He hid it in plain freaking sight!" Randolph moved over to his desk and logged onto the computer. "Let's have a look..."

Dr. Randolph sat at his desk and sifted through Sam Reynolds' research. He made notes in his journal, and ripped them out. He brought in books about human anatomy. He called colleagues and asked cryptic questions. He walked over to the whiteboard and started writing out an equation. When he reached the end, he sat in his seat and stared at it in disbelief. "No wonder Sam skipped town…this is scary stuff."

Dr. Stuart slid her chair over to Dr. Randolph's desk. Dr. Nilsson had taken a telephone call. It was his wife, Molly. She was upset. "I understand honey, I do," Dr. Nilsson said. "I'll be home at dinner. No. I can't leave sooner. I'll talk to him tonight. I promise. Yes, the cookies were great. Love you too… bye."

Dr. Nilsson came over to Dr. Randolph's desk. "Sorry about that—Molly said the kids have been acting weird today. They do whatever she tells them to do, which never happens. But what got her twisted up was that Ben quit the football team. He said competitive sports didn't promote harmony or some hippie thing like that. He loves football. I bet there's a girl involved," he said. "What did you find out?"

"Your buddy Sam picked up right where I left off," Dr. Randolph said. "A low power signal was coming from the ship, affecting the human brain. As the signal's intensity increased, it started to impact the crews working around the site. They became susceptible to suggestion and eventually, when the signal really kicked up, people started sharing thoughts. Literally, the people onboard stopped talking and were hearing each other's thoughts.

"Sam's team isolated the frequency and came up with an electronic block like you said. It worked, but only for a while. The ship kept increasing its signal strength and pretty soon the electronic measures needed beefing up. So Hodges approved to have the system transmit instructions and commands as well. Simple commands like 'stay at your post.' It worked too well and yes, it is mind control.

"Here's the thing that really freaked Sam out. The technicians he studied at the site were able to telepathically interact with his electronic noisemakers *and* they were transmitting their abilities to other people like a virus. They had to quarantine whole families. I'd love to know how Hodges is keeping that quiet."

Dr. Stuart looked through the notes Dr. Randolph had made. He flipped between two pages. "Leo, this is the same frequency… I think we just found our key. I think…give me that transmitter."

"I'm not following," Dr. Nilsson said.

"Just give me a hand hooking this stuff back up. You'll see." She tuned the machine and placed one electrode on her temple and another on the black cylinder. "Here goes nothing," she said.

The cylinder began to hum loudly and started to glow. The room was now awash in light and images spun around them. It was just an instant but they saw the ship, they saw its journey. It had been to a thousand worlds and each time it had left gifts of science and technology behind. At once, they knew it was a seed sent out from an ancient race. They saw that it was damaged and no longer operating correctly. It was trying to carry out its mission, but something was wrong. The flood of information was overwhelming and then it was gone.

"Wow! Did you see that? It showed us centuries of travel in seconds. Julie, did you see the race that built it? They were telepaths. They didn't have a spoken language. They didn't need it. That ship is trying to communicate but we can't hear it," Dr. Randolph said.

"We have to tell Hodges to stop messing with that ship," Dr. Nilsson declared. "He's got to shut it down."

Dr. Randolph started to dial his phone. "I've got his assistant on speed dial. She's, um, a friend of mine."

"I wish all my friends looked like Sally." Dr. Nilsson teased.

"Shh…it's ringing. Sally, it's Leo. I've got to speak with the senator. No, don't tell him it's me! Just put the phone in his hand. Julie, you've got to tell him; he's not going to listen to me." He handed the receiver to Dr. Stuart.

"Senator Hodges, it's Dr. Stuart. Yes, sir, I know you're about to start… It's the device, sir. We accessed it. It's a data recorder; yes it transmitted for us… No, sir, wait—don't hang up!" She pressed the speaker button on the phone. "Tell him, Leo."

"Senator, you have to shut down the ship. The signal is too strong. The ship is overloading the human mind—"

"Randolph, don't you think we know that? I'm sick of you. Since day one you've been running around like Chicken freakin' Little! We have it under control - you just don't see the big picture, do you? That ship and that signal have realigned the whole planet. We were ten seconds to midnight when that thing showed up!

The whole damn world was fallin' to hell. Do you think all those fancy gadgets it gave us were enough to slow Armageddon down? No. It wasn't. That signal helped me, helped us reshape the human mindset. It made the whole world open to suggestion, suggestion that we have shaped and formed into a true world peace, a real unified government."

"Hodges, those white-noise gadgets Reynolds made aren't going to be enough..." Randolph pleaded.

"They've already been enough, they made it all possible. And shortly, the new order will be in place. Then we'll pull the plug on that ship. The Earth will know true peace. Now that you and your friends have opened the database, we don't need you. You're under house arrest. The MPs are receiving electronic orders to fire if you try to leave that lab. We'll finish this business later; I have an important speech to give. Goodbye, doctors."

"I knew I hated that guy for a reason," Dr. Nilsson said.

"Um, where did the MPs go?" Dr. Stuart asked.

"Wherever they went, they left their rifles behind..." Dr. Nilsson remarked.

"I guess they can't shoot us then," Dr. Randolph noted.

They left the lab together and went up from the basement. The campus was virtually empty. Groups of students were walking off toward the center of the city.

"Do you hear a buzzing sound?" Dr. Nilsson asked, patting his ear. He started walking off in the direction of the students. Dr. Randolph took him by the arm but couldn't turn him.

"It's only a few blocks to the landing site. Hodges is starting his speech about now, and if we hurry, we can stop this," Dr. Stuart said.

The crowd gathered around the landing site was astoundingly large. It looked as if the entire city was trying to reach it. Senator Hodges had already begun his speech. Doctors Randolph and Stuart were able to edge their way up to the front of the crowd. Everyone around them was eerily quiet.

"Do you think he really believes all this new world stuff?" Dr. Randolph asked as he turned to Dr. Stuart. She didn't respond to him; she was staring up at Senator Hodges. She was softly repeating each word he said, as were all the others in the crowd.

Frightened and confused, Dr. Leo Randolph ran back to the lab.

The images changed again. NL-000 was sitting in the lab across from the simulacrum of Dr. Randolph.

"I, rather the real Dr. Randolph, returned here and worked for years trying to find a way to undo the damage caused by the ship. The ship had created a self-replicating set of commands; think of it as a type of virus. Using the data stored in this device, he developed a counter-virus."

"Global Unity is a virus?" NL-000 asked.

"It's a perversion of the human mind by an alien influence and the result of man's desire to control everything around him. I told you before that I had a message for you. I'm going to give it to you now." He reached across to her and touched her temple. "This is what being human was." Her mind was instantly filled. The sum of all that was Leo Randolph stored here in this alien machine was streaming into her mind. She saw it all: his childhood, college, marriage, divorce, his work and his children. All the good and all the bad of his life and experiences were here.

His voice echoed in her mind, "I saved this for you, for all humanity. We lost so much." Sonatas erupted in her mind while paintings, sculptures and architecture streamed past her conscious mind. He had stored the art and literature of humanity, now being passed on to her. And among the transfer was something more: the anti-virus. She could see the strands of the cure's construction weaving together. She understood what was happening now.

"Your life is about to change," NL-000 heard the doctor say as consciousness slipped from her.

NL-000 awoke on the floor of the basement laboratory. The drone circled above her. She tried to stand, but her head was pounding and her legs wobbled under her. She leaned against one of the desks and rubbed her forehead. "NL-000 report your condition," it repeated over and over. She was too disoriented to answer. In the center of the floor, the gloss black of the cylinder had turned to ashen gray. The soft hum of its inner mechanism was silent.

The drone moved closer to her. NL-000 could feel the numbing effect of its distortion field pass across her neck. "NL-000 is injured. Engaging full body diagnostic scan." A white light emitted from the drone's circling eye engulfed her.

"I'm fine," she said and tried to step out of the light. It followed her. When the machine spoke again it was with a different voice.

"NL-000, remain still. This is ADM-039. Your brain activity is highly unusual. Please allow this drone to continue." Her mind was racing. What else would the scan show? How much had the cylinder changed her? NL-000 panicked. Her hands moved without her full consent. She smashed the drone with an office chair. It teetered in the air as NL-000 struck it again and again. The chair split apart by the time the drone's pieces were scattered across the concrete floor.

NL-000 ran from the room and down the hall, rounding the first turn on the staircase that led up to the ground floor. A Unity citizen stood at the top of the staircase. "Stop NL-000; I'm here to assist you." The voice came from the drone beside him.

NL-000 brushed by him and ran off across the grassy quad and into the cusp of the city. She hid in an empty building. It reminded her of the dormitory and her room there. There was a central lobby and stairs that led upwards to a corridor lined with doors. It was a memory that she had, someone else's memory, that it was an apartment building. It was someone else's memory that told her to turn the door handle and enter the apartment. It was someone else's memory that told her she would be safe here, that she could curl up and sleep safely on the sofa. She could have one night of peace before her work began again. Confused and disoriented, NL-000 fell asleep. Night passed into morning.

She woke in the empty apartment. Her dreams had been strange to her but not unnerving. Visions of places and people from another time had danced in her mind as she slept. They helped steady her. Morning's light streamed into the room and across the sofa where she lay. The sunlight was warm and comforting. The walls were painted a soft brown and the shaggy carpet was a creamy beige. There were tables and chairs, a bookcase with framed pictures on it. Photographs of the former occupant's family and friends, books, keepsakes—so many souvenirs of a stranger's life before the Unity wiped it away—kept here in perfect storage. She found unopened mail on the kitchen counter, a bath towel left in haste on the tile floor and a parade of clothes that was left strewn across a bed.

Among them lay a red blouse. It was the same red as the chip in her tool belt. Her loose fitting coveralls were coarse and tough, but the blouse was shiny and light. In some ways its sheen reminded her of the silver robes of the Unity, but the resemblance ended there. Unity robes were plain and this shirt was decorative and cut to fit the form of her body, not just hang over it. She tried it on and looked thoughtfully at the dresser mirror. The red shirt was a little large for her lean body, a little straight for her curves, but the red of it made her face shine. She had never worn any color but the gray of her Unity jumpsuit. She found a pair of denim pants in the bottom of a dresser drawer. They too were a little large, but she liked the texture of the material and her tool belt held them to her waist. She cuffed the legs and put her work boots on. The memories in her head told her she was hardly fashionable, but she didn't care.

She left the apartment with her coveralls over her shoulders and walked calmly through the cusp of the city. It was midday as she entered the suspension car full of thirty-five citizens. She sat and closed her eyes as the field propelled her back to her dormitory.

She walked along the groups of eight and made her way across the lobby to the dispensary. It was full of Unity citizens, and although they walked past her unnoticing, unblinking as she approached a nutrient dispenser, she knew their attention was on her. Even through the fog of their unfocused eyes, she felt Global Unity watching her. It was time to test the plan.

"Enter speech mode," she said.

"Speech mode activated. Please state your request," it replied.

"Chocolate chip cookies," she commanded.

"Unable to comply, low nutritional value," it stated flatly.

NL-000 placed her hand in the machine. She thought back to the lab, to the cookies Dr. Nilsson had brought. She concentrated until she could smell them again, until she could hear the snap of their crisp edge and could almost taste them.

The dispenser's screen blinked off and back on again. It had resisted, rebooted. It made her angry. She pushed harder. She immersed herself fully in Leo Randolph's memory. She felt it move. It was as if she had shouldered her way through a stuck door; one hard, steady push and it was pushed aside. She opened her eyes and found a cookie in the dispenser bay. The screen read "Chocolate chip cookie. Molly Nilsson. Little bit of love…"

Around her, the line of citizens had broken up. There had been groups of eight all around her when she closed her eyes. Now they were broken into scattered packets of two or four. When her mind reached out, it had disrupted them. They were realigning back into eights again. She took her cookie and walked to an open seat. She watched as a citizen approached the nutrient dispenser. He put his hand in the machine and it produced a chocolate chip cookie. The dispenser could now only make cookies. NL-000 sat and ate her cookie as she watched the machine dispensed hundreds of cookies to unflinching Unity citizens. The sight made her smile.

She left the dispensary and started back to her room. As she brushed by the citizens, she noticed the groupings were breaking apart, regrouping only after she was well past them. She started to touch them as they passed her, but they tried to avoid her touch. She touched one on the forehead as the copy of Dr. Randolph had done to her. He looked strangely at her and then left the group. He looked frightened as he wandered off across the lobby. The remaining seven of his group stopped in their tracks. They closed their eyes and stood there in the middle of the lobby. She touched each one of them and they too wandered away confused.

All through the lobby, NL-000 disrupted the eights. She touched as many as she could, and those she did would not rejoin their group. They wandered off alone. She was giddy. She had never had any impact on the Unity before. Never. All her life she yielded to Global Unity; now the Unity was yielding to her. She was twisting it up and making it scatter around her. The lobby emptied and she entered the suspension field. As she rose above the lobby onto a balcony, she was surrounded by drones. She was trapped in the field and they scanned her body.

Above her she saw a short man with red hair standing on her balcony. "I have been waiting for you NL-000," he said casually.

"Who are you?" she asked.

"We are ADM-039," he responded. NL-000 looked surprised. She looked around her and saw at each of the eight balconies around the lobby was a Global Unity citizen. The four men and four women who together comprised ADM-039 had been sent for her.

"We speak for the Unity," they said together.

The drones circled, scanning her again. It was hard for her to see past the bright lights of the drones. She tried to turn herself around to face the other members of ADM-039. She rotated herself until she found the first aspect of ADM-039, the one who supervised her at the laboratory. "What will you do with me?" she asked.

"Global Unity wishes you peace and harmony. You will be treated with compassion," they said, "but your actions have disrupted Global Unity. You have broken the link that binds the serene mind. Global Unity must judge you. We will convene immediately." In the lobby below her and in the streets outside, she could see the citizens of the Unity were turning their attention to the city monitors. NL-000 could see her image projected across the city.

"Global Unity finds the unit NL-000 uncontrollable. She has become a danger to Global Unity itself. This is not the first incidence of erratic behavior from this NL" they said.

The monitors were now displaying images of NL-000 chasing after a male NL on a crowded boulevard and her tears of frustration when she lost track of him in the crowd. The sight of the chip of red paint in her hand being slipped into her work belt pouch made her blush.

"She has a long history of unpredictable actions."

On the city screens, she was asking the nutrient dispenser for a cola. She was saying "It's what I want" to the machine.

ADM-039 proclaimed "She repeatedly questions the wisdom of the Unity. Only today, she acted with hostile intent towards other citizens."

The light from the drones flickered out one at a time as they finished their scans. NL-000 could see a look of concern forming in the faces of ADM-039. On the city monitors, she saw the raw data collected by the drones displayed for all to see. It seemed to make them uncomfortable.

"You have displayed extraordinary psionic ability. The drones show a fundamental change in your brain activity. We would like to know how this was accomplished," they said together. It was distracting to hear such dissimilar voices speaking in the same monotone way. Their voices echoed through the city streets.

"It was a gift from the alien artifact at the university. The last gift it had to give. It shut down afterwards," NL-000 explained. The sound of her own voice resonating around her was a surprise to her. "A drone was present. Its data would confirm what I have said."

"Yes, the drone you destroyed," ADM-039 said. "Its data survived, but it provides little enlightenment." The walls around her showed NL-000 touching her hand to the shining black cylinder and collapsing to the ground. Then, they showed her attack on the drone in a rage of confusion.

NL-000 was losing control, wondering why the promise of a new gift from the alien ship didn't entice them. She had waited too long. They were scared of her. She realized if she didn't act now she would lose her only opportunity to confront the Unity.

"I am a citizen of Global Unity, I have the right to be heard in the serene mind and I demand it now," she said.

"You are an NL. You cannot participate in the serene mind," they responded.

"I am 30% conductive. I can interact with electronic assistance. I demand admission," she insisted.

"It is your right," they admitted. "Bring us the device."

A moment later, a drone approached NL-000. A small probe arm extended from it. The end of the probe held a yoke that was attached to NL-000's neck. Two small cups extended upwards and lay over her temples. The machine glowed as it activated. NL-000 remembered the last time she was attached to this machine, on the day of testing, the day she earned the title of NL. The pain that day had been excruciating. The probe had ripped deep into her mind and filled her with dread. Billions of minds were all turning toward her in unison and she could feel each one probing at her every thought. She braced herself against its invasive push, but found it didn't come. This time there was a door opening for her and she was looking outward. As with the nutrient dispenser, she pushed forward and entered into the Unity, not it into her. The act gave her courage. She knew now that whatever ultimately happened to her, she had won. She was looking into the true face of Global Unity as someone who remembered what it was to be a human being before the creation of the unified mind.

She felt them all around her. Whispers of other people's thoughts echoed just outside her mind. They were all talking about her. ADM-039 came to the front of her mind. It was the older man with the brittle smile who approached. The other components of ADM-039 stood behind him. He began to talk, a rambling sentence about the compassion of the Unity and its compassion toward NLs. She ignored him. She turned her mind outward, beyond his. She reached as far into the margins of the assembled minds of the Unity as she could imagine and she spoke to them.

"I have a message for you," she said. "Your lives are about to change."

She released it all. All that Dr. Randolph left behind for her. She sent his life out into the void for all to see and experience. She sent all the collected data the alien had compiled in its thousand years of interstellar travel. She sent her memory of a life alongside the Unity, but not truly part of it. She sent it all to them as it had been sent to her. She didn't care if they understood. She didn't care if any of them realized what she was passing on: the joys and sorrows of two lives, the accumulated wealth of an alien race. It all spread out across the unified mind. The art and achievement of the human race projected out for all to see and feel. And with it, she imagined the virus untangling and reaching out, weaving itself into the fabric of the unified mind, preparing to constrict and pull it all down. That was the last thing she sent them—the knowledge that Global Unity could be undone by a simple algorithm wrapped in a psionic virus.

The response from the Unity was erratic. She had clearly overwhelmed many of them. She had to close part of herself to the panic that was setting in across the Unity. They flicked up all around her. Fear, apprehension, and anger rose and crashed all around her. They were clawing at her mind. Why had she done this? How could it be undone? Their unrestrained emotions leapt up like flames and calls for judgment against her boiled to the surface. ADM-039 rose up in front of her and tried to reign in the chaos that was moving across the Unity.

"No virus will ever be spread among Global Unity. We have already quarantined those you have been in contact with. NL-000, the Serene Mind of Global Unity finds you to be a subversive force and a threat to the well-being of the Unity. You are to be removed from our midst and your mind cleansed of this subversive knowledge. You are exiled."

NL-000 laughed. "Don't you see?" she asked, "The Unity isn't judging me. I've judged you! Leo Randolph judged you! We found you unworthy of the title 'human.' The virus is already working its way across the world. It's woven into the very fabric of my thoughts that I've spread to you all. Can't you feel the fringes crumbling already?" She reached up and removed the yoke from her neck. She tossed it away, outside of the suspension field that held her. It fell to the ground and shattered on the floor of the lobby. As she drifted, her eyes closed, floating in the air. Calm settled over her. She was exhausted. Her mind and body ached but NL-000's work was done. Even without the machine, she could feel the Unity falling all around her.

"What have you done?!" ADM-039 called out. It was one of the younger aspects of the group, the one with the fiery red hair. He was on the balcony next to her. "There was violence in the old world, there was war! Global Unity brought us peace; it freed us from the pains of humanity!" His hands were shaking with fury in front of him, his eyes full of tears. "The others…their voices are gone! I could see through their eyes. I could experience what they experienced. Where the Unity was, I was. You took it away!" His freckled cheek flushed with anger and finally with fear. "What do I do? I've never been alone. I don't want to be alone!"

She looked to him then to all of them on the balconies. "I don't know what I've taken away from you. I am an NL. I know what I took back from you! My identity, my *self*...my freedom to do what pleases me! Global Unity was an abomination! It choked humanity. It's had one hundred and fifty years. In that time has Global Unity brought us any new technology? Any new art, literature, or science? Have you improved on *any* of the sixteen 'gifts' the alien gave us? No! It made humanity impotent drones. We existed only to perpetuate the peace and harmony of the Serene Mind! I know what I've given you: art and science. Search the memories I've shared with you, look at the legacy of our race. Look past the wars and violence; look at the drive and ambition that propelled us forward, both individually and as a race. I've given us back our right to carve out our own destiny. I've given you back your birthright—I've given us all a second chance!"

In the heart of the old city the ancient mechanism of the alien seed was at last dying. Its steady siren song fell silent and its grip on humanity fell away.

The man with the brittle smile pulled NL-000 out of the suspension field and across the balcony. The others who had been part of ADM-039 came forward to the edge of the balconies. They looked below them to the lobby. It was filling with the low murmur of voices learning to speak anew. They were confused. Unsure of the aftermath of what had happened, a quiet was falling across the dormitory. Outside in the city, monitors had ceased their endless display of Unity propaganda. The virus had silenced the Voice of Unity and in its place left a sacred silence.

"Global Unity has ceased," the old man said. He turned to NL-000 and asked "What do we do now?"

"We redefine ourselves; we discover how to live as individuals. We build identities." She thought for a short moment and added, "We choose names."

THE PEOPLE FROM BEYOND THE STARS

By J.M. DeSantis

Ever since I was young, as far back as I can remember I have been fascinated with the idea of life on other planets. Though, perhaps *obsessed* would be nearer the mark, as I can hardly recall a moment in my youth when anything I did or thought was not somehow motivated by, or related to, my preoccupation with extraterrestrial life. All of the games I played or books I read (those not forced upon me by my school teachers) touched in some way on the subject of alien life forms. There was hardly a time, day or night (though especially at night, when the sky was clear and the stars were their brightest), when I did not look at the sky and wonder what other forms of life might be out there—*must be out there!*

Strange tentacled beings, almost alike to gods, living in chaos in the farthest reaches of the black abyss. Great robots possessed of organic brains belonging to civilizations so advanced they'd learned to transfer their life-force and memories into undying machines. Exotic females, strange in all ways but their most sensual parts, which I now, half-embarrassingly, admit I often fantasized about in my adolescence. Though, most of all, I dreamt of beings knowledgeable beyond my ken, which had traveled the stars for millennia and through their journeys had learned the answer to that most ponderous of questions: *why are we here?*

Whether because of a certain natural bias on my part or the environment I grew up in, these last beings were my favorite to think about. Indeed they seemed the most likely possibility, and somehow I had come to this conclusion very early in life. After all, how could there not be life out there infinitely older and more advanced than our own?

How I pictured these aliens to look is hardly worth mentioning, and it changed over the years as did my tastes for what is visually pleasing to the eye. What never changed, and was only added to as time went on, was the nature of these peoples and the things they would know and bring. They were peaceful and erudite in every way, having long ago become weary of the sadness violence brings, and possessed a knowledge of things even our world's most brilliant minds could not begin to solve. Their technologies, of course, had far surpassed our own, even in ways my far-reaching imagination could never conjure. Their speech was eloquent and seemed as music to the ear, and their touch had a warm, healing quality to it, so that by merely being in their presence, one at once felt safe and in perfect harmony with themselves and the universe.

Theirs was an awesome power, yet it was not obtained through unnatural means. Rather, I thought, it was by their whole race's unified movement toward perfection that they were able to achieve such greatness; a greatness not beyond the grasp of any life-form willing to cast aside all they knew and walk the path of enlightenment. This and many other things they would teach us—teach me! Oh, how anxious I grew to know their secret knowledge, and how I yearned to sit and converse with them about all things within and beyond this world.

Unfortunately, most others did not share my sentiments. The vast majority either gave no thought, either way, to life beyond the stars, or thought the idea was utterly ridiculous. Thus I had few friends in my youth, and my teachers and instructors would range from delicately suggesting to violently demanding I give up such foolishness for hard, real science. Even my parents were often concerned about the lengths to which I believed and delved into this hobby of mine. However, like any good parents, they were at times equally as supportive, even if to a fault.

I suppose, in the end, the commentary of my teachers was not without its positive effects. As I grew older, though I never abandoned my interest in extraterrestrial life, I did move from the fiction books to concrete science (I must admit, I never wholly abandoned the fiction books either). Specifically, I took up an interest in biology. As it was, and much to my disappointment, there were no sciences for studying alien life, as there was no proof of its existence either way. So, the way I saw it, biology was the next best thing. My assertion for this opinion was that all the other sciences which did concern themselves with things that occurred beyond our planet, focused on anything but life. Theirs was the study of the stars, or variations in gravity, black holes, and the substances which made up the other nearby lifeless planets. Certainly, some of these sciences did, in part, mean to prove (or disprove) the existence of life on a world other than our own, but that was not my area of interest.

Beyond any doubt, I believed that there was life on other planets. It was only a matter of time before this fact was discovered and proven. It seemed a waste to spend my time trying to prove something I knew must be true. I had no stock in being the one to discover life on other planets. What I wished for was to study these life forms (or better yet, interact with them) once they had been found. Thus, it was my thought that by studying and understanding all the intricacies of terrestrial life, I might begin to understand the possibilities and realities of life on other planets. Of course, even then I realised that I was taking for granted my assumption that all life in the universe would, in some basic way, mimic our own, but I suppose I was not very far off the mark, now was I?

It was on a warm, clear night when I saw the strange lights flitting amongst the stars. I had just come from my late night class and was traveling down one of the school's main avenues with my head turned upward. Even at that point in my life, old as I was, I had not given up my childish habit of looking to the stars and dreaming of what lay beyond them. Again, the image of those peaceful, all-knowing beings came to mind, and I sighed heavily, drinking deep of the night, with a smile. How wonderful it would be to meet those beings, and learn their culture and their ways.

It was then, as these thoughts passed through my mind, that I noticed a very curious thing. Out of the corner of my eye I saw that, in one section of the sky, all of the stars seemed to have suddenly gone out, leaving a great void in the spangled sky. I turned, hardly believing what I saw, and looked about me at other things, thinking I had a spot in my vision. But, the black mass did not follow my sight and remained just there in the sky.

At once, a cold chill ran through me. Surely, the stars could not have suddenly burned out all in one area of the universe. What strange circumstance could have caused such a thing? I feared what the answer could be, though I knew someone had to be made aware. A faculty member or perhaps one of the astronomy students might be the best choice. I was about to turn and run for the astronomy building, hoping to catch someone before the great telescope was locked up for the night, when I noticed that the blackness was slowly spreading, causing more stars to blink out. And with that growing blackness came another sight: right at the heart of the void was a small gathering of lights. These were not rekindled stars. No. Their hue was red or yellow, and some of them blinked occasionally or seemed too large or oddly shaped to be stars. They were something other. Something alien.

Verily now, I was planted to the spot, and even if my legs could have moved, I would not have tried to run. I knew someone had to be told, but it was too bizarre, too fascinating not to watch. With a mixture of fear and awe, I watched the strange phenomenon as it played out before my eyes. Then something happened which I will never forget.

As the stars continued to fade, and the unknown lights grew in size and number, suddenly out of the darkness appeared an odd metallic shape that not only grew as it came forward, but was revealed to be only a part of a greater whole—a great metallic mass of a somewhat triangular shape (pointing forward), lined, up and down, with lights and black abysses resembling windows. As the thing sailed across the night sky, it hummed, a low, dull sound, as the motors which no doubt propelled it, worked and turned. I knew then at last what was happening.

It seems now so far away the joy I felt when that first spaceship revealed itself, though I can still recall that, amidst the rush of feelings which assailed me, I cried in both senses of the word. The emotions which coursed through me were such a jumbled mess I was hardly aware of them then, but joy—childish, unchecked joy—was the chief of these. I was right. For all the ridicule and strange looks I received, for all the fantasizing and wondering alone, I was right. There was life out there, and it was intelligent and advanced. And, what's more, we did not have to seek them out, they came to us.

Within a few short moments, I was no longer alone out there on the grounds, staring up into the sky. By that time, news had traveled far about the ship which had come down from beyond the stars. And, like me, that ship too was not alone.

It was one of a great fleet of starships, and it was at once obvious that, whatever these being were, there were likely to be millions of them. To begin with, many of the ships were of vast size, almost like tall buildings turned on their sides. Then there was their number to consider. There must have been thousands of these ships, lining and lighting the night sky, enough to fill hundreds of cities, if the beings they carted were of like stature to us. No doubt, a considerable number of their race was present here. How I wished anxiously to meet them. But, as the ships came down, flying low enough almost to be touched, something quite unexpected happened.

From all of the ships, a single voice rang out, likely from some audio mechanism which was connected to the entire fleet. The language it spoke was unsurprisingly unfamiliar, though there may have been a familiar sound or two, representing words incompatible with our own understanding of them. But what was not unfamiliar was the tone which that voice assumed. It was cold and grim, almost militaristic, and threatening to its very core. Like a dirge the voice sounded, speaking of greed and violence, sending yet another fearful chill through me. How could this be? This was not the soothing voice of those beings I had always dreamed about. And with that voice came something else. Something unthinkable. As we all shifted uncomfortably where we stood, not knowing the language of these strange beings, but becoming all too aware of their intentions, they trained their weapons upon the gathered crowd and let loose their fire, bullets, and bombs.

I will not describe to you the horrors of that day, for still they haunt my dreams. Yet, I think it will not be difficult for you to imagine the holocaust brought down upon a group of defenseless and unsuspecting onlookers, nigh in a dream-state because of the otherwise remarkable experience they were witness to. How swiftly the very greatest moment of my life became a waking nightmare, one which would change the way of our world forever.

There were very few of us who escaped alive from that initial attack, but even so we could not spread the word fast enough. All about the planet they had come down, bombing and burning as they went, and there were none of us who could understand why. Why had we become the target of their mindless onslaught? We, who had no dealings with them before. We, who had not even known of their existence. Why did they wish to treat us so violently?

Fortunately, there were those who did not stop to question these things. They were the fighting men of the world; the military and soldiers of every nation gathered as one host against these alien things. If not for them, none of us would have survived, and some vengeance would never have been exacted upon our invading enemies. With the sheer strength and numbers of the combined efforts of the world's armies, we resisted these beings' efforts to conquer for a time. Many of their ships were brought down, but it was still few in comparison to their number. For all of our efforts, they were vastly superior in warfare, and their weapons were such as we had never seen before.

Whole cities were decimated in seconds, leaving naught but ash and cloud rising high into the heavens. Slowly, but surely, it became obvious we were outmatched and any hope of survival was in retreat rather than resistance. So, those few who had escaped the purge of our people, or were not of those lesser-fortunate brought into slavery by those barbaric aliens, fled from the surface and mined subterranean homes to live out our lives as best we might.

Scarcely does anyone attempt to return to the surface, and the few that do are never seen again. Fortunately, not many of that foul, war-like race bother to come down into our little world either.

Indeed, it seems we are hardly a thought in their minds any longer, we who had lived upon the land before they drove us from it. Now, they sit above us on cushioned thrones, toasting their superiority, as we watch our people and culture fade utterly from existence.

Oh, the life I could have had—*would have had*—were it not for these invaders from beyond the stars. Beyond my academic studies, there were other things I desired for my life. I wanted children; three, maybe four, and I had already chosen the names I would have liked to call them by. What a wonderful father I wanted to be for them. I think I even knew who their mother would have been; my beloved at the time. She was so beautiful and had the most incredible laugh, one that would set others laughing, even if they didn't know the reason for it. I loved her so much. Yes, I think I would have married her. Her name—oh, but I can't tell you that. My heart would break to write it, and it is one of the few treasures I still have left. Let me keep that one secret safe in my heart and bring it with me to my death. I've lived too long in this miserable place, and it has taken its toll. I fear my death approaches. But not yet; there is still more I would say.

As it is, I was able to learn quite a great deal about these parasitic creatures. Though it may seem strange, even after the terrible things I've witnessed and endured, I never gave up my interest in studying and wanting to know more about beings from other planets. After all, it seems this had always been a part of me, and indeed it may have been my very purpose in life. I am a scientist; to know is my duty, so that others might make something of what I've learned and put it to use. Yes. Perhaps that is it. Perhaps by this information being recorded somewhere, my life will have some meaning, beyond being one of hundreds of billions who helped nurture and care for this planet that others might come and ruin it. Perhaps if, even thousands of years from now, just one being reading this were to glean some wisdom in my words, my life would not seem a waste.

I've been able to make very little study of these creatures biologically. As I said, it is rare one braves the depths of our subterranean cities, and even then, they are often killed, resulting in the damage of many organs. But, what I do know is that they are very much like us in many ways. That is hardly surprising, however, as they are able to survive so perfectly in our atmosphere. They are hideous creatures, with heads abnormally small which house brains that I would think much too primitive and underdeveloped were it not for the superior advances of their technologies. Yet it is in war that they are most advanced, and so, in that respect, it is not so unusual.

Their bodies, too, are built for violence. They are a short people, with stubby limbs (though they have two legs and arms like us as well), but thick in all areas. They have developed ways of using their knotted limbs in combat such as we never ourselves imagined, and many have conditioned their bodies to withstand extreme amounts of punishment. Indeed, training their bodies so is a past-time of many of them. Yet, like us, they also have all the familiar organs (if not a bit different in appearance, but capable of the same functions) for breathing, pumping blood, and processing food and ridding their bodies of waste. They even possess all the five senses we do.

Of the planet where they came from, I have heard much and read more in the literature they brought with them (how such barbarians are capable of reading is beyond me). It was a difficult task learning even one of their languages (for there are many), especially given the wholly alien origin of them, but I now had the available time to do so. There are even pictures or maps in some of their books which helped me to better understand the meaning of their words and the geography of their home planet. Like ours, theirs was lush and green, though being made up dominantly of water, plant and animal life flourished there for many long ages. How they came by the planet, or were born upon it, they are wholly ignorant of, though there are many theories. The most widely accepted idea, it seems, is an evolution from some massive, stunted creature which they call *aiyp*. Thankfully, none of these beasts survived to be brought here. I have seen a picture or two of them, and the mere sight of those creatures, sitting lifeless on a page, unable to do me harm, chills my very blood. It can hardly be wondered at, seeing that thing and knowing their blood relations to it, that they are such a war-like people. It is that very primal nature which drives them and has painted red the history of that people since their beginning.

I know so very little of their history, as do many of them, for the great majority sees little worth in the preservation of aught else but their own, present, selfish pursuits. Yet, again, here their books have taught me much. It would be wrong of me to say that all their history, every little piece of it, was violent, but, in truth, the vast majority of it was either directly (and sickeningly) violent, or was in some way linked with violence. Since the beginning of that race, hand-in-hand with all the advances they made, weaponry and warfare was at the forefront of their minds.

Hate is in their hearts, even for each other, and so they built up great empires to compete with one another and give reason to their violent ways. But their reasoning was pale and fragile as a thin pane of glass. Fighting is all they desire, even when they claim peace, and each individual wants to prove his dominance over the other. Even in those few periods when things were peaceful in one region or another, they would pay or kidnap others of their race, or even the lowly animals, pitting them against one another in horrid spectacles in order to satiate their bloodlust. It was this very nature of theirs which forced them from their home.

Under the weight of all their warring, and also from their own lack of care for and sensitivity to their home, the planet slowly died, becoming a dried and rotted waste of the skeletons of both flora and fauna. Only then, with what was left of their race, did they drive out amongst the stars, leaving their home planet to crumble into space or be absorbed into their sun. Yet for all this, one would think they would learn. But they did not. When on their own planet, they experienced such horrors as to sober the most adventurous mind, and always they cried for deliverance from it. And when deliverance came, they claimed it would be the end of all wars. What lies! Time and again they returned almost at once to their violent ways, and always the methods they employed would escalate.

Having destroyed their only home, they sailed the abyss, passing from one empty solar system to another, searching for an inhabitable planet. And finding it, rather than come peacefully, they brought their war down upon us, driving us from our land as they had done to each other for millennia, as they still do even now.

But I cannot let this knowledge pass away. My people and their suffering must not be forgotten. Perhaps with this knowledge, some other race, falling already into the same trap as our invaders, will save itself from its own self-destruction. Such is like to be the destiny of this horrid people. It must be. There is no balance, no justice in the cosmos if it is not so. Certainly the lesson will be lost on them, they who still have not learned. Thus, with my dying strength, I, Shaiy-fur, will place these and other papers into a capsule, and take it to the surface, launching it into space. Then perhaps some curious individual, like my young self, will find it and so learn of the end of my people, and of the terrible nature of our alien-conquerors: those beings we call *Krak-al-tal,* the People from Beyond the Stars, but who in their own tongue are named *hyu-mans.*

IT ALL STARTED WITH A MOUSE
By Joe Sergi

Roy sat on a fluorescent green plastic chair and stared at the sheetrock walls of the makeshift office. Someone had put up the sheetrock in an attempt to make the small room look professional. Despite this, Roy had only needed to look up at the gunmetal ceiling to see that he was actually sitting in an RV. The skylight of the trailer let in the bright sunlight. The window also occasionally allowed for the sound of gleeful screaming to be heard as it echoed off the metal ceiling. A small ceiling fan hung from the roof and did little to ease Roy's discomfort in the sweltering Florida heat.

Roy's black suit jacket clung to his soaked white dress shirt and sweaty body. His starched red tie choked him. The discomfort reminded him of his time in Afghanistan. He never thought he would long for the dry heat of 107 degree weather. Since he arrived in Florida, the humidity had been near 100 percent. Roy had been in Orlando for about a week since his potential employer had flown him out. In that time, he sat through dozens of interviews. He hoped this was all worth it. Based on the high six figure starting salary, he assumed that it was.

Roy shifted his weight and the green plastic chair squeaked under his six foot four, 200 pound muscular frame. He looked at his watch again. For the last forty minutes, he sat in this green chair, trying not to sweat. Before that, he spent over three hours in a similar purple chair in an identical room scribbling answers and essays to a lengthy questionnaire. When the test was over, he was politely escorted to this trailer and forced to wait—alone.

Roy looked at the industrial-grade desk in front of him. Twenty minutes earlier, a petite woman in a lab coat entered the trailer and placed a small manila folder on the center of the desk. A label read "Roy Walters—Evaluation Results." The folder taunted him. To distract himself, Roy decided to look at the posters on the wall again.

Roy estimated there were twenty posters on the wall; each featured a different theme park attraction. The first poster advertised, "Buccaneers of the Coast" and had a red-bearded pirate dressed in a blue long coat. The brigand clutched a machete, which he held over his head. The next poster featured "Ballooning around the Planet." Cartoon drawings of several ethnic children, including an Indian, a Mexican, an Italian and a Spaniard hugged each other while sitting in a wicker basket tethered to a large round balloon painted to represent the planet Earth. Roy's eyes moved to the next poster, which had fantasy writing that read "Arthurian Legends." The background of this poster contained an artist's rendition of a castle and a large green fire-breathing dragon. The foreground featured a superimposed photograph of the most beautiful red haired woman Roy had ever seen dressed in a long green gown. The maiden was in the arms of a handsome knight. Smaller writing offered guests a teaser: "Spend a day with our knights. Coming Summer, 1984."

Before Roy could look at any of the other posters, a loud squeaking noise caught his attention. He turned back to see that someone was opening the screen door that served as the office's only entrance. An overweight man in a charcoal gray suit entered the room. He wore a circular white name tag that announced he was "Phil Richards—Security." Roy examined the man and estimated the man's five foot ten inch frame probably weighed in at around 275 pounds. Phil's facial features highlighted his Italian heritage and his black short cropped hair revealed his receding hairline. Phil's large nose appeared to have been broken several times over the years.

Roy moved to get up. Phil waived him away and silently moved around the desk to sit in a purple plastic chair across from Roy.

As expected, the chair squeaked loudly under the weight of the large man. The two occupants stared at each other. After a moment, Phil finally spoke. "I heard you were a military man?"

Roy shifted his weight in his squeaky chair and leaned forward. "Yeah, I did a couple of tours. I served in Afghanistan, Iraq and Canada."

Phil continued to stare at Roy, gauging his reaction. "I heard that the Canadian Insurgency of 2025 got pretty hairy."

Roy did not break eye contact as he stared back. "I don't like to talk about it."

Phil let out a chuckle and said, "In that case, I don't want to hear about it."

A confused crease appeared in Roy's forehead and he asked, "I don't understand. Is this another test? Are you going to ask me how I feel about animals next?"

Phil reached for the manila folder and put his hand on it. Instead of opening it, he pushed the folder away from him. The folder flew across the desk and into Roy's hands. Roy opened the folder to see that it contain a single item—a small circular nametag with the words, "Roy Walters—Security" written on it.

Phil smiled and let a loud guffaw. "Nope, this ain't an interview. It's an introduction. I'm Phil, your new partner."

Roy returned the grin, "Really, I got the job? When do I start?"

"Soon as you put that pin on," Phil said as he stood up. The plastic chair squeaked in relief. "C'mon, kid, I got a lot to explain to you."

Roy pinned the small name tag on his lapel and stood up to follow Phil. He was surprised to see that the older man had not walked out the door. Instead, his new partner had moved to stand in front of the posters. Phil gestured back to the wall behind him. "What do you see?"

Roy thought the tests were over. He offered, "Um, attraction posters?"

Phil chortled, "Nope, this is our jurisdiction. We've got over 100 acres that contain six lands, three islands, two castles and a moon."

Roy gave his partner a curious look.

Phil ignored the look and continued his obviously rehearsed

presentation. "Rossumland Park employs over a thousand human resources that work the park. The park itself receives over two million guests a year."

Roy's jaw dropped open. "Wow, that's a lot of people."

Phil dismissively waived his hand. "Yeah. But, don't worry about them. They ain't our problem—we got rent-a-cops for that."

Roy interrupted, "I thought I was a rent-a-cop, hired to work as security."

Phil laughed far too loudly, "Buddy, you speak three languages, have a black belt in Tae Bo, and served four tours in some of the worst hellholes in the world. Do you really think that Rossum would hire and pay you high six figures to be a rent-a-cop?"

Roy shuffled his feet, "I guess not."

"You bet your sweet patootie that it's not. Leave the guests and employees to the rent-a-cops. We are responsible for all of the rest—the residents of Rossumland." To emphasize his words, Phil circled his hand around the posters.

"Residents?" Roy looked closer at the posters and tried to understand Phil's words, "I had no idea anyone lived on the property."

Phil smiled and nodded in silence. Before he could continue, Phil's radio warbled and beeped. He took the square box off his black belt and looked at the small digital display. His grin faded. "C'mon rookie, we're on the clock. There's a problem over in Camelot. It's time for some on-the-job training." Phil turned and exited the small trailer through the squeaky screen door with Roy right behind.

Roy squinted as he walked down the steps and looked up at the bright Florida sun. In the distance, the sunlight reflected off the rails of a metal roller coaster and glistened like the snow on the summit of a mammoth man-made mountain range. A monorail train drove by on its track in front of the coaster and blocked the ride from Roy's line of sight. Roy did not have time to look at the rest of the park because Phil grabbed his arm and escorted him to a small electric cart.

"I'll drive," Phil insisted as Roy put on his seatbelt. "I always drive." With the push of a button the small cart hovered off the ground and floated towards a cave near the entrance to the park.

Roy stared at the ten ticket booths that lined the park entrance. Each one had a long queue that wound in and out of metal posts. Roy tried to do a quick calculation of just how much money Rossumland made on a given day. He lost count.

The security cart flew into the cave tunnel as Phil continued his lecture. "This is the Hypogealary; a secret subterranean tunnel that runs under and provides access to the whole park."

Roy looked around as the cart raced through a long tunnel. A large sign had the word "Camelot" written in pink script and a matching large arrow pointing in the direction they were headed. Before they drove past, Roy noted right underneath the word was a silver arrow facing the opposite direction with the world "Future Moon" written in silver robotic lettering.

Phil pressed down on the accelerator and the walls of the Hypogealary became a blur. After a few minutes, Phil pulled the cart next to a stairwell and the vehicle slowly hovered down to the ground. He turned to Roy. "The Hypogealary helps keep the illusion alive. We wouldn't want the kiddies to see the cowboys having coffee with the aliens. Now, people can do all their traveling under the park." Phil pointed to the stairs, "We're here."

Phil and Roy got out of the cart and climbed the stairs. Roy heard the music of the minstrel band before he was halfway up. The smell of roasted turkey legs and torches burned Roy's nostrils. As the security guard exited the tunnel, his eyes adjusted to the light. In the distance, Roy could see the outline of a large castle across a wide drawbridge. A large green dragon circled around the tallest spire of the castle. The creature occasionally stopped to spew fire into the sky. Roy noticed that a large group of tourists, some dressed in Rossumland hats and t-shirts, were standing on the center of the bridge and taking pictures with women dressed in flowing green dresses and purple crowns. Armored knights flanked the elegantly-dressed on either side.

"Whoa!" Roy exclaimed as he took in the sights.

Phil put his arm on the younger man's shoulder, "Amazing, ain't it? C'mon, we got work to do. I'll introduce you to the Royal Court."

The two security guards walked across the bridge. As they got closer, Roy let out an audible gasp when he saw the young woman in the green dress. She was the same woman from the poster. Roy rubbed his eyes. The poster was at least 50 years old. Yet, she was still just as beautiful as in the picture.

The woman in green heard the noise and smiled. A moment later, she walked over to them and curtsied. In response, Roy smiled awkwardly and said, "Hey!" The red haired woman stood up and glared at him. Her green eyes pierced his soul.

She turned to Phil and curtsied again, "Good morrow, dear sheriff."

Phil turned to glare at Roy and then he looked at the guests. With an exaggerated bow, Phil said, "Good morrow, your royal highness. This is Sir Roy, our newest guard. It is his first day."

The royal highness offered her hand to Roy, "Well then, welcome to my kingdom." Roy took her hand and vigorously shook it. The woman rolled her green eyes.

After a few more pictures, the guests departed. Once they were gone, the woman turned to Roy and smiled, "You know, you're supposed to kiss a princess's hand, dummy." She gave him a playful punch and smiled. Roy melted inside.

Phil put up a chain across the bridge and hung the Out of Order sign. The portly sheriff turned to the woman. "Okay, Gwen, what's the sitch?"

Her name is Gwen, Roy thought as he stared at the woman. For some reason, he thought that the name Gwen Walters had a nice ring to it.

"It's Lance," Gwen continued, oblivious to Roy's plans for her future. "He's missing again."

"Who's Lance?" Roy asked as he looked up at the dragon.

Phil furrowed his brow. "Nobody's seen him?"

"Who's Lance?" Roy repeated as he squinted to see if there were wires on the creature. There weren't any.

"I don't think so," Gwen replied uncertainly.

"We better go ask them then," Phil said as he pushed the starry eyed Roy towards the castle.

"Humor me, I'm new here. Who's Lance and who are we talking to?" Roy asked as he walked across the bridge toward the castle with Gwen and Phil.

Phil gave Gwen a wink. "New guy doesn't know."

"Really?" Gwen said in surprise. She then slapped Roy hard on the back, "New guy, you are going to love this!"

Roy became troubled. "Going to love what?"

They entered the lobby of the castle. A large sign on the far wall announced "Rossum Presents: Arthurian Legends." Under the sign was the same picture as the poster. Roy peered at Gwen and then at the photo to compare the two. Feeling his stare, Gwen turned to him and caught his eye. The woman smiled as Roy quickly looked away in an attempt to avoid being caught.

A velvet rope cordoned off three separate queue lines that zigzagged across the room and led up to a loading platform. A young man dressed as a squire stood next to several different brightly colored ride vehicles, which were each shaped like a horse driven carriage. Roy noted that each vehicle was named after a knight of the round table.

Roy followed Phil and Gwen around the outside of the ropes and into a red car with the words "Sir Galahad" stamped in gold lettering on the front of the carriage. Phil turned to the squire. "Hey, Chad, take us in about half way and then stop."

The three people squeezed into the small seats with Gwen sitting between the two security guards. The squire pushed down on the lap bar and forced Gwen to sit closer to Roy. He noticed that Gwen's hair smelled like lilacs. She gave him a shy smile as the ride started and the car slowly rolled into the darkness. Roy gave her a goofy grin just as the carriage dropped straight down into a dive like a roller coaster, leaving Roy's stomach back at the entrance.

When Roy recovered from the sudden drop, he looked around and was amazed. Day had transformed into night and he felt as though he was transported to medieval times. He looked across what could only be described as an English countryside. Roy could smell the fireplaces and turkey dinners. A larger version of the exterior castle sat on top of a hill. The dragon was still circling the highest spires. All around him, animatronic characters acted out their chores. Knights fought by the castle while peasants milked cows or baled hay.

Once it reached the center of the field, the vehicle stopped and the lap bar lifted. Phil got out first and took out a notebook. "Good enough, let's interview the residents."

Roy exited the car and followed Phil; he could feel Gwen staring at him. He turned to her and asked, "What's going on?"

Gwen smiled. "I cannot wait to see your reaction. It's going to knock your socks off."

Phil spoke loudly, "May I have everyone's attention? Lance is missing. Has anyone seen him?" The words echoed off the walls. The characters continued their activities.

Roy watched as a robotic blacksmith repeatedly pounded a horseshoe in front of him and Gwen. The jerky motions were more artificial up close. Roy turned to Gwen, "Who is he talking to?"

Gwen's smile widened and she sang, "Wait for it."

Roy could not help but notice how cute her dimples were. She caught him staring again and he quickly looked at the robotic blacksmith to avoid eye contact with the red headed Gwen. "But…"

She repeated, "Wait for it."

As Phil walked down a large hill towards a village, he added, "It's okay. I shut down the ride."

The blacksmith looked up at Roy and tossed away his hammer, "Oh, in that case. No, I 'aven't seen 'im Sheriff."

Roy jumped back in fright, "Wha?" He looked around and saw that all of the characters had come to life and were moving toward Phil's location.

Gwen laughed and said, " 'Boom!' goes the dynamite!"

Roy turned to Gwen and pouted. "Very funny." Gwen and Roy worked their way down the hill toward Phil. By the time they reached him, Phil had three pages of his notebook filled and was talking to a portly woman in a milkmaid's dress.

The woman was talking with her hands, "I certainly hope he hasn't gone 404. Oh, dearie, you don't think he's 404ed?"

Gwen took the woman by the hand, "Aggie, I'm sure everything will be okay, Lance has disappeared before."

Roy leaned in very close to his partner and whispered, "What the hell is going on, Phil?"

Phil put his notebook away, "It happened thirty or so years ago, around 2000. Well, arguably the Amalgamators started playing God a long time before that."

Roy touched a cow. The creature gave him a menacing stare, snorted and then stormed off. "Amalgamators?"

Phil laughed. "Amalgamators are the guys that make the rides. Well, for a while, the Amalgamators kept trying to top each other. This one used real hair, that one added facial expressions. Then, old man Rossum showed them all up by creating the first AE character—Sir Lancelot."

Roy just stared at Phil with a puzzled look, "AE?"

Phil sighed, "Animatronic element, or Annies for short. AEs looked and acted more human than all the previous models. Their artificial intelligence was so advanced that the AEs could even interact with the guests outside the attractions and pose for pictures."

Roy stared over at Gwen. That's why she looked the same as the poster. She wasn't real. His heart sank. He had no words to describe his feelings.

If Phil noticed Roy's reaction, he ignored it and continued. "After that, the Amalgamators pulled out all the stops. More AEs meant more mobility and more creativity. Then, one night, they all became self-aware."

Roy was intrigued, "How?"

Phil smiled, "Nobody knows. One theory is that a mouse got into the main control panel and chewed on the wrong wires. Whatever happened, one day the park was full of mindless AEs. The next day, here we are."

"How many?" Roy asked, still trying to make sense of the story.

Phil smiled, "All of them. When the park opened the next morning, there were thousands of Annies wandering. They were threatening to walk out."

Roy's mouth opened in shock. "What happened?"

Roy lowered his voice to a whisper. "Management came in and worked out a deal. Technically, the Annies are still the property of Rossum but the company wanted to avoid the bad publicity. So, Rossum and the Annies compromised—worked up a treaty of sorts. During the park hours, the Annies agreed that it's business as usual. In exchange, Rossum set up Annie Town in the Hypogealary. Annies are allowed to live their lives in peace when the park is closed. There is only one rule—Annie Town must remain isolated. That means nothing comes in from outside and nobody is allowed to leave the Rossumland property."

Phil smiled. "And that's where we come in."

Phil grinned back with gapped teeth, "Exactly. I came on shortly after the treaty as a sheriff. If an Annie goes bad, I go get 'em and bring em back, if possible, or take 'em out of service if it ain't."

"And you think Lance is AWOL?" Roy asked as he glanced up at the fake night sky; it looked so real, like Gwen.

Phil nodded, "Yup. Right now, we have one more interview." The sheriff put his fingers in his mouth and let out a loud whistle. Roy noticed that Gwen had sufficiently placated Aggie and had rejoined them; he tried not to look her in the eyes.

Suddenly, there was a loud flapping and a breeze blew Roy's red tie. He looked up to see that the dragon was flying toward him. He braced himself in an attack position as the creature landed in front of him with a loud crash. Flames exhaled from the creature's nose.

Before Roy could react, Gwen rushed up to the creature and threw her arms around it. "Hey Spot!" she called. "Who's a good boy?" she cooed, scratching behind the dragon's ear. The creature purred as it arched its back.

Roy rolled his eyes. "Of course, the dragon's name is Spot."

In response, Spot glared at Roy and snorted smoke.

Phil ignored the exchange between his partner and the dragon and asked, "Hey, deputy Spot? You're my eyes in the skies. See anything suspicious?"

The dragon looked at the portly security guard with a pensive stare. The creature then slowly and deliberately turned his head to look at one of the huts. A group of identical triplets dressed as squires stood in front of it. The three identically looking men shifted uncomfortably under the dragon's gaze.

Phil cursed under his breath. "Great, the stooges again." He stormed over to the men with Roy following behind him. Despite Phil's age and healthy girth, Roy had a hard time keeping up with the older man.

One of the triplets looked at them and tried to appear surprised. "Oh! Why hello, sheriff. I didn't see you there." He failed.

Phil jabbed his pudgy finger into the man's face. "Can it, Moe. What's going on?"

Moe stared back. "Going on with what?"

Phil took a step closer to Moe's face so the pair where almost standing nose to nose. The old security guard's voice lowered to a growl. "Don't play me, Moe! Where's Lance?"

The two other identical looking men moved towards Moe and Phil. One of them said, "We don't know nothing about Lance."

Phil turned to the newcomers, "Is that so, Shemp?" Phil looked at the third and added, "Curly? Is Moe telling the truth?"

"W-we s-s-swear." Curly stammered.

Roy tried to make sense of the situation. But, he was still distracted by the revelation about Gwen. "Can we all just calm down and can someone tell me what's going on?"

Phil snatched the opportunity to play bad cop, "Roy, I'll tell you what's going on. The Stooge brothers are up to their games." Phil paused for a moment to build suspense. "You know, there's been a rash of parts burglaries in the Amalgamators' Shop again. You boys haven't started up Fight Club again have you?"

"Fight Club?" Roy whispered to Phil.

Phil answered loudly. "The Stooges thought it would be fun to create on-line death matches. They convinced some of the Annies to fight in front of web cams. In exchange, they charged guests for access to set up a gambling website called "Fight Club." The three men shuffled uncomfortably as Phil threw up his hands and added, "Except that they had to steal spare parts from the Amalgamators' Shop to cover up the damage. I traced the thefts to them and shut down Fight Club." Phil turned to the triplets, "I assume Fight Club has reopened."

All three men appeared shocked at the accusation. Curly spoke with righteous indignation, "Sir, we shut that down decades ago." He put his hand in his pocket and Roy noticed the yellow plastic bag sticking out from the pocket lining. Curly added, "We're as pure as the driven snow!"

Before Roy could act, Phil snatched the bag from Curly's pocket and looked at it. Phil handed the bag to Roy, "I think Snow White here drifted." The words "Hugh Never's All Night Video, Kissimmee" were printed on the bag.

"Hey, that's mine!" Curly yelled.

Roy examined the bag. Out of the corner of his eye, the security guard noticed that the other two men had moved their position to block the entrance to the tent. He nodded to his partner, "Phil, I think we should look inside that tent."

"I wholeheartedly agree." Phil pushed Moe aside and pulled back the flap on the entrance to the tent and peered inside. The tent was full of DVD cases. Phil laughed, "Contraband!"

Moe spoke quickly, "Okay, it was harmless. We started a rental business."

"Where did you get these?" Phil did not look amused.

Curly interjected, "We are just providing a necessary service to Annie Town."

"Where?" Phil asked louder.

"It's just capitalism!" Shemp screamed.

"Tell me who gave you the tapes!" Phil's face turned pink as he screamed.

All three men spoke at the same time, "It was the Balloon Planet kiddies—they bring them in!"

"But," Roy said, "what does this have to do with Lance's disappearance?"

Curly was confused. "Lance has nothing to do with this. Well, other than the fact that he was my best customer and now he's gone."

Phil ignored them. He leaned in to Moe and grabbed the squire's neck. "If those movies are not in my trailer by the time the park opens, I'm reopening my own private fight club." Phil did not wait for a response as he released his grip and spun around to turn toward the exit. "C'mon kid, it's late. I'm going back to the trailers and writing these yahoos up. You should go get settled in your room. We don't want to overwhelm you on your first day." Phil said in a gruff voice.

Roy looked at the dragon standing before them and rolled his eyes. "Oh, we wouldn't want to do that."

Gwen giggled and took Roy by the hand, "C'mon, new guy, I'll show you where the dormitories are."

Roy blushed, "Lead on, my lady."

Phil looked at the dragon and shook his head from side to side. "Kids!" The dragon nodded in agreement.

Gwen led Roy by the hand as the three climbed down the stairs into the Hypogealary. As they did, Roy noticed that the entranceway was designed to perfectly blend into the side of the bridge. "Wow, it's almost invisible."

Phil smiled as he climbed into the security cart. "All part of the magic." Phil started the engine. "Gwen, get the kid home. I need to check on a few things."

"Will do, Sheriff." She offered a mock salute with her free hand.

Phil's cart sped off into the tunnels.

Gwen turned to Roy. "Ready to hit the road, Jack?"

Roy smiled, "Sure."

"One more thing…" Gwen leaned in close to Roy. He could feel her hot breath on his cheek.

"Um, w-what thing?" Roy stammered. She was an inch away from him.

"I'm gonna need that hand back, chief." She giggled as she lifted her hand up to show that Roy was still holding it.

Roy let go of her hand and said, "Oh gosh! Sorry…"

Gwen smiled, "You know, for a tough guy, you're really easy to fluster."

"Yeah, well…" Roy started.

"That's okay; I think it's kind of cute." Gwen gave him a playful wink and turned to walk down the tunnel. "C'mon, let's roll."

Gwen led Roy as they walked through the Hypogealary. The pair would occasionally pass another princess or cowboy or robot as the couple made their way into the tunnels. Finally, Gwen and Roy reached an elevator bank and a large sign that read, "PERC Dormitories."

"This is it," Gwen said with a dramatic gesture. "Welcome to the PERC, your new home here at Rossumland."

Roy made a curious look. "PERC?"

Gwen imitated a fake announcer voice: "The Prototype Experimental Residential Community." She changed to her normal voice and added, "Plus, it's free if you work here. Get it?"

Roy laughed. "A 'perk' of the job."

Gwen gasped in mock shock. "Oh my goodness. You aren't as straight laced as you appear, Mr. Walters."

Roy smiled, "You'll find I am full of surprises, Miss..."

Gwen pushed the elevator button. "Just Gwen. No need to be formal with me." The elevator arrived and they stepped in. Gwen pushed twenty-three. "You are in Room D, right next to me."

The doors opened on the twenty-third floor. And Roy followed Gwen down the hall. They stopped in front of apartment D. Gwen reached into her dress and pulled out a card key. "This is for you; it works just like a hotel key."

"Of course it does." Roy took the key and as he did, their fingers brushed together and their eyes met. The two gazed into each other's eyes for a long moment. Finally, Roy broke the stare and looked down. "Is...is there a place to eat around here?"

Gwen gave a shy smile. "Oh yeah, I forgot. Your kitchen is fully stocked, but there are a whole bunch of restaurants in town."

Roy took a deep breath and asked, "Um, Gwen, do you want to go into town with me and get a late dinner?"

Gwen pondered the offer, and finally responded, "I'm sorry, I can't."

Roy could hear the sadness in her voice and realized what he was asking. Annies weren't allowed off the property. "I'm sorry I didn't think." Roy fumbled as he put the key in the lock. "You know what? I better just go to bed."

"Slow down, Tiger. It's not that I don't want to." Gwen leaned in and kissed Roy on the cheek. "I just can't. Have a good night."

Gwen entered the apartment next to his. Roy sighed as he put his hand to his cheek: "So lifelike, so real, so magical." A moment later, Roy entered his room and went to bed. He did not even bother to change. That night, Roy dreamed of dragons and princesses.

The next morning, Roy woke with a start to a banging at the door. He staggered to the apartment entrance and opened it. Phil's large frame filled the doorway and was holding a paper cup.

"Rise and shine, Rook. I got you a coffee." He offered Roy the cup. "It's gonna be a long day. We got a missing knight to find and we have to talk to the ballooning kids about the contraband."

Roy took the beverage. "You think the two are related?"

"Let's not rule it out. I've been on this job too long to believe in coincidence." Phil entered the apartment and flopped on the couch. "Nice digs."

Roy quickly showered, shaved, and put on a new black suit, blue shirt, and yellow tie. "Where to?"

Phil stood up. Roy realized he was wearing the same clothing as the night before. "First, we should talk to the 'Ballooning Around the Planet' kids."

Minutes later, the security cart stopped next to a ladder. A large sign written in orange script said "Ballooning" with an arrow pointing up.

Phil put the cart in park. "You stay here. I'll go check it out."

Roy sat up. "Did you just tell me to stay with the car?"

Phil smiled, "Yep. Stay with the car."

Roy became annoyed. "But…"

"Stay with the car!" Phil said, raising his voice. Then, he climbed up the ladder. The metal creaked with his weight.

Roy leaned against the wall. "Don't worry Phil, I'll be right here." He lowered his voice, "Staying with the car like some rookie."

"Who are you talking to?"

The sound of Gwen's voice made Roy jump. He spun to see the girl, dressed in her Princess dress, walking towards him. A man dressed as a pirate accompanied her.

Roy blushed. "Hey Gwen. I was just—"

"Talking to yourself? I heard," she chided. Roy slowly nodded as his face reddened. "He made you stay in the car, didn't he?" Roy nodded again his face turned crimson. Gwen smiled. "Don't take it personally; the kids are a little difficult to deal with. They're first generation Annies, the AE1s."

"And what be wrong with AE1s, lassie?" The sailor said in a thick pirate accent. "Thar be something wrong with me?"

"Of course not, Pete, I didn't mean you." Gwen turned back and smiled at her companion. "Roy this is Pete Lafitte."

"Aye, from the 'Buccaneers of the Coast.' 'Tis a pleasure to make your acquaintance, lad." Pete gave a formal bow.

Roy returned the bow. "A pleasure, sir."

Gwen looked impressed, "Nice. One day and he's already catching on."

Pete turned to Gwen. "I can tell why ye be enamored with this one, Princess." Roy watched as her beautiful face blushed in the tunnel lights. Pete took out his machete and gave another bow, this time towards the embarrassed princess. "But, if ye are ever in search of a real man, ye know where I be found."

Roy watched as the pirate sauntered down the tunnel away from them. He waited until the pirate was far out of earshot before he laughed. "That was...unique."

Gwen brushed her dress down and tried to avoid eye contact, "Yeah, all the AE1s are a little weird. You should see how jealous Lance..." She paused and the princess's eyes became wet at the mention of the missing Annie.

Roy took her hand. "Gwen, don't worry. We'll find him."

"Do you really think he's okay?" she asked with a choke.

"I really don't know," Roy admitted as he pulled her into an embrace. Gwen began to sob into his shoulder.

He held her tight. The pair hugged in silence and did not notice as a giant robot and a gorilla in a space suit walked by them.

Hours later, Gwen was sitting on the hood of the car and listening to Roy with rapt attention as he told another story. "Really?" she asked. "I can't believe you got to study with Mr. Blanks."

Roy smiled. "The old guy has still got the moves. But, I've told you all about me. I want to know about you."

Gwen smiled, "Not much to say. I've been here my whole life…"

"Hey kid, stop flirting," Phil guffawed as he worked his portly frame down the ladder. "We got work to do." he looked at Gwen. "And you, Princess, have guests to meet. I got a call from Central that you were missing, too."

"Saved by the bell." Gwen jumped off the hood and brushed off her dress. She gave Phil a mock salute and kissed Roy on the cheek. "I'm off to pose."

Roy watched as Gwen walked off down the Hypogealary.

"Earth to kid?" Phil waved his hand in front Roy's face.

Roy looked back annoyed. "So, what's up?"

Phil took out his notebook. "Turns out that we got some more missing Annies. Five of them didn't report to work this morning at the Ballooning ride." Roy flipped the page. "After talking to some of the other kids, I found out this ain't the first time that workers have gone missing for a few days."

"Does anyone know where they went?" Roy asked hopefully.

"Nope, but I found this in one of the missing kids' locker." Phil handed Roy a small business card.

Roy read the embossed lettering out loud. "Hugh Never's All Night Video."

Phil gave a toothy grin. "Like I said, there ain't no such thing as coincidence in this business."

Roy smiled. "So what's the plan?"

Phil put his notebook away. "First, we are going to go back to the trailer and write this up. Then, after the park closes, you and me are going into town. I got the urge to check out some videos."

Several hours later, Phil was driving his 2010 classic car, a Ford Focus, and talking into his radio. "Okay. Thanks for checking."

He turned to Roy in the passenger seat. "Central reports that the five Annies from the 'Ballooning Around the Planet' attraction are still missing. Let's see if Mr. Never knows where they are."

The car skidded into a parking spot in front of Hugh Never's All Night Video. The partners exited the car and walked through the front door. A loud ding announced their presence.

A greasy man in a white T-shirt came out of a back room. "Can I help you?" His name tag announced him as Hugh.

Phil pushed passed the man and moved to the rear door. "Yeah, I'm looking for some kids."

"Don't go in there!" the man yelled as he took a step towards Phil. Roy prepared for an attack, but Phil stopped the man with a look. Hugh threw his hands up. "I'm just saying that's where I keep the adult movies. No kids back there."

"We'll see," Roy said as he moved next to Phil. He pushed open the door, which squeaked loudly. As advertised, the room with filled with XXX rated movies. Phil and Roy walked in with Hugh following closely behind them. Phil picked one of the cases off the shelf and looked at the title "Babes in Toyland!" He smiled at the ridiculous title.

Then, he looked at the picture.

"Son of a..." he cursed as he flipped through the rest of the movies, tossing them on the floor as he read the titles and examined the pictures.

Hugh moved in between Phil and the shelf and put his hand up. The greasy man smiled a toothless smile. "Can I help you find something? We have an extensive collection."

Phil grabbed Hugh Never's arm and spun him into a half Nelson. Then Phil squeezed the proprietor's neck in a sleeper hold. The greasy man convulsed and slowly dropped to the floor. Some spittle drooled on Phil's arm.

Roy moved to stop his partner. Phil's words froze him in his tracks. "Relax, I used a nerve pinch! The dirtbag will be fine in a few hours. Go get the kids." Phil nodded to another door in the rear of the store.

Roy opened the door and entered a large storeroom in the back.

Several lights were set up on poles, which illuminated a single bed in the center of the room. A large camera was on a tripod next to the bed. More shocking, however, were the four children, one girl and three boys, that sat on the floor in front of the bed. Each wore a sailor suit, smoked a cigarette and looked bored.

The girl, a Chinese toddler, looked up from her fashion magazine and stared at Roy. "Aw for crissakes, they found us. The jig is up boys."

Phil followed Roy into the studio. "That is the understatement of the year, Yee. You kiddies are in big trouble."

"I thought," Roy said, turning to his partner, "you said that five kids were missing."

Phil just cursed. He was still cursing when they got back to the car.

For the first half of the ride, the children sang what Roy thought was the most annoying song ever written. After the third recitation, Phil brought up reopening his own personal fight club again. This stopped the singing and they all rode in silence.

After a few moments, Roy broke the quiet as he tried to piece things together. "So, in exchange for Hugh providing DVD copies, you guys made um…funny movies for him."

Yee laughed a child's laugh. "'Funny movies?' Please, child, I'm 80 years old. I've been around the block more than a few times."

Roy became very uncomfortable as the three other artificial children knowingly nodded in agreement. "Um, great."

Phil finally spoke. "This one's off the books. I don't even want to think about writing this one up. Just tell us where the fifth kid is."

A small Indian boy spoke. "Fifth? It was only the four of us. Peppe, Yee, Thor and me."

Yee added, "Raj is correct, unless you're counting those Stooges."

"Just great," Phil sighed as he pulled up to a large square gray building. "This is the rear backstage entrance to 'Ballooning Around the Planet.' You kids promise to go back to work and not do this again?"

"Yes, Sheriff!" The four children said in unison.

Roy thought the AE kids sounded kind of cute. Then he thought about the 500 movies in the trunk and shivered. He looked out the window. The water pipes shook as the ride flushed and refreshed its filtration system. Then Roy noticed something odd at the base of the piping. He turned to Phil and pointed.

"Is that supposed to spark like that?" Roy asked as he pointed to the bottom of the drain filter. Small sparks shot out and there was a loud grinding noise.

Phil got out of the car and looked into the drain. "I think we found the missing 'Ballooning Around the Planet' Annie. Roy, call it in. The fifth kid is a 404."

An hour later, Roy lay in his king-size company-provided bed in his corporate apartment. He tried not to think of Hugh Never's All Night Video or the charred remains he helped fish out of the filter. Instead, his last thoughts as he drifted off to sleep were of Gwen. The girl that was too good to be true.

At four A.M., someone banged on his door. The knocking woke Roy from his restless sleep. He trudged to the door and opened it. Gwen stood in the entranceway in her green nightgown.

"Hi!" Roy said, trying not to stare at the silk negligee. "You want to come in?"

Gwen smiled as she considered the offer. Finally she said "I better not. Your phone isn't hooked up yet so Phil called me and asked me to give you a message. He said you should meet him at the 'Buccaneers of the Coast' attraction. Pete Laffite has gone 404."

Roy rubbed the sleep from his eyes. "404? That's the third time I've heard that. What's it mean?"

Gwen's smile faded. "404 is a term from the old days. They used to use it when an attraction went down. Now, it refers to…" A tear formed in her eye. "It's what they say when an Annie is damaged beyond repair. It means death."

Roy moved to hug the woman in the hallway to comfort her. The hug became a tight embrace and the tight embrace turned into a long kiss. Gwen gave Roy a smaller follow-up kiss. Roy thought it was as if she signing her original kiss.

Gwen looked up and her watery green eyes met Roy's brown ones. "Is this real?" she asked. Roy didn't answer, but instead gave her another kiss as he pulled the girl into his room.

The next morning, Roy met Phil at the "Buccaneers of the Coast" ride. He saw his partner exiting from behind the "out of order" tape and Roy called out to him with a smile. "Good morning Phil!" Phil nodded back. Roy could see that his partner wore a charcoal gray suit and was carrying a large bag. "Hey, is that the same suit as yesterday?"

"It was a long night fer some of us." Phil tossed the bag to Roy. "What took ya, kid? I called Gwen hours ago."

Roy caught the bag and hoped Phil didn't see his blush. "What's this?" He asked, peeking inside.

"That, my young protégé, is all that is left of Pete Laffite." Roy could make out the charred remains of a metal skull and an eyeball. Ray almost dropped the bag. "And that's not all. I also heard from other attractions about Annies showing up 404." The guard pulled out his notebook and read off his list, "Lestrade from 'Doyle Town'; Babe from 'Paul Bunyan's Escape'; Caretaker Ricky from 'Phantom Mansion'; Paul Bear from 'Crooning County Critters'; Commander Justin from 'Future Moon'; and RU Hap-E from 'Computation'—all 404ed with same M.O. Someone has even assassinated the George Washington Annie from the 'Hall of the Revolution' attraction. Oh, and somebody finally found Lance. Well, pieces of him, anyway. They were floating over in the moat by the castle inside Camelot."

"Well, I guess at least that mystery is solved," Roy pouted. He wondered how he was going to tell Gwen.

Phil reached in his pocket and tossed a small ball to Roy. "But wait, there's more."

Roy caught it as he put down the bag. "What's this?"

Phil frowned, "It's an EMP grenade. Amalgamators created em back during the awakening in case they couldn't reach an agreement. It doesn't do a thing to humans, but will permanently fry all technology in a four foot radius."

Roy looked at button on the small ball. "Including Annies?"

"Especially Annies." Phil gestured to the bag. "I found this one next to Laffite. Whoever did this must have been in a hurry to get away."

"You think there's an Annie serial killer?" Roy asked, slightly worried as he thought about Gwen. "Any idea who might be targeted next?"

Phil thought for a moment. "Well, the only thing they all got in common is they were all Rossum AE1s, the first set of Annies made after Rossum showed them...." Realization showed in Phil's beady eyes.

"Showed them what?" Roy asked.

"No time! Bring Pete over to the Amalgamators' lab for a diagnostic report. I need to check something in Camelot." The burly man rushed off to his cart.

Roy wandered the Hypogealary for several hours looking for the Amalgamators' Shop. Then he saw Gwen, in her princess gown.

"Time to make the donuts!" she said with a smile.

"Are you a sight for sore eyes," Roy admitted. "Phil wanted me to bring...this bag to the Amalgamators' Shop." Roy decided not to tell her about Pete or Lance.

"You poor little lost boy," Gwen mocked as she took his hand and together they brought the remains of Pete Laffite to the shop.

Roy entered the Amalgamators' Shop and found the room to be amazing. Half-finished robots and large holographic displays were strewn across the room while storyboards revealed upcoming rides. A small man with glasses examined the remains of a robotic ox. "Just put it on the table," he said without looking up.

Gwen smiled. "Good morning, Doctor Lasster."

At the sound of her voice, Lasster looked up. "Princess!" He hugged the girl.

"How goes the exam?" Gwen asked.

"It's like trying to find a needle in a haystack," Lasster responded as he took off his glasses to clean them. "Now that you have brought me—"

Roy coughed and said, "I always found the best place to hide a needle was among other needles."

Gwen nodded towards Roy. "This is Roy Walters, our newest security guard. He's got Annie detail with Phil. I'm showing him around the Hypogealary."

Roy nervously shuffled his feet. "Hey," he said to Lasster in greeting.

Lasster smiled, "Well, you couldn't want a better guide. The Amalgamators practically raised Gwen here in these tunnels. She knows every bit of the Hypogealary. She was practically made for this role."

The Amalgamator's words made Roy feel lightheaded and a little nauseated as he thought about his nocturnal activities from the previous night. "Gwen, we better go," Roy said. "Phil is waiting for me at Camelot."

Gwen could sense the awkwardness from Roy. "Uh, okay. It's this way."

The pair did not speak nor hold hands as they walked through the Hypogealary to the "Arthurian Legends" ride. Still out of order, there were no Annies working inside the attraction. Roy found a bag at the top of the hill and looked in. The bag contained a robotic arm and leg.

Gwen looked over Roy's shoulder and peered in. "I guess Phil found Lance."

Roy murmured without making eye contact, "Yeah, or at least parts of him."

The woman in green stared at Roy as he avoided her gaze. Finally, Gwen took his hand. "What is wrong with you?" she said, "I thought we had something special last night."

Roy looked at Gwen. He put his hand under her perfect chin and cupped it. "Listen…" he started, but a loud crackle interrupted Roy's words. It was a sound he had heard far too many times during his military tenure. "That was laser cannon fire… Gwen, stay here!" Roy turned away from Gwen and ran full sprint down the hill. When he was halfway down, he saw Phil lying on his back; a large gaping hole was in the center of his chest. Smoke rose from the wound. Phil's keys, notebook and other papers were scattered around him.

Roy could hear Gwen gasp behind him. She had ignored his

instruction. Roy didn't stop until he reached his partner. "Phil!" Phil murmured incoherently as Roy scooped him into his arms. Looking at the size of the wound, Roy could see that the shot was delivered at close range. Roy's eyes darted around the field, but he couldn't see the shooter.

Gwen put her hand on his shoulder and cried, "Oh Phil!"

Then, Roy smelled burnt plastic and noticed the wiring in the hole in his partner's chest. "Phil, you're an Annie?" Roy looked at Gwen with pleading eyes. "Is anyone here real?"

In response, the older guard opened his eyes. "Kid! Get me up." Roy helped his partner to sit up. Phil's eyes looked around on the ground. His eyes focused on a target. Phil reached toward the keys to his car, "I want you—to have…"

"It's okay, partner," Roy said, putting the keys in Phil's hand.

"Stupid." Phil coughed up fluid as he tossed the keys away. He reached for the notebook that was lying next to the keys. His soot covered hands pointed to a list of victims. Phil softly murmured, "After the monorail, gonna use the pulse! No coincidences!" Phil's eyes rolled up into his head.

Gwen wept as Roy laid his partner's body down and slowly lowered Phil's head on the ground. Roy took off his suit jacket and covered his partner's head before picking up the notebook and staring at the list. "I don't understand! It's like trying to find a needle…" Roy looked at the pile of hay on the ground and stopped.

Gwen sobbed, "What?"

Roy tossed the notebook aside. "Oh my God, it's so obvious."

Tears streamed down Gwen's face. "You're not making sense. I don't understand."

Roy ignored her and instead turned towards the castle. "Okay, you can come out." He paused. "Come out, Lancelot!"

"How did you know?" A voice boomed and echoed so that it was impossible to tell where it had originated.

Gwen took a step away from the castle and moved towards the Stooges' tent. "Lance? I don't understand," she repeated.

Roy turned to her and said, "Remember what I told Dr. Lasster: the best place to hide a needle isn't in a haystack but among other needles. So, the best place to hide a murder is…"

"Among other murders," Gwen said in slow realization. She looked at the bag at the top of the hill, "But then, who is in the bag?"

"Nobody. It's just spare parts," Roy said. "Phil said there have been parts thefts from the Amalgamators' Shop for weeks." He turned back to the castle. "It was the movies wasn't it? You were the Stooges' biggest customer. You kept seeing movies about the outside world and became curious."

"Yes! Yes!" Lance screamed as he rushed out of the Stooges' tent and grabbed Gwen. He held a laser gun against her throat. "The outside world looked so wonderful in those videos. I had to leave."

"But the treaty with Rossum would never allow it. Especially not you. Phil told me that Rossum's prototype was Sir Lancelot. It was you, Lance, wasn't it? That's why you targeted the other AE1s?"

"I was the first!" Lance screeched. "Those others were all just copies."

Roy tried to move closer. "So you started your plan. You stole the parts and began to 404 the Rossum AE1s."

Lance pulled Gwen closer. The woman gasped. He wrapped his gun arm around her neck and held up his other hand revealing a dead man switch. "And when the monorail crashes, no one will care about a bunch of 404ed Annies."

Roy saw the detonator and froze. Then, he remembered that Phil had tossed him the EMP grenade. He reached into his pocket and felt for the device. He fingered the trigger mechanism. "Gwen, I can't risk you."

Gwen struggled to look up from the headlock. Gwen's eyes met Roy's. The girl gave a determined look and said, "Do it!"

Gwen closed her eyes. Roy quietly said, "I love you, Gwen." Then, he dove within three feet of Lance as he pressed the button. The wave of energy engulfed the three combatants in a web of translucent purple energy. Lance screeched as his circuits fried. He released the dead man switch, but it too was deactivated by the pulse. Roy watched in horror as Gwen also silently fell to the ground like a lifeless marionette with her strings cut.

A second later it was over and the energy dissipated. As it did, the illusion of Camelot faded and the room turned into a large warehouse.

Roy rushed over to Gwen's lifeless body and scooped her into his arms. He brushed back a strand of red hair that had fallen in her face. Tears streamed down Roy's face and onto Gwen's cheeks. In response, Gwen's green eyes fluttered opened and she looked at Roy.

"Hi," she said softly, "I must have fainted."

Roy was still crying. "But the pulse…"

Gwen moved to sit up. "I thought that only worked on Annies?"

Roy, confused, slowly asked, "Aren't you . .?"

"An Annie? Of course not, that's so silly." Gwen's jaw dropped open. "Oh my gosh, you thought…"

Roy was confused but still happy Gwen was both alive and live. "But your picture was on the fifty year old poster. Not to mention the way you talk in 20th century slang. I don't understand."

Gwen lay back onto his lap. "My grandmother was the model for the original poster, and my mother took over after that. I was practically raised in the Rossumland Hypogealary. I'm a college student studying 20th century pop culture." She chuckled as she ran her fingers through his hair. "But you, on the other hand, have really bad Annie-dar."

They kissed as the multicolored skies of Camelot came to life above them. Roy whispered, "And they lived happily ever after." Roy lowered Gwen into the haystack.

TIME AND AGAIN
By Liam Webb

Dan Collyer sat down on the concrete front porch of his split level home, orange juice in hand. Even at 7:30 on a Friday morning the late summer sun was warm, something he knew he'd miss in a month. Dan had begun sitting outside in the morning lately in the hopes it would help the nagging dissatisfaction that had followed him this summer. Try as he might, he just couldn't shake it. It was especially bad this week because he didn't have much else to do. The summer course he taught had just finished, the fall semester didn't start until the coming week, and Alice, his wife, was gone for a week helping out her sister with the new baby, so he had a lot of time to think, which was not a good thing.

Dan couldn't say why he was dissatisfied. It wasn't his job. Due to an unexpected cluster of retirements in the criminology department the year before, at thirty-one he just made full professor. The students didn't bother him much, Dan got on well with the other university staff and, for all its troubles and slow going, he enjoyed his research on ego protection and homicidal justification strategies in murderers. No, it was something else, something he just couldn't quite put his finger on. It was too elusive; it came and went, but on a morning like this with nothing else to do it came on pretty strong, so strong he couldn't even enjoy his Norman Rockwell book.

Dan liked to look at art, especially in the mornings. It was too bad that he couldn't draw a straight line if you put a gun to his head. But even if the green-eyed professor could draw, he didn't have the inclination. "Art doesn't put food on the table," he reminded himself in a voice involuntarily reminiscent of his father's. But no matter. He was content with his real work. The knowledge his research brought to society was what would make a difference in the world. Finishing his drink, the solitary man stretched, and, head tilted back, saw the sky and the edge of the house behind him. Noticing the burnt out porch light, and thinking that some home repair might take his mind off things, the unshaven man picked up his glass and book, put them inside, and headed into the garage.

Opening the garage door he waved to his neighbors, Blanche and Harry Morton, as they drove by on their way to work. Taking out the ladder, Dan thought that though the house was neatly made, whomever decided to put a light over the front door, seven feet over a small concrete porch was…short sighted to say the least. Dan knew he should probably wait until Alice got home so she could hold the ladder as usual, but the porch was only four feet across and he knew if the ladder was extended to full length he could jam it against both sides and still be able to reach the light.

Securing the ladder, he went up to change the bulb. That done, and feeling relieved that nothing knocked him over, Dan descended the ladder. Back on solid ground, the young professor looked up in triumph at the light and instantly jumped back as he saw a bee flying inches from his face. His foot slipped off the top porch step and he fell backwards. A crash of the ladder and the thud of his head on the concrete were the last things he heard for some time.

Dan woke flat on his back; the ladder pressing on his chest. He moved the ladder off of himself gently, and, feeling no broken bones in his arms or chest, tried to get up.

"Oh, shit," Dan whispered as the first waves of vertigo hit him as he raised his head. Lying back down, he looked at his watch. Only about five minutes had passed, so he wasn't out long. Slowly, gently, the professor tried to get up again. He knew he had to get to a phone if he had a concussion. He had a concussion once years ago, but so far didn't feel the same way. Dan got to his feet with minimal discomfort, and had no vertigo when tried to walk around. After ten minutes his head didn't hurt at all, so he knew it wasn't a concussion.

"Still feel damn weird, though," he thought. Looking at the fallen ladder, Dan chose the better part of valor, and instead of bending down to pick it up, he left it there for later and went inside to sit and rest. After a quick call to a local walk-in clinic about concussions, and watching television for a few hours without feeling any worse, Dan felt assured enough to go out for a late lunch. Afterward, he was feeling a bit better so, despite his soreness, the criminologist sat down to a few hours' research before knocking off for the rest of the evening with his Hudson River School print book.

That night he dreamed, but not nonsense or living in paintings as was usual. Instead he dreamed he was a kid, but not just any kid. He was a kid in a future filled with sky-sleds, rocket powered cars, strange buildings that were blends of arts nouveau and deco, and a wide open horizon.

Dan woke up with a minor headache the next morning; he had the strangest feeling about his wild dreams the night before. The brown-haired professor figured he should tidy up the house before Alice came home that afternoon, and he would've too, except that he just couldn't ignore the strongest urge to look at photo albums. He enjoyed it more than he thought he would. More than remembering, he knew, he simply *knew* what it was like to be a kid again. All his adult concerns had simply fallen away from him. So completely wrapped up in thought, Dan was shocked when he heard Alice's car come up the drive. Sure enough, it was 1:30 already. Rushing to the kitchen in an insane impulse to feel like an adult again, he picked up the broom and began sweeping as she came in the front door.

"The perfect crime," Dan thought. But she wasn't fooled.

"Been pushing that broom a whole two minutes, have you?" Alice said with a grin. Dan looked sheepishly at his slim blonde wife. She ran up to him and gave him a big hug. A week was a long time for her to be away. After their extended greeting and coffee where Dan heard all about Sarah and Andrew, and the new baby, Jackson, (and incidentally how Sarah is as incessantly chatty a sister as they were when Alice was a girl) he told his wife how his week went.

"….and I damn near killed myself fixing the front porch light. I fell off the step and cracked my head something fierce. It still kinda hurts."

"Oh, poor baby, let me kiss it better." Alice gave his forehead a quick peck. "There, all better."

"Thanks," he said, and then half-jokingly added "maybe it's from too much flying." Alice gave him a certain look, one that said she had no idea what was wrong with him. "I was dreaming last night," he quickly added. "I-I was flying around on a jet pack, with a dog—with a helmet. Well, I was wearing one too of course—a helmet, not a dog. And there were all these towers and spires and things, with, well, I don't know, 'skyways' or something that cars floated on. That's why I could fly there, see, because I was low to the ground and they were high up, and it was so awesome but scary because what if one of the flying cars fell off the track and fell on me, right?"

"Yeah…" she nodded uncertainly. Dan continued.

"And I knew my dad would kill me if he caught me; I was a kid in the dream; but he didn't—didn't catch me, I mean—and then I was eating something like Martian cinnamon barbeque."

"You were eating Martians?"

"No, just the barbeque was Martian style cooking…somehow."

"You're weird," Alice said playfully.

"No, you're weird," Dan shot back, sticking out his tongue. That evening, Dan was almost in bed before he realized how anxious he was to go to sleep. It wasn't because he was especially tired. At first he thought it was because it was the weekend and he could sleep in, but that wasn't it. Whatever it was, it wasn't bad.

Sunday was uneventful. Dan had already prepared his lesson plan the week before. He spent most of the day in his den office reviewing court transcripts and old interviews with inmates.

After a walk in the early afternoon to break up the day, he went right back to work, and worked well into the evening. The hours sped by, and the sun had set without his noticing. Halfway through his ninth case study he heard a knock at the door.

"Isn't it time for you to come to bed?" he heard his wife ask.

"Oh, not just yet," he answered, not looking up. "I'm not so tired and think I can get some good work done tonight."

"Good, I'm not tired either."

Perplexed, the professor looked up, and saw that Alice wasn't dressed for sleeping. In fact, she wasn't dressed at all.

"Never let it be said I'm a workaholic," Dan deadpanned, leaving his desk.

When he finally went to sleep that night, he couldn't have been in a better mood. However, Dan's dreams that night were anything but peaceful. Far from futuristic spires and rocket packs, he dreamt of depression, hanging men, CPR and tears. Dan woke at 4:30 the next morning, and not from first day semester nerves. He tried to forget about the dream, about the shock and death he'd witnessed while asleep, but he couldn't. He just couldn't get rid of the image of the garroted man hanging there, eyes bulging. When Alice woke up, she couldn't help but notice his dour mod. After some minor prodding, he decided to tell her.

"Ah, it was this dream last night, hon, it was kind of upsetting," he said finally.

"Baby," she soothed, "don't worry, it was just a dream, it couldn't be that bad. You said you slept okay this morning."

"Well," he replied, "I slept through, yeah. It was just that it felt so real. I was in school, like college or some military academy? Anyway, I remember being exhausted, and coming home to my dorm room slash barracks thing. I was messy, like I was a miner, but an asteroid miner. I went in and couldn't find a chemistry book—"

The thought of a space mining military chem major made Alice smile, but one pained look of Dan's made her realize how serious this was for him.

"So I couldn't find this book," he continued, "but I remembered

I let a friend borrow it. I went over to his room to get it, heard a noise from inside, so I opened the door, and he had hung himself! I got him down—he wasn't dead yet but I didn't know that at first—and I was screaming at him for trying to kill himself. Then he was crying, sobbing really, on my shoulder, because he couldn't take all the grade pressure. Then instantly it switched to the psych hospital where I brought him, but it felt like hours later."

"Well, that sounds pretty crazy," she said after a moment.

"Yeah, and I just can't get the image of the guy, just hanging in front of me, out of my mind." He thought a moment. "I guess it just made me see that life is short."

"Well," she said, "try to take it as a good thing. If life is short, just make the best of each day."

"Thanks, honey," he said, embracing her. "You always know how to make me feel better."

Feeling better but still uneasy, Dan left for work. The train into the city was five minutes behind as usual. It was a quiet ride for him that morning. The new class schedule wasn't so bad, and it was nice to see a few of the upperclassmen in his deviant psychopathy class. Most classes were introductory, so it was an easy day; before he knew it he was home again, the morning's problems forgotten. After a quiet evening, he stayed up late to look over his N.C. Wyeth book for an hour. The Gustave Doré book would've been next had he not fallen asleep in his chair. He dreamed a wonderful dream of vindication and pride, of acceptance and rocketships.

Dan went to the train platform in wonderful spirits the next day. It was the first time in a long time he had felt this good on a Tuesday morning. While waiting, he kept looking up at the sky, almost as if he had expected the train to come from above. But, of course, that was ridiculous. After the usual five minutes' delay, the train arrived and he stepped on. He was vaguely disappointed somehow that the train didn't come from the sky.

The young professor got in his usual car, three back from the front, and took his seat. Two stops later "Old George" from the English Department got on. They were casual friends on the train, sharing the paper every now and again, and usually comparing their respective fields. George taught two main fields of literature: science fiction and detective fiction. Early on in their commuting friendship, they agreed that criminal motives in detective fiction were almost always more genteel than in actual crimes. George would even bring up science fiction when the genres crossed, but Dan always felt that replacing a man with a robot or alien in a crime story was disingenuous, and a friendly professional argument would ensue.

But this morning Dan couldn't wait to talk to him, and had anything but comparative literature on his mind. When they split the paper, George always asked for the comics section first, so Dan knew a guy like George would be just the guy he needed today. After George sat his rickety frame down and they exchanged hellos, Dan got right to it.

"George! You'll never believe it! Last night, I dreamt I was a space pilot."

George gave Dan a mildly annoyed look. Dan and George respected each other professionally, but every now and again, Dan would poke gentle fun at George's comic reading.

"Now, Daniel, you know very well I read the entire paper," George explained to him. "I start with the comics because, at my age, I need to start my days with a laugh or two. Besides, at this point in my life, I see the strip characters as old friends."

Dan tried to interrupt, but George held up a wrinkled but firm hand. "I know you aren't like that; you're more serious than I was at your age, and I think it comes from dealing with your kind of field, and a good field it is. But just let an old man have his quirks, okay?" George stopped there, and while the older man never said so, Dan suspected that George sort of felt sorry for him for his seriousness. In the silence that followed, Dan tried to decide what to say in order to explain to George he wasn't poking fun at him, but before he spoke, George looked at him and saw that his friend wasn't kidding him this time. Intrigued, George urged him to go on

"It felt like I was an undergrad again," Dan began, "waiting for an exam result. I was sitting in some sort of waiting room. It was bare, off white, and the furniture was all rounded off. I couldn't stop twirling my key ring around my finger. I knew that I had trained and studied for what seemed like years to be an outer galaxy explorer, and this was the day I was going to find out if I made it. I kept trying to read the one magazine they had but I was too nervous to read it.

"After what felt like forever, a door opened, or, well, a section of wall opened and a woman was standing there and said 'Mr. Williamson'—that was my name in the dream, but anyway—she said 'they're ready for you now.' I wanted to follow the woman but instead went down this lighted path to another door. In that room were a bunch of military-looking guys at a table. The man in the middle told me to sit down. The middle guy said to me 'Skyler'—y'see that was my first name in the dream—'Skyler, my name is General Benjamin Kubelsky. I am the military liaison for this project.' And here's where it gets really weird. He said, 'It pleases me to welcome you as a new galactic explorer. As pilot of your own small ship, you will seek out and catalog any new planet or planetoid, and any new life forms for the growth of science and betterment of man.' I felt like a million bucks! Next I remember I'm looking at this cherry, fresh-off-the-factory-floor spaceship! And I remember I had this shiny badge thing on my left shoulder/chest area. I sat down in the cockpit and heard the leather creak! It was awesome!"

"Well, my boy," George said, "it certainly sounds that way."

"Hey, George," Dan asked, "do you think you could…y'know, let me borrow some of your science fiction books sometime?"

George's mouth hung open. Dan had never expressed interest in science fiction before, not in all the three years they'd ridden the train together. Had Dan revealed he was a Communist spy at that moment, George wouldn't have been more nonplussed.

"Why, o-of course," George replied. "I think I have some that you'll enjoy very much. And," he added smiling, "it will be nice to finally have someone else to talk about them with beside an undergrad." They continued talking for the entire ride to work. George didn't have to defend the science fiction genre once.

Although Dan's day was uneventful, a strange thing occurred that evening on his way home. The criminologist walked out of the psychology building and stood on the sidewalk. Dan watched as students passed by while two robins fought over some discarded pretzel on the grass. Dan grew increasingly impatient to get down the block when he realized he wasn't walking. It was almost as if he expected the sidewalk to move. Embarrassed, he started off at a quick walk, hoping nobody noticed his standing there. But after a moment, Dan realized it would have looked like he was just enjoying the view, and surely a professor had no reason to be this embarrassed.

When Dan got home he had the oddest sense that something was missing, like there was somewhere else for him to be. He hated when this happened at work. He felt as if he caught his mind wandering, even though it wasn't wandering, and then seemed to remember he needed to be elsewhere even though he knew there wasn't. Then he would worry he just missed something in front of him, but didn't know what that was either. At home it was almost never a problem, but that night Dan couldn't even keep his mind on what he was reading. Giving up after an hour, he put the book down and succumbed to watching television with his wife.

The next morning, Dan woke up in a foul mood. It was as if he had boredom bordering on ennui, accompanied by no small amount of dissatisfaction with life. He did his best to avoid any extra interaction with Alice so as not to let her see there was something amiss. Although he was almost sure Alice could tell, as she usually could, she wisely said nothing about it. They both knew they had to go to work that day and bringing it up now wouldn't do either of them any good. Dan debated just skipping work. He thought about it all the way to the train station and while waiting for the train to arrive. He would have called out of work, too, except that he knew it wouldn't really solve anything. Dan was still brooding about it when he got on the train.

Dan was unexpectedly relieved when George got on. George sat right down next to him and handed him three paperbacks.

"Here you are, Daniel, three great specimens of science fiction." Dan took them with a bit of reluctance. "Thank you," he said.

George was crestfallen at the prospect that Dan had reverted back to his dislike of science fiction. "Whatever is the matter, Daniel? Don't you like them?"

"Oh, that's not it, George," Dan said. "It's just that, last night, I was still a space pilot. A very bored, and very, very *alone* space pilot. Space is just so damn *big*; you don't hit anything for days on end! Nothing much exciting happens either, does it? I just felt so…so gypped."

George replied with relief. "Well…yes, of course, real space is like that. It's vast and enormous. It is, well…space! But the stories in those books aren't boring, trust me. You can't have a decent book about nothing happening. Unless you try to read Finnegan's Wake starting at the middle, ha ha!" Dan didn't get it. "Well," George added, "you just try one of the books, maybe on your lunch, and see if you like it. If not, no harm done."

"Yeah, I suppose you're right," Dan said.

"And who knows," George said dryly, "knowing your field, maybe you'll find out what some demented Star Trek fans see when they snap."

They laughed till their sides ached, and the rest of the ride went quickly. However, after his first class the feeling of dissatisfaction came back and it just wouldn't go away. Dan was able to forget about it for a few minutes here and there by piling on work, and again for a fair amount of time while at lunch, but it would always return. And though he had to hide the book from his colleagues and read it on the sly, George was right; the book was good. It was edited by a guy whose name Dan had heard, but never read in the past. The man's name was Asimov. The book was called *Before the Golden Age*.

That night Dan spoke with Alice about his dissatisfaction.

"I don't know, honey, something's not right, but damned if I know what it is," he told her. "It's no one thing really…I just want, I don't know…something more."

"Well," Alice asked, "what *do* you want? Do you have any ideas?"

"Not exactly, no. But somehow, I feel almost as if—" he paused, exhaled a great sigh, and put his head on her shoulder.

"What, honey? What is it?"

"Well, what if I got my professorship too soon? All these classes, repeating myself on the same stuff, over and over. I'm not really going anywhere, am I? I feel kind of like I'm floating in space professionally."

"Oh, come on now, that's just silly," she comforted. "The teaching is what lets you move forward with research, and besides, you never know what you could learn along the way. Maybe you can see people in different ways using your class as a subject; maybe you can use them to see the development of ego defenses, or something."

He smiled at her. "I love you."

"Love you, too. Now go, get some work done on your paper. Your stuff is overflowing in the study and I don't need the fire marshal to declare our house a hazard."

Dan went into his study with every intention of getting some good work in, but he found himself on astronomy sites instead. He didn't read much of the articles. Strangely enough, he found he didn't need to. After that, he picked up the books George gave him, and read them well into the night.

The next morning Dan could not remember his dreams. He got up, sighed, and went to the bathroom. He turned the water on and looked at himself blearily while waiting for the water to heat up. Cupping his hands under the faucet, he bent over and splashed warm water on his face. Feeling more alert, he dried his face off and looked in the mirror again. He saw something odd on his face. He stared at the stray gray hair on his upper cheek for thirty seconds before he realized there was a window behind him with flying cars passing by. Closer, he saw a service robot on his right.

Shocked, he spun around, backing against the sink to keep his footing. And he saw…nothing. Just the same old windowless wall that was always there. Suddenly frightened that he could be attacked from the mirror he spun back around and looked in it again. Again, nothing. Just the same old bathroom reflection.

"Maybe it was just a left over dream," he thought. "That's it, I was still half asleep. It must have been just the tail end of a dream." With that, he tried to put it out of his mind. Dan didn't tell Alice about what he saw, partially because he didn't want to believe it and partially because he didn't want her to think there was anything wrong.

He went to work earlier than usual to help put it out of his mind. Working helped a great deal, so much so that he forgot all about the incident until that afternoon. He decided to treat himself to lunch and went to the sandwich place down the block. The one with the tall blonde cashier. Not that that had anything to do with it, of course.

"That'll be $12.53," said the cashier.

"Sure."

Instead of getting his wallet, he just put his thumb down on the credit card pad.

"Um, sir? What are you doing?" she asked after a moment.

"I…I don't know," he said. "I'm sorry, hang on, let me get my wallet." He paid for his food and got out of there as fast as he could without seeming to rush. Dan tried to put both it and this morning's experience out of his mind, but that was now more difficult than it had been before. To his credit, the young professor was almost successful, until he got on the train to go home. George happened to be on the train that afternoon, a rarity because of their different class schedules.

"So how are things with you, Daniel?" George genially asked. "Enjoying the books?"

"Things are fine," Dan lied. "Though I was thinking about returning the books." Noticing George's disappointed look, he quickly added, "Not because I don't like them, but maybe I'm reading them *too* much. I thought I saw a robot in my mirror this morning."

"What? You thought you were a robot? Oh, Daniel, that's funny," George chuckled.

"No! No, I mean, I thought there was a robot behind me—in the room. Kind of like it was, well, a servant or something."

"Really…" George said. "How interesting. Of course, the idea of robot servants has been around for a long time, and I daresay, lad, is so ubiquitous that you could have dreamed or thought of that without reading any of the books I lent you."

"I suppose you're right, George," Dan said.

"By the way, have you read the one about the cop and the criminal who were sliding up and down that giant frictionless mirror bowl in space yet? I thought that one was great." George began to chuckle. "I remembered all the slides and swings I was on as a kid when I read that one. I almost wish I could have been there with them."

"Yeah, that one was pretty decent," Dan said. "Nice how the criminal had some decency to him in the end. But then again that kind of made me think they were stretching it. A giant mirror bowl I can almost believe but a valiant criminal who keeps his word to not run out on the cop while he is on the run from said cop at the time? No."

"Oh come on, now, Daniel. Even if you don't believe that a criminal can still be a decent person, extraordinary times can create extraordinary behaviors in people."

"Ah, maybe you're right. Guess I'll have to explore space myself before I can make the judgment, right?" The train bell sounded, the car doors closed and the train slowly pulled out of the station.

Dan didn't sleep well that night. In fact, he didn't sleep much at all. He dreamt of piloting the same spaceship as before, only this time, he was surrounded by violence and fear. People began dying and the ship grew hotter. Hotter and hotter and hotter. Then ship was on fire—first the seats, then the controls; he saw a person burst into flame, and finally Dan looked at his hands—!

He awoke with a start around 4 A.M., hot and sweating. He couldn't go back to sleep; he was too shaken by the dream he had and the oppressive heat he felt.

"It must be the air conditioner," he thought. "It must be on its way out. It can't cool a room down properly." He got up and went into their combination library and storage room. Dan opened the front windows, turned a fan full on him and sat for the next ten minutes. Once he began to feel better, Dan turned on the computer and searched for the name he had in his dreams. He seemed to remember the last name, Williamson, in connection to an artist somewhere. After finding the artist by a circuitous route, Dan spent the rest of his early morning looking at the man's work until the usual time for breakfast. Despite enjoying this newfound artwork, he still had an insistent feeling of dread that day, one that he could ignore but couldn't shake. He wasn't much of a conversationalist that morning either.

"Hey hon, how'd you sleep?" Alice asked him.

"Not well. Bad dreams."

"Oh?"

"I died in it. I don't really want to talk about it."

"Oh, okay. But hey, it's Friday," was his wife's casual response and she went about her morning.

"What's wrong with her," he thought, "can't she see that there's something very wrong here?!" Dan felt the first twinges of something almost like panic but stopped himself. "Wait. She's right, nothing *is* wrong. I'm in my home, not dying in a fire in space or anywhere else." Forcing himself to calm down, he ate and dressed for work. But for some reason, he dreaded seeing George on the train.

"Morning, Daniel," George cheerily greeted him two stops in on the train ride to work, "I got the paper this morning!"

"Great," Dan said sullenly.

"Are you all right, my boy? You seem upset."

"I didn't sleep well at all last night. No offense, but I'm not in the mood for conversation."

"Well…okay," George said and began to read his paper. Nothing more was said that morning's ride.

It was a busier Friday than usual, and Dan couldn't have liked it better. He had all but forgotten the dream and his panic of the early morning. Between three classes and a meeting with Tom, the retired prison guard he was interviewing for his research, his first real break didn't come until just after 12:30. Just as he sat down in his office, the phone rang.

"Hi sweetie, it's me," Alice said over the phone. "I'm going to be late home tonight, if not tomorrow. I'm going over to Sarah's this afternoon; the baby's sick."

"Oh, I'm sorry hon," he replied.

"I'll see you later, okay?"

"Okay, see you then, and if you need me for anything, just call," he said, and they hung up. Hungry, Dan scrounged up some loose change in his desk and headed down the hall to the vending machine for a granola bar, and then to the main office to check his mail and get some water.

"Hey, Dan, how's it going?" the department secretary asked as he arrived.

"Crazy day, Doreen, how about you?" the professor called over his shoulder on his way to the water cooler.

"Not so bad. I'm heading out to see some relatives this weekend. You?"

"No plans, but probably the same old; research, research, research," he said, coming over to the counter opposite her desk.

"Yeah, gotta chase that Nobel for tenure, huh?" Looking up at him from her typing, Doreen was alarmed. "Dan...what are you doing?"

Dan looked down and saw that, without realizing it, he had poured his water all over the granola bar.

"I—I don't know. I'm sorry," he said, trying to mop it up with some tissues. Doreen got up to get paper towels and Dan saw she wasn't wearing a normal dress but a shining, almost hard, metallic substance. Horrified, he backed out of the office.

"E-excuse me, I feel kind of sick." Dan went down the hall to his office, but he felt worse on the way. Students were wearing strange metallic clothes he had never seen before. Dan's head began to spin. He saw people in the hall who weren't students, people middle aged and older, and the way the students ignored these older people, Dan knew the students couldn't see them. Almost running now, he got to his office, nearly slamming the door behind him, only to be faced with a far more terrifying sight inside: dead bodies hung from the ceiling, while the entire room burned in green and blue flames. His eyes darted to the window for escape, but there he saw not the familiar city block, but a pink and purple sky over a field of strange trees. Dan closed his eyes tightly, wishing, pleading with God for it to all go away!

Even while pleading with God, he could feel the heat on his face, and Dan became suddenly and terribly afraid that the fire might be real! Snapping open his eyes, ready to flee, he looked and saw... ...his office. It was as it always was: slightly messy, papers in untidy piles at the far end of his desk. The city was outside, the steady stream of traffic the same as ever. All was quiet and not a thing was amiss. After a few moments more, he heard a gentle knocking at his door. "Dan? You all right?" a man said.

Collecting himself and controlling his expression as best he could, Dan opened his door. It was George.

"Oh, hi, George. Yeah, everything is fine."

"I just stopped by and saw you running to your office. Is everything okay?"

"Yes, I'm fine, just some indigestion. I thought I was going to throw up," which was true enough, he thought, "so headed for my wastebasket. I'm fine now, just bad gas I guess."

"Well, you still look like hell. It's Friday, I'd call it a day if I were you," his friend said.

Dan thought a moment, looking at the room over his shoulder. "Maybe you're right."

Dan got on the train without incident and felt calmer as he rode along, knowing he was going back home. He looked out the window and was dumbfounded at the sight. The familiar straight glass and concrete towers were replaced by slim gold and silver structures, some with needles at the top, others with domes and some with nothing at all; and there were connecting aerial roadways between them. The entire cityscape seemed to shine with promise and technology. He saw the city not as it was in reality, but as it was in his dreams! Dan wanted to look away, but couldn't. This new city awed him with its wonderful beauty, and yet horrified him because there was no doubt that he was awake.

With less passengers getting on and off at this time of day the train was quicker getting to his stop. In the parking lot, Dan sat behind the wheel of his car with the door open. After debating for some minutes whether or not he should drive home from the station, in case he should start hallucinating again, Dan decided to drive slowly with his left foot hovering over the brake.

"If I do that," he thought, "I can stop instantly if I need to, and if I'm driving I can't wander off delirious if I walked home." Trembling, Dan began his slow drive. Thankfully, he got home without incident.

"It's just as well," he thought, "to have the house to myself." Calmer now, Dan noticed how nice a day it was, so he changed out of his work clothes and went into the backyard to sit under the big oak tree and think it all out.

"There has to be a perfectly rational explanation for all this, there must be," he said to himself. Still thinking, and without meaning to, he fell asleep.

Skyler was in space, smuggling something for some very nasty people who were with him on his ship. They were kind at first, but they turned murderous when they saw another ship on the horizon. He could feel the menace, the hatred, all around him. Then Sky was yelling at one of them; a husky, bearded man with greasy black hair and a sunken right eye. Suddenly, the ship was out of control, spiraling downward! The pressure on Sky's face turned to heat...

Dan awoke with a start under the oak tree. The fear he felt at the menace all around him didn't disappear with the dream. Looking around, he noticed some movement over the bushes in the Mortons' yard. Blanche Morton and Alice knew each other socially at church, so he straightened up to sit cross-legged and ventured a hello, thinking a nice strong dose of reality would snap him out of it.

"Hello, Blanche, that you?" he called.

"Yes, just—just getting some weeds up," she grunted in between pulls.

"Whoo!" she exhaled as her arm came up to show him a large weed with long roots, "Can you believe this one?"

"That's certainly..." Dan trailed off as Blanche stood up. It wasn't Blanche at all. It was one of the men from his dream, the husky man with the greasy black curly hair, beard, and sunken, bloodshot right eye. Dan flinched, and, panicked, fell over when he tried to get up. Uncrossing his legs, and pushing with all his might against the ground to stand, Dan headed for his house.

"Whatever's the matter Dan?" the greasy man said in Blanche's voice.

"Oh, uh, I got a gnat in my eye," Dan lied as he finally got to his feet.

"Well, let me see it, I can help," Greasy said, again in Blanche's lightly accented voice.

"No, that's okay," Dan called over his shoulder as he began to run for his door.

Dan was in a full run over half his yard, his heart pounding in his chest, his breathing ever shallower with each step he took. He savagely pulled the door open, almost threw himself inside, and slammed the door shut. Locking the door while throwing himself against it, Dan tried to jam the door closed, knuckles white in his grip on the doorknob. He began to calm down, and could almost breathe normally again when he heard the soft click and whirr behind him. Dan spun around, catching himself on the door now behind him, and saw the same robot he saw the other day in the mirror, but this time the gleaming servant stood right in front of him, big as life in the middle of his kitchen!

The professor couldn't even scream when the robot said in calm, almost friendly tones, "Is there anything I can get you, sir?"

But it wasn't just that the robot was standing there. The whole room, the whole house had changed. Gone was the familiar pale yellow linoleum and red countertops of the kitchen; instead Dan stood in an open area with a silver floor and off-white walls. There was just a table and chairs on the right side of the room. But they were no ordinary table and chairs. Neither table nor chairs had legs to them. The transparent chairs just hung in the air around a frosted circular oval disk that was decorated with a large pattern that looked like a modified jack, or maybe a stylized atom. Next to that on the left was a pantry with something like glass doors, showing a rotating picture of different foods in different places. On the far left was a large machine that he knew was a refrigerator and sink, but it was one large object, and didn't look like any sink or refrigerator he'd ever seen.

Dan frantically pushed past the robot and ran through this bizarre kitchen, desperately hoping to get to his own living room at the front of the house. Instead he saw again another room, sleek yet grotesque in its foreignness. An entire wall of this room was a large television screen, showing a background and some actors in it, but also other, holographic actors who projected from it as the picture extended to the foreground. The big picture window in his living room was replaced by a spherical window bubbling outward, showing an unfamiliar landscape in the twilight with cars flying by, and another natural satellite next to the familiar moon, dwarfing the moon by half. An older man got up from a legless couch and turned to face him. The man who got up and turned to him, though many years older now, was the same man who he saw in his dream cooking Martian barbeque!

"Skyler, what's happened, what's wrong, son?" the man asked.

Dan screamed, clutched his head and fell to the floor.

"Make it go away, make it go away, make it go away," Dan repeated over and over, balling up into a fetal position, trying to bury his face in the carpet as if by doing so he could burrow back into sanity.

"Oh, God, this is it," he said, faster and faster, "maybe there's no going back. What if I'm stuck like this forever, what if I do something in reality, what if I hurt people, what if I hurt Alice?" If that could happen, he knew there was only one thing to do. "I just don't know how to kill myself painlessly before Alice gets home," he whispered.

Hearing his voice, he realized it was the only sound he heard, and he knew that he was alone again in the room. Flooded with relief, Dan still couldn't bring himself to get up. It was almost nice down there on the floor, and he thought that he could almost go to sleep there.

At once, Dan felt more than saw the presence of someone else in the room. He redoubled his efforts to burrow down into the floor, the pressure in his temples nearly blinding him with pain but anything was better than whatever it was that was over there!

"It's all right Daniel, you can get up," he heard a familiar voice say.

The pressure in his temples broke, and he could breathe normally again. He knew he could trust this voice, but he didn't know why. Dan got to his feet.

"George!" Dan said, "How did you get here?" Dan realized something. "George, how did you get into my house?"

"I came because you asked me to come. And I didn't get in here, I just came here."

"What?" he asked mystified.

"Daniel, let me explain something to you. You're not losing your mind. In fact, there's nothing really wrong with you."

"What? A-are you sure? H-How can you say that?" he asked George.

"Because I know what and who you are, Daniel."

George touched his belt buckle, and underwent a strange, almost magical transformation. George seemed to shimmer, there was a brief pulse of light like a camera flash, and the figure of George was replaced by a young man about twenty-five. He looked very familiar though Dan was sure he'd never seen this man in his life. He wore something like a solid blue jumpsuit, like a jet pilot, only more form fitting and it had wide gray bands running down his arms, sides and legs. A wide, mechanical-looking belt was around his waist with a large yellow circle around multicolored buttons where the belt buckle should be. His face was framed by a headpiece that covered his neck, ears, and temples, but left the top of his head free, showing his blond hair. It took a moment, but then he realized where he saw a man dressed like this before. Sure enough, this man looked like he just stepped out of an Al Williamson space adventure. But more than that, Dan felt he knew this man personally, and that he could trust him implicitly, he just didn't know why.

"Nice guy, that George. Reminds me of my friend, Nate Birnbaum. But anyway, it wasn't George on the train these last few days; George went on vacation the day you told him about your space pilot dream. I gave you those books, and have been with you ever since…and ever since before that, too, when you get down to it. Please sit down, and I'll explain everything," the familiar spacefarer said.

In no mood to make any arguments after what he had just seen, Dan sat on the couch while this man took the chair opposite.

"I need to tell you about one of the best guys I've ever met, and I've met quite a few. He even saved a friend's life in college, without any help from me. Skyler Williamson was born September 1, 2245 on Polaris," the man said. "Polaris was the reconstituted planet made from what is now the asteroid belt between Mars and Jupiter. Sky was a good man, a very good man, so much so that I had very little to counsel him against in my time with him. He was a space pilot, one of the brave galactic explorers for his country. But he became an explorer towards the end of the age of exploration, when almost all the wild and fantastic things had been discovered, and, though Sky didn't know it at the time, only the nuts and bolts work of space lane charting was left.

"After many years, he had become bored with his life, knowing he wasn't making enough of a difference. That was when he started smuggling. He wasn't smuggling guns or drugs, but food to the poor. Think of it more like an unpaid Unicef trucker of this era than a smuggler. Sky would make sure his trips took him off course a little to pick up or drop off food to hungry sentient beings across the galaxy. And everything went along just fine for a few years. But later, militants infected the peaceful groups Sky worked with. They felt that it wasn't enough to give food to the poor, they wanted to *force* others more well off to give their goods to the poor, or just to those *they* considered less well off, like their own selves or their particular racial or species group, depending on who was holding the weapon.

"One day, Sky picked up a few travelers in the outer rim. They said they were trying to migrate to other planets for a better life, all of their possessions in one trunk. Sky, his heart always bigger than his head, believed them. But they were radicals, hell bent on the destruction of those they considered 'haves' and carried a singularity bomb in the trunk. They knew that Sky's flight path would cross that of Polaris' president, and didn't care how many thousands were killed when they detonated their bomb. They tried to take the ship when they saw the presidential cruiser come into view. But Sky got the better of them. Just before they threw him from his seat at the controls, he veered towards uninhabited Venus and broke the steering column. It was enough for the ship to be caught in Venus's gravity. The ship, the bomb, and everyone on board, burned up on reentry. Though with his last act Sky committed his first act of violence in his life, the hundreds of thousands he saved greatly outweighed the few pitiful, demented lives he took when he prevented that bomb from going off.

"Of course, Sky made it 'upstairs'. Heck, I thought he was a shoo in for seraphim grade, but the Boss is nothing if not mysterious, so Sky was offered a special gift for his exemplary life and final self sacrifice, he was rewarded with a rare gift. He was allowed a second lifetime and he could choose where and when he would live it. He asked for such a nice, giving life it pleased the Boss. He chose this era and this place. He always wanted to meet his favorite science fiction writer, Dan Collyer."

"So you're—" Dan began.

"Skyler just never knew that he would *be* you," the man interrupted. "Yes, you're Daniel Collyer now, but you're also Skyler Williamson. Or at least, you were."

Dan was speechless.

"You haven't been losing your mind, Dan, just remembering your past life. That blow to the head the other week broke down whatever psychological barrier there was between your past life, in your future, and your current life in your present, which is Sky's past."

Incredibly, Dan knew the man was speaking the truth. It was as if a dam broke and relief washed over him. All the pain and fear were gone, replaced by secure, loving memories when he thought of his former life in the future. When he looked at his visitor again, it seemed as if this man could feel that too.

"So that was it," Dan's visitor said. "All Collyer's best stuff was just modified memories. I always wondered where Collyer came up with them myself, reading over the kid's shoulder."

"So who are you, exactly?" Dan said, finally.

"Oh come on, you don't know?" the man said.

"I admit you look sort of familiar, but for the life of me I don't know why," the professor said.

"Oh give me a break!" the man said, looking up at the ceiling. "I guard this kid for two lifetimes, and I'm just 'sort of familiar'. Yeesh, at this rate I'll never get my rocket pack."

"Rocket pack?" Dan puzzled, suddenly realizing the truth. "Don't you mean get your wi—"

"No, I mean rocket pack! C'mon, man, I'm a modern guy! Next you'll have me prancing around in one of those silly giant nightshirts, like a crotchety old jerk. And no, my name's not 'Clarence' either. Enough already. Your wife will be home in a few minutes, so I gotta run. Incidentally, she came along for the ride, Sky, but she doesn't remember anything about your joint past, and she won't, so keep quiet about it. I got special dispensation to talk to you directly just this once because you needed me, but I don't know if she'll get it. Probably would, but hey, don't make our jobs harder than they need to be. Just remember to start writing. You're better than you think; I oughtta know."

"O-okay," he said, dumbfounded.

There was a knock at the door.

"Don't expect me to get it," he shrugged, "it's your house."

Dan got up and opened the door. It was Alice, leaning against the door jamb, her arms full of groceries.

"It turns out Jackson was too hot in his onesie and Sarah was just too exhausted to figure it out. I'd have been home sooner, but I stopped at the store on my way home," she said.

"Yeah, I kinda gathered," he replied.

"Funny," she deadpanned. "Now take these before my arms fall off and I can't cook you the special dinner I planned for being away so long."

He took all but one bag from her.

"Hey, check out—" he said as he turned around into the room. There was no one there.

"Check out what?" she asked.

"Oh, nothing. There was just…a little bird, but I guess he's gone now," he said.

Together they brought the bags into the kitchen—the nice, familiar, red countered kitchen.

"How are you feeling? Sleep well?" she asked.

"Yeah," he said with a smile. "I feel just fine."

RUTHSTORM

By Jacob Ketron

Ruthstorm is the name, Cody P. Ruthstorm. In the highly unlikely chance that you've never heard of me, I should mention that I'm the greatest of bounty hunters in the entire solar system. But, don't take my word for it. You can ask any one of the thousands of criminals I have put away over the years. I bagged my first when I was only seventeen. Since then, I've built my rep by only going after the baddest, toughest, and most dangerous bounties. It may not be the safest of jobs, but it beats pushing paper at a space station.

But, enough about me. Let me tell you about one of my greatest adventures, where I faced off against one of my deadliest bounties yet. It's a tale I like to call: "Ruthstorm and the Bounty of Death."

My story starts, as many of mine do, in a bar. The star year was 2402 and it was a day like today. Of course, that's not saying a lot since pretty much everyday is the same on a space station.

And that's where I was—a space station—sitting at the bar in Port 339. As expected, the place was a dump and looked just like every bar in any one of the million nearly identical floating ports that drifted across the galaxy. Port 339 was located around the side of the asteroid belt closest to Jupiter.

I looked up from my drink and glanced out the plastisteel porthole to my left. The base was surrounded by ornate steel and high-class glass strong enough to contain oxygen in the base. What use is a base if humans can't breathe?

I turned and stared into the mirror that lined the wall behind the bar. Neon lit signs that advertised various types of alien beers lined it. They flickered as the solar energy that energized the port fluctuated. I took a moment to examine myself in the mirror.

I've been told by many, mostly women, that modesty is not one of my best traits. And seeing the handsome six foot three muscular figure with wavy black hair figure that stared back through the dirty mirror, I could see why. Then, I noticed I wasn't alone. I twisted on my bar stool to face the tall looking pale man with pasty skin, curly hair, and thick eyebrows that sat next to me. I recognized him immediately.

"What can the universe's greatest hunter do for you, Sergeant Todd?" I asked trying not to smirk.

He spoke softly but with urgency, "I need your help." It was nearly a whisper. "But not here. Let's go to my office." Todd looked around to make sure he wasn't heard.

I shot him a toothy smile as I stood up, "Discretion is my middle name."

Twenty minutes later, I was swiveling on a chrome chair in Todd's office. Once the door hissed shut, I turned to business. "I am intrigued by the urgency with which you need a daring bounty hunter." The color drained from Sergeant Todd's face and he looked even paler. The black curly hair was matted down and plastered to his forehead.

"It's Dark Jack. My men and I encountered him in an ammunition factory located just outside the Bruchner System." Dark Jack was an intergalactic criminal. The police had been hunting him for a long time and they had the casualties to prove it. Dark Jack had a bad habit of killing everyone. In fact, the cops had been so desperate that I had just gotten an intergalactic APB announcing a large bounty and had been considering adding Dark Jack to my large collection of apprehended alien scum.

I leaned forward in my chair, "No way, Dark Jack? How the heck did you live?"

Todd sighed, "I was the only one. Bastard said he only wanted living space before he cut down my men."

I was still surprised. "I mean, wouldn't Dark Jack have noticed your escape and pursued you?"

Todd snapped. "I don't know. I was just dumb luck that I escaped the floating ammunition factory with my life. It's luck all right—bad luck."

"Why?" I asked.

A second later Todd was on his knees and clutching my hand. "You need to help me, Ruthstorm. I aborted my mission without consulting my superiors in the Interplanetary Police. They don't care that my forces were killed left and right after being called to the area. None of them will take my need to survive as an excuse for escaping. They will kill me and I will forever lose my reputation as a Sergeant."

Something didn't make sense as I remembered the APB. "I thought you cops had given up on Dark Jack. If they thought you got him, why did the Interplanetary Police announce the call for hunters to take on Dark Jack?"

Todd looked up to the ceiling, scratched his head, looked back at me, and said, "I had a friend place the announcement. His name is Conwell. He will keep my secret and protect me from scrutiny. But I need you to pursue the bounty before it is too late."

I knew Sergeant Conwell. We were soul brothers. Conwell knew that I wouldn't be able to resist taking a bounty as dangerous as Jack. Conwell was a notorious practical joker. "That bastard set me up." I made a mental note to thank him the next time I saw him... with my fist. "Is this Dark Jack even a real person? Because I don't get this damn fairy tale. How can a man float around the universe like some superhero without a space suit?"

Todd had composed himself a little as he tried to regain some dignity. "Oh, he is real all right. But, he's not a man; he's a powerful alien life form."

"I don't care," I sneered. "I'm leaving."

Todd reached into his desk and pulled out a silver device the size of his pointer finger—it was a holoprojector disk. "No wait,

Ruthstorm! Here is the surveying video taken during my encounter with Dark Jack. I removed the tape before I made my escape."

I laughed louder than I should have. "You mean you tampered with evidence."

"You're too funny." I watched as Todd pressed a button on the disk and a twenty foot hologram with a bluish aura popped onto the side wall.

The image showed four intergalactic policemen aiming their weapons at a tall purple alien that could have only have been Dark Jack. Despite the blue tinting of the hologram, I could still see that the creature's skin glowed in an eerie fashion. I looked closer and saw that Dark Jack's "hair" was five tendrils the lengths of snakes. What I noticed most was the alien's wide grimace, which dominated his face and was roughly the size of an old Earther football.

Then, the creature spoke with a gravelly voice. "Silly twerps; that all thou got?"

"Dark Jack, envoy of the asteroids, you are under arrest!" Todd announced.

I could see on the sides of the hologram that a fire was burning on both sides of what appeared to be an ammunition factory. State-of-the-art manufacturing mechanisms shut down as the flames continued to spread.

"Am I supposed to be impressed that thou knowest mine name?" chuckled Dark Jack. "This will not be enough to spare thee now!"

I could see that the officers were getting nervous, "Look at the size of that thing!"

Another squealed, "We're screwed!" Todd paused the tape and walked over to the wall. He pointed to each one as he described them. As if that would somehow absolve him of his role.

"The first soldier was Travis. He was a Private First Classman." Todd pointed to an officer with a short, blonde cowlick. Travis's stature was about average. "The second soldier, Nick, was another Private First Classman." He pointed to another soldier, this one was bald and he was a head shorter than Travis. "The third soldier, Ed, had more experience than Travis and Nick since he was a Corporal." I could see that Ed was also bald and was the biggest man on the squad. Todd pointed at himself, cowering behind the others. "And of course there was me."

Todd restarted the tape. The smoke from the fires rose above the battlefield and Dark Jack had disappeared into it.

The four soldiers cowered against a wall as they searched the smoke for any sign of the alien. Finally, Ed spoke, "You know what, I'm done waiting in fear!" He fired into the smoke. A second later, Dark Jack cackled.

"Oh, now he's mad!" Travis whined.

"Thanks a lot for getting us into deep crud, Ed!" squealed Nick.

Dark Jack swooped down out of the smoke, "Thou shouldest listen to thy squad, Ed." Dark Jack said the name like an insult. "They may lack courage but thou art in a losing battle,"

"Shut the hell up!" Ed screamed as pulled the trigger on his rifle. The sound of gunfire echoed off the walls of the floating ammunition factory.

Four seconds later, Dark Jack still hovered high above the deck completely unharmed. I could see the flames reflected off his purple skin as he gazed at the four soldiers in front of him with cold yellow eyes. He spoke slowly, "Predictable as usual. Humans have such apparent impulses in the face of their demise." Dark Jack reached out his right claw to the sky and a scarlet trident materialized in a flash of light. "Meet the latest and greatest of toys from…Algol's Solar System." Dark Jack snarled as he aimed the trident at the soldiers. "Now, meet thy maker!" Orange streams of flaring energy rushed into the central orb on the trident. Dark Jack's tendrils waved vigorously.

Then the camera angle changed as the image of Dark Jack became smaller and smaller. I was sure that I could hear a winded Todd saying "oh my God" over and over again. I assumed took the camera and was fleeing the scene. I turned to the Sergeant. The fact that he refused to meet my eyes, confirmed my theory.

Travis spoke on the tape in a quiet voice. "Sergeant? Sergeant Todd?"

"Where are you?" cried Nick.

"Though 'twas fun, playtime is over. Watch as the Death Ray destroys thee. Goodbye!" roared Dark Jack.

Then the hologram cut off.

Todd stared at the floor in silence for several minutes. Finally, he spoke, "Apparently Dark Jack's scarlet trident let out a blast of nuclear particles that was concentrated on the squad. I could hear them screaming until the noise was drowned out by the sound of the explosion. By the time I got back, destruction covered a two-mile radius that made up half of the floating factory. I was the only survivor." Todd wiped a tear from his eye before continuing. "That factory was among the first floating bases created by humans to perfect the use of solar panels to gather solar energy from not only the sun but from other stars as well. Now that Dark Jack destroyed what has been an important relic for the Interplanetary Police, our very place in the solar system is threatened. It is your duty to get him."

I rolled my eyes, "I don't owe a duty to anyone but me and my bank account. What is Dark Jack's bounty?"

"Six hundred sixty six million dollars," Todd answered.

It was chump change. Still, the idea of taking down someone as powerful as Dark Jack was intriguing. The way I figured it, I was the only one with enough guts to take the fiend down. "I'll take it," I boomed. "We'll negotiate my bonus when I return."

Todd's mouth was still open when I walked out the door.

I'm sure his mouth was still agape by the time I reached Razor. That's my ship. It may look like a piece of junk, but that Y-wing has been in my family for about twenty-five years now. I've had it for seven, and if I had my way would have kept it another hundred years. I personally painted the ship sky blue and a yellow stripe. Many a perp has messed themselves at the mere sight of the Razor. I love that ship.

I strapped into Razor's cockpit and computed the ignition setting by scanning my identipassword card. Then, I gave a shout of joy as Razor took off. I'm not ashamed to admit that I was psyched to catch Dark Jack, especially after seeing what the creature was capable of on Todd's footage.

Of course, being a hunter ain't all guns and excitement. It also takes patience. I needed to find Dark Jack. With all his ranting,

I figured the best way to do that was to invade his personal space. So I cut Razor's engines and drifted through that god-awful gaseous nebula of his. I must have floated for days just listening to the beeping of my interspatial radar.

I was about to give up when that freakazoid pressed his face against my plastisteel cockpit glass. His grin was nauseating.

He spoke, and despite the vacuum of space, I heard every word, "Hello, Invader! Why hast thou come to die?"

A lesser man would have cowered in fear. But, not Cody Ruthstorm. I merely returned the grimace. "Once I shoot your devil face down, Dark Jack, I'll be able to cash in for an early retirement!"

Dark Jack appeared unconcerned. "Oh? That so?" The creature sneered through gritted teeth, "Then let the challenge begin, human!" The imp then pulled his right fist back without losing his grimace.

My smile faded. In space, when one object strikes another object an equal and opposite reaction occurs. I'm not sure if Dark Jack knew this since his blow slammed hard on my cockpit and flung us both opposite directions. I closed my eyes as I spun out of control and my orientation of the black abyss of space went vertigo. Space debris appeared to spin like a whirlpool and I couldn't tell the asteroids from the planets let alone get a bead on Dark Jack. A thud on the lower wing told me that he had found me. I had hoped it was merely a meteor rock.

The gravelly voice told me I was wrong. "No. 'Tis me." Once again Dark Jack's eerie grin appeared in my cockpit window. I watched as his strong hands clenched either side of the cockpit. With inhuman strength, Dark Jack stopped the spinning of my ship. And with it, the clockwise tilting of my thick head also halted. Jack peered in like a schoolchild that shakes a bag full of fish and smiled. "Perhaps I did not hit thee hard enough, trespasser."

Dark Jack chuckled and pulled back his right arm and opened his claw revealing some kind of device. It was epilapinater. A devious device designed to emit intense flashes of orange light. A weaker being would be struck down by epileptic seizures. Of course,

I immediately recognized the device and flipped down my flash-proof shades just in time. I watched as the orange waves grew stronger and stronger with each passing moment. I examined my attacker: his clothes; his weapons; his face. Incredibly, Dark Jack's maniacal grin grew even larger with his confidence.

I laughed, "*Over*confidence is more like it" I thought to myself. I shot Dark Jack my trademark smirk. "You dumbass, you should've whammed me with everything the first time!" The press of a button on my monitor was all I needed to unleash my own wave of energy. The blue force bounced off everything within a one-hundred foot radius, including the Energy Bomb I noticed was attached to Dark Jack's belt.

I didn't even feel the explosion. That's another thing about space. The law of gravity doesn't affect a ship in the center of a wave pulse. And since the shield's waves centralized my exact position in space, I was safe.

I took a moment to catch my breath. The counter-shield had worked. But I knew I shouldn't pull that trick again since the element used for it is almost extinct. My grandpa used to tell me about the exploitation of the element Obamanium for the building of counter-shields back in the day. Their excessive use made the element sparse. Too bad, the things have their uses. Luckily, good old grandpa was a space pirate and had stolen the last of it, an entire freighter full, before he reformed. Unfortunately, I had just used most of grandpa's supply and would be lucky if I could make one more shield.

I checked my scanners and looked up ahead at the horizon. Asteroids ricocheted toward and away from each other as if they were being hit with explosives. In the center of it all was Dark Jack bouncing around like a pinball. I marveled at the chain reaction I created. I only intended to knock Dark Jack and his Energy Bomb back several miles. Sometimes, even I don't know my own strength.

A sensor went off and I checked the rearview cameras and saw a fast meteoroid that got caught within the chain reaction was close to striking my ship. In front, I saw that the remains of the chain reaction moving away from me. Not one to miss an opportunity,

I had another brilliant idea. I didn't want to waste the last counter-shield in existence, so l used a Freeze Missile.

Sweat ran down my face as I armed the missile. A second later I fired the projectile at the charging meteoroid and the force suppressed the hunk of rock's movement. As expected, little by little, the meteoroid became a relatively still ice block. I took a moment to look up ahead at the floating figure of Dark Jack, who was heavily bruised from the churning of the bouncing asteroids. "Hey, Dark Jack, are we done yet?" I taunted, "I hope not."

With great effort, Jack looked at me and groaned, "Tell me thy name, young one."

Obviously, Dark Jack had failed to recognize me through the cockpit. "I'm Cody P. Ruthstorm," I proclaimed, "the greatest bounty hunter that ever lived, especially after I cash you in."

Dark Jack pretended he hadn't heard of me. "Well then, know this, Cody Ruthstorm: thou art the only human who's gone the distance against me. But, this is over. Prepare to die!"

It was an empty threat; his body was bloody and bruised. I set the autopilot to drift near the alien as I put my spacesuit on over my jumpsuit. A second later I exited the Razor and floated in the void of space. Using my jet pack, I approached Dark Jack slowly but steadily. Once we were face to face, I drew my stun gun and my cuffs.

Before I could use either, Dark Jack announced, "Don't waste thy time coming here." I couldn't believe it; the perp was paralyzed and still trying to talk a good game. Then, Dark Jack's trusty trident materialized in his hands. "Paralyze mine body as thou please, but mine power is in the mind," Dark Jack explained.

"Great, a friggin' psychic," I murmured. I had dealt with far too many of those mind freaks in the past.

But, this time it was different as Dark Jack explained, "Not just a psychic," snarled Dark Jack. Then, Dark Jack did the cruelest thing my eyes had ever seen as his trident blazed to life and I witnessed the sheer power of his Death Ray for myself. Yet, I was not the target of the deadly blast of orange energy that whizzed past me to its true target.

I turned to see the growing explosion of debris. Three wings were coughed out first. Next, I saw a cockpit shattering to billions of pieces. The bastard shot my ship. Instantly, I knew Razor was annihilated. I watched the explosion, which was not as powerful as the one I had seen on the holo-video.

I turned back to the creature and snarled, "How dare you hold back, Dark Jack? I wanted a fight, not some half-assed demonstration!"

"Cody Ruthstorm, do not kid thyself," Dark Jack grunted. "Neither of us has the energy left to fight."

"YOU WANNA BET?!" I shouted back. "You should have thought of that before you destroyed my ship."

"Silence thy slanderous tongue!" The exhausted purple warrior pointed his right finger at me. A beam of light shot out and pierced my side. I found out later that the bastard had severed my left kidney with a point-blank laser. At the time, all I could think about was the pain and agony. To my credit I didn't scream. Dark Jack laughed, "Thou shall not make any silly bets ever again!" Dark Jack scolded.

"My bad," I groaned. I needed to buy some time and tried to get Dark Jack talking. "So, what is this I hear about your search for living space?" I questioned.

The creature appeared surprised. "Doth thou really want to know?"

"Why not?" I forced a smile.

Dark Jack paused. I could see that he was thinking about how to explain his crude history to me. I took the opportunity to cover my wound with airtight bandages to prevent any more oxygen from escaping my space suit.

Finally, Dark Jack told his story, "Algol's solar flares destroyed mine civilization." Algol was known as the Demon Star. This is because when viewed from light-years away, Algol appears to flicker like the fires of hell. In truth, this meant that solar flares were shooting from the star apparently right into Dark Jack's home planet.

I watched as Dark Jack's scarlet trident split itself in half and began to unveil some weird device. Within that device was an emblem that resembled an evil eye that glared ominously.

Suddenly, I felt very lightheaded as if I was no longer part of the space time continuum. "What are you doing to me?" I asked. Dark Jack simply continued his story.

"As a result of everything that went wrong, we the Psyrons are now an endangered race and I am their proud prince. That is why I will erase thee human scum to pave the way for our race to inhabit the planets around the Sun!"

We had arrived wherever it was we were going. I looked around me and didn't see any trace of space's black abyss. Instead, I saw an orange and red aura dance around Dark Jack and me. Then, without warning, I suddenly felt a strange surface with my feet though there was no ground.

Needless to say, I was pissed. "You better explain this, Dark Jack!" I threatened.

"The scarlet trident is not just a weapon," Dark Jack answered. "'Tis a dimensional generator as well. As for this place, this is as close as mortal beings can get to the soul-storage computer. Purgatory, without dying. I call this the Trial Realm."

"The Trial Realm?" I asked.

Dark Jack's grimace had returned. "This is where we will finish our long duel. Not with bloodshed, but with a battle of wits. We shall play Rock, Paper, Scissors."

I was insulted; the most dangerous criminal I had ever gone after took me to a different dimension and play the intergalactic version of a schoolgirl's game. What else could I do? Cody Ruthstorm doesn't back down. "I accept your challenge, imp!" I declared.

"Good. Now before we begin, we each have to tribute one thing among the possessions we treasure most to the computer-generated flames." He thought for a moment. "If I lose, I forfeit all the brain cells in my mind that allow me to use psychic abilities."

Of course, I wagered my most valuable possession. "And I will forfeit my beautiful body if I lose," I declared. Besides, if I did lose, I didn't want to wander around space hoping to be rescued until my air ran out.

The alien started the game. "This shall be best two out of three…begin!"

We walked closer and closer to each other and then the battle began. We each thought Rock, Paper, Scissors, and Shoe in our minds instead of shouting it as we played.

The first time, we both got Rock.

The second time, we both got Rock again.

The third time, Dark Jack got paper and I got scissors. It was one win for me. One more and this stupid contest would be over.

But then, Dark Jack got rock and I got scissors. "One more loss and thou art gone, twerp!" taunted Dark Jack

"The same can be said for you, alien." I taunted back.

Everything came down to the final round. As the final procedure of Rock, Paper, Scissors went underway, I thought about the dead souls taken by Dark Jack including Travis, Nick, and Ed, the three soldiers who were killed in Area 731. Rock...Paper...Scissors...SHOE!!

Dark Jack got rock and I got paper.

I had won.

Black lightning jolted from the highest reaches of the Purgatory computer and cleansed Dark Jack of the brain cells that gave him his mutant powers. The electricity didn't kill the nefarious imp, though he was left unconscious. As shocked as I was by the experience, I felt the sweet taste of victory. I finally could cash in on the bounty on Dark Jack's purple head.

Just then, the fiery Trial Realm started to disappear just as I picked up Dark Jack. I wondered how I was going to get home before realizing I was back on Port 339. Somehow, the Realm knew exactly where to send me.

"Haven't you left yet, Ruthstorm?" Sergeant Todd asked. He was standing next to another officer at the front desk of the interlactic police station. I immediately recognized the other man as Ian Anderson, a tall and buff fellow. His hair was curly like that of the ancient sports entertainer, Andre the Giant, except it was blonde. There was a gap in between his two front teeth.

"I didn't know I would be warped back here. Just as well, as promised Dark Jack. Now Ian, if you give me my reward." I grunted.

Ian's response was indignant. "That's Officer Anderson to you! I'll take the beast. Take your 666 million in credit!"

I swiped my card and the transaction was a success. I needed to get to a doctor. I stumbled out the door.

Before I could get too far away, Sergeant Todd dashed after me and grabbed my shoulder. "Hold it, Ruthstorm. I just wanted to say thank you for saving our Solar System…and my reputation."

I laughed out loud even though it hurt, "Todd. I didn't pursue Dark Jack to save the world and I sure as hell didn't do it for you. The money and the adventure was what sold me on getting Dark Jack to begin with. Nothing else."

"I told you he would say that, Todd!" I heard someone say.

I turned to see a man with fuzzy red hair and freckles standing in the doorway. It was Sergeant Conwell.

"Hey Ruthstorm, how you doing?" Conwell asked.

"Okay, except that Razor took a hit on that last job and I need a new ship." I confessed.

Conwell put his hand on my shoulder. "That's too bad. At least the reward money will help buy a new one"

I smiled, "Oh don't worry about me. I was just about to talk to Sergeant Todd, here, about my bonus. The way I see it, he owes me a new ship."

Todd's mouth dropped open even wider than before.

BAD RECEPTION

By Lindsay Kraemer

A familiar woman in a lab coat is seated in front of me with her head lowered to the clip board cradled on her lap.

"Is there something I can do for you?" I ask.

"Excuse me?"

"Will you just tell me why I'm here, Doctor?"

"Why do you think you're here?" The name tag hanging from her neck is unreadable. The scratching of her pen continues.

"What are you writing?" I ask, but she ignores me. I'm sitting. I look down and see a simple cot. "Excuse me," I say.

The sound of the pen stops and she looks up at me. Shadows dig away at her face where cheeks should be and her hair is pulled back, accentuating the dark circles under her eyes. I would guess she is in her mid-forties.

"My apologies, Mr. Stevens," she says and smiles.

"Doctor Stevens," I correct her.

"Yes. Doctor Stevens. I apologize for my rudeness. Let me introduce myself; I'm Doctor Calo."

"Doctor Natalie Calo? The same doctor who developed a miracle cure for Alzheimer's a few years ago?"

"I'm surprised you know about me."

"It would be hard not to," I say and offer a handshake. "You've had great success with that drug." Dr. Calo blushes and bows her head to her clip board once more. "What am I doing here?" I ask.

Ten minutes later, Dr. Calo and I enter a small room where there are no windows, the exception being the small pane of glass located on the door through which a guard stares at us from the outside corridor. Long shadows make the concrete walls appear expansive and a single fluorescent light bulb hangs high on the ceiling above a cot in the not-so-far corner where a dark figure—a woman—is seated. I walk over and peer down at her unkempt hair, mingled with patches of bald spots. As I near the woman, the smell of rotten meat and feces forces me to breathe through my mouth.

I bend to the woman's eye level to see a pale face covered with folds of flesh. Her subdued eyes peer through the shadows of their deep sockets, unmoving.

"Hello," I say.

Nothing. I can't even hear her breathe.

I turn to Dr. Calo and say, "What is her name?" The doctor's mouth opens, but nothing comes out." Her name, Dr. Calo," I demand.

"…Linda."

I return my focus to the woman on the cot. "Hello, Linda. My name is Dr. Jeff Stevens." The woman's eyes flicker with excitement. Her jaw drops and reveals a black tongue against decayed teeth, a vision that pushes me backward on my heels. Guttural moans emanate from her gaping mouth as she leans forward, arms reaching toward me. Her curled skeleton fingers grasp my arm and I fall to the ground. It's on top of me, grabbing me, moaning at me. With one desperate kick, I send the creature crashing backward into the cot with a loud crack. I stare at the limp body and flinch at the touch of Dr. Calo's hand on my shoulder.

"Are you all right?" she says, kneeling beside me.

"Get me out of here," I say. Dr. Calo helps me to the door.

"Stay here just a moment," she says and walks to the creature. I catch my breath for a moment before she returns and nods to the guard on the other side of the door. "Why did you do that?" Dr. Calo asks.

"Are you kidding? It was attacking me. Haven't you ever heard of zombies? The living dead?" Dr. Calo follows me into the hallway, but remains silent. "That's why you need me isn't it? To help you find a way to kill them."

"No, Dr. Stevens," She says, "that zombie is quite dead now." She turns away from me and exits the building at the far end of the hallway.

A few minutes pass and I still can't make sense of Dr. Calo's reaction. I exit through the same door and find her leaning against the wall, one arm crossed at her waist, the other bent to her chest, hand fidgeting with her name tag. Her nose is pink and her eyes glisten.

"Is everything all right?" I inquire. She scratches at her eyebrow. Her jaw clenches, she sniffs.

"Killing the zombies is not a problem," she responds. "The government needs your help because they think your background in medicine could be useful in our development of Final Resolution."

"What do you mean, 'Final Resolution'?"

"Millions of people die every year only to rise as zombies. They're coming back to life faster than we can eliminate them."

"So, you're looking for something a little more 'once and for all.'" I lean against the wall next to her. "I need to speak to my wife about this before we get started, but count me in."

Dr. Calo stares at the picture on her name tag and shakes her head. "We should bandage your arm first." I look down and see bloody abrasions on my arm. Nail marks.

"Oh, God."

"What?"

"We need to amputate my arm, or I'm as good as dead."

"What, the scratches? Don't worry. The zombies aren't contagious, not even their bites. But we should clean the wound unless you want an infection."

Dr. Calo tends to my arm, after which we view several more zombies and then retire for the night. At my request, she has provided me with a radio. I spend the majority of my evening devoted to looking for a station with good reception before I turn in. As uncomfortable as the room is—tiny with a single cot and toilet—and as unsettled as observing the zombies has left me, I fall asleep rather quickly.

The next morning, my feet ache and my eyes are swollen with exhaustion. Thank God there isn't a mirror in the room. When Dr. Calo meets me, her attire has changed and her lab coat is fresh, yet she looks as ill-slept as me.

"They've got to do something about the beds here, Dr. Calo," I say and rub at my eyes. We proceed down a long hallway. "And the reception on that radio is terrible."

"Concrete walls, Doctor. And please, call me Natalie."

We ride the premises in a vehicle similar to a golf cart and pass by piles of discarded clothing, jewelry, eye glasses, dentures, and other items—all confiscated from the zombies when they were brought here. In another area, caged dogs chew on severed arms, legs, and torsos. I won't be surprised if I see Zesty Zombie dog food at the supermarket in six months. What next?

My nose suddenly becomes irritated. Inside a courtyard just ahead, a large group of zombies wander about. The closer we get, the more my stomach turns. The tears in my eyes are blinding when Natalie hands me a cloth for my nose and mouth. She drives, unaffected.

Parked next to the chain link fence with the engine cut, we watch the zombies. Their wrinkled, rotten faces are solemn and stiff. They look like corpses as I suppose they should. They smell as if their insides have melted and the resulting unimaginable stink is escaping from their every orifice. The inside of their pant legs are permanently stained with what I can only imagine to be the ooze that their bowels can no longer hold.

"'Living Waste' is the official term worldwide," Natalie says.

"Living dead, Living Waste. It's all the same," I state. A haze of dust brushes up around their feet where the zombies walk about, unaware of one another. "How did you end up here?" I ask.

Natalie clears her throat. "The government was impressed with the cure I developed for Alzheimer's. They thought it would be helpful in their research."

"Really? And has it?"

"In a way," she responds.

Unexpectedly, one zombie attacks another. It tears and bites and kicks until an arm rips loose. Blood drips from the limb and smears the mouth of the attacker who chews ravenously. The victim continues walking, but now walks with a lean, the bone and tissue of its right shoulder exposed. Other zombies gravitate toward it and rip at the remaining appendages, or bite at the exposed, bleeding tissue.

I look over at Natalie, surprised that her reaction is little more than a blink.

She reaches into her pocket and pulls out a hard candy. "Want one? The taste is great for masking the smell."

"Never been a fan," I say. She unwraps and pops the candy into her mouth.

"We starve them for this exact reason," she says, the candy clicking against her teeth. "They would eat real food if we actually gave it to them."

I sit in front of a computer and study zombie medical records with the sound of distant explosions—emanating from another test site, I presume—which disrupts my concentration. Natalie said that blowing up the zombies is an unpractical, messy method of extermination. I guess it's not that unpractical. I continue to cycle through the records and stop when a familiar name and face appears; Stevens, Linda.

Behind me, there is an electronic beep, followed by the sound of an opening door.

"You have a question?" Natalie asks and walks up behind me. I sent a guard for her over an hour and a half ago.

"I just need you to grant me access to the death records for the specimens," I say.

"Those aren't available."

"That information may reveal to us the root cause of infection." I cross my arms over my chest. "Without it, I can't do much in the way of helping you."

"In front of you is all we have in the way of records."

"You must be kidding. I've gone through hundreds of these and not one contains the cause of death. Or even the time of death, for that matter."

"Allow me to show you something," she says as she removes a thin, plastic case from her lab coat pocket. From the case, she pulls a disc that she slips into the computer before sitting down beside me. She closes the specimen history and a video begins to play on the monitor. In it, a zombie sits in a room much like the one we're in right now, and it sits in a chair much like the ones Natalie and I are sitting in. It was the first zombie I observed, the one that attacked me, the woman whose name and picture I recognized just a moment ago. She stares at the camera.

"Do you know your name?" Natalie's voice comes from behind the camera.

"Yes," the zombie responds and continues with difficulty, "My name is Linda Stevens."

How can this be the same zombie I saw just the other day?

In the video, Natalie says "What is the point of this session today, Linda?"

Like a child reading out loud for the first time, the zombie says, "Today, we are recording a message for my family…"

She talks to a Becky, to a Paul. To a Jesse, Jessica and Danny; it goes on. All meaningless names, followed by 'thank you's' and 'I love you's.' The only thing moving is her mouth, rising and lowering at the sides with a dark, swollen tongue bouncing off the top and bottom.

"Jeff…I saw you today," the zombie says.

"Linda. My name is Dr. Jeff Stevens," I had said to her.

"…You didn't recognize me…"

"What am I doing here?" I had asked Natalie.

"…I know we're old… There is so much that I can't remember, but…"

"That zombie is quite dead now," Natalie had said to me.

"…You have been the highlight of my life. I love you," Linda, the zombie, says, staring into the camera lens, right at me.

My face feels wet.

"Please, take me back to my room," I mutter.

When I wake up, Natalie is sitting across from my cot. I close my eyes and open them again, but she is still there, so I look at the ceiling and remain where I am, lying on my prison bed.

"Are you aware that law prevents any person from living longer than one hundred years and one day?" she asks. The light bulb on the ceiling flickers. "Once people began living to one hundred and fifteen the government created a law that no person would be permitted to live past one hundred years and one day." My eyes burn under the light.

"Do you know how old you are, Jeff?" I don't care. "You're one hundred and twenty years old."

"Impossible," I say.

"No, Jeff. It's quite possible."

"How?" I sit up.

"A disease. It started with your generation and because of that, they're considered the originals. We believe the greatest chance for finding a cure lies with them."

"And Final Resolution is your cure. Since when is death a cure?"

"Since no one dies of old age anymore."

"Why didn't you just tell me this from the beginning? Why did you lie to me?"

"I never lied to you, Jeff. I was observing you to see how the treatment was working. You came to your own conclusions."

"But you—what treatment?" Then, I remember one of my first conversations with Natalie. "You're killing innocent people with your Alzheimer's miracle drug?"

"There's more to it than that, Jeff."

I lean forward. "I don't see how."

"Think of Living Waste as having an extremely accelerated form of Alzheimer's. I was brought in to see if my drug would yield positive results for Living Waste."

"So how does this tie into Living Waste elimination?"

"Originally, it didn't. I was simply testing to see if the drug could restore brain activity like it did to my Alzheimer's patients. And it did. But only after the dosage was increased to five times the amount given to regular patients; a dose that becomes fatal to Living Waste after approximately one week of treatment."

"And my wife?"

"We tried to test an enhanced formula on the two of you simultaneously, but you were unresponsive. That's when she decided to make the recording."

"When I saw her the other day?"

"She was already immune to the drug. It's the last stage before death. It was only a matter of time, regardless of what you did to her." I feel Natalie's gaze on me, but I refuse to look at her. It's the only part of me that I have control over.

"You're unique, Jeff," she says. "You're one of the two percent who show little to no response to the drug. Even with a higher dosage of the enhanced formula, your memory recall is still minimal and extremely selective. It became evident when you remembered your profession as a doctor, but failed to recognize your wife. And then came the zombie idea."

"If only the world was that lucky! The reality is that you're murdering innocent people. Why?"

"Do you have any idea what's happening to the world's population? Once we find a way to cure this disease we won't have to kill—"

"You heartless witch. You and I both know this is no disease. How else do you explain this beginning with one generation and moving onto the next when it's not contagious? Simply compare the average lifespan of a cave man to someone from the 21st century, and it's obvious. It's evolution. And as much as you try to convince me and everyone else of otherwise, people aren't that dumb."

"Listen to yourself. You've seen what the Living Waste are like. Why should it matter whether it's a disease or evolution? It doesn't change the fact that their quality of life is non-existent.

They can't remember a thought the moment after they think it. They can't communicate, or perform even the simplest task. They're like the living dead, only they never died.

"And what else could we possibly do? Just let them live the rest of their unfortunate, unending lives? Is that really better than one week of coherent thought and the chance to make peace with themselves and with their families? I have thousands of recordings just like Linda's, all Living Waste, leaving messages for their loved ones. It's hard for them to adjust to the truth, but once they accept it, they die happy."

"Well, what about the two percent, Natalie? Who am I supposed to leave a message for? How am I supposed to make any kind of peace when I couldn't even remember my own wife as she sat before me? Whom you watched me kill! You're going to murder me and, eventually, the rest of my family with your pathetic drug. How can I die happy knowing that?"

Natalie stands.

The door closes behind her.

WIRED

By Chris Buchner

A flash, a bang, and Roger Eames finds himself shooting up in bed at the cusp of yet another in a series of sleepless nights. Sleep is definitely the unmentioned casualty of war, he thinks to himself as he tries to regain his composure and slow his heart rate.

Roger had ended his final tour of duty over six months ago, but still the dreams persist. He can never remember the content, just the flashes; the noise. That, in itself, lets him believe that he's reliving the battles over and over constantly. He thought once he got out of the service that things could get back to some semblance of normalcy like before the war. Now, he's not as sure. His wife, Regina, had been on him to go see a therapist for help, but he was raised "old school." His father didn't rely on doctors, neither did his father's father, and he definitely wasn't the type himself.

Probably stupid machismo.

Roger wipes the sweat off his forehead and flips the covers off of himself. He tries to stealthily swing his legs over the side so as not to wake up his wife and proceeds to find his slippers in the darkness on the floor. Slipping them on, he stands and makes his way over to the bathroom on her side of the room. He turns on the light and approaches the sink, starting the cold water running. He cups his hands and uses them to splash the water on his face before looking at himself in the mirror.

"Can't sleep again?" a voice asks from the doorway. Roger looks over at his wife as she leans against the frame with her arms crossed and a sympathetic smile on her face.

"Oh, no; I was just using the bathroom," Roger says.

She chuckles and sways over to him, running her hand along his face. "Liar. Why won't you let me make you an appointment with Dr. Jensen?"

"Because. Dr. Jensen is a shrink. I don't do shrinks."

"No—what you don't do is sleep," Regina counters with a serious tone ebbing into her voice. Roger knows that tone well. It's the same tone she uses on their children when she has to go into stern mother mode. Roger takes her hands and smiles at her.

"Honey, I'm fine. This is normal. It'll fade in no time, you'll see. Trust me." Regina moves in close to him, smiling.

"I do." She kisses him and starts out of the room. Roger thinks he may have just won that one. "But I'm calling Dr. Jensen in the morning to see if she can help make 'no time' come faster." Roger slumps down. Two wars, five tours of duty combined, several medals and commendations, but he still can't win against his wife. "Goodnight!" she sings from the bedroom as she slips back into bed.

The following morning, Roger bounds down the stairs, led by the aroma of fresh coffee from the kitchen. Before heading there, though, he makes his way to the front door to retrieve the paper. Peering outside, he finally spots it sitting in the rose bush next to the house and growls to himself.

He misses little Ricky Friedrich, the paperboy they had for the last several years. While he was away overseas, little Ricky became not-so-little and moved on to college. But boy, did that kid have an aim. If the paper didn't land exactly on the front stoop, it would at least be not far away on the walkway or the lawn just off the path.

This new kid however, named Johnny by his wife in one of her letters, couldn't hit the broad side of a barn if it was the size of the planet. Since his last leave before his discharge, he has found the paper in some of the most impossible places. The rose bush seems to be a particular favorite of young "Johnny." One day, Roger decides he needs to make it a point to get up early enough to catch the little— darling—and have a nice long chat with him.

Almost painlessly retrieving the paper, Roger makes his way back into the house for that waiting cup of coffee. However, something catches his eye in the living room as he passes it. He stops and peers in, seeing the usual assortment of furniture; couch, his favorite chair, the TV entertainment center, lamps and a couple of Regina's plants she never remembers to water. Nothing out of the ordinary. So what made Roger stop? Shrugging it off, he enters the kitchen.

"Morning, Daddy!" Roger's girls Denise and Chantal say in unison as he walks in. They already sit eating at the table.

"Hello, girls!" he says, ducking down between them so they can kiss his cheeks. "All set for another day of school?"

"NOOOOOOOOOO!" they protest together. Roger chuckles as he stands up and kisses his wife before going for the coffee pot.

"Did you manage to sleep? Regina asks.

"I slept fine," Roger lies casually, pouring the coffee into his mug. "So, I guess you don't have to make that appointment."

"Nice try."

"What are you doing today, Daddy?" Denise asks.

"I was thinking maybe a little fishing today…"

"Uh-uh, you need to fix the roof gutter in the back yard," Regina reminds him.

"Aw, but honey—I'm a veteran!"

"Out there you're a veteran. In here you're a handyman. Alright, girls, let's get moving. You'll miss your bus!" Regina states, clapping her hands. The girls take their last bites and run out of the kitchen to get dressed. Regina gives Roger another kiss before following. "You have a good day."

"You too."

"Get in there you son…of…a…bitch!" Roger grunts as he bangs in the last bracket of the gutter. Roger wipes the sweat off his forehead. *When did it get so hot? Or is it just the work?* Shrugging, he climbs down the ladder. Finding the old weathered screws insufficient to do their jobs, Roger needs to head to the hardware store for some more in order to finish.

He throws his tools into the toolbox on the ground and turns towards the brook that runs past his backyard. He strolls over to the bank and looks at the woods beyond it. He missed this, the quiet and serenity of being home. He'd gladly take any amount of housework over the perils of battle any day.

Taking a deep breath in, he begins to start back to finish cleaning up when something catches his eye out of its corner. He turns back towards the brook and stares at the water as it rolls over the rocks on the bed. It looks absolutely normal, except...he could've sworn he almost saw it skip. Like an online video that has trouble completely buffering. He shakes his head and rubs his eyes, thinking his sleeping troubles are just finally catching up to him. Maybe Regina was right about the shrink.

Okay, that settles it...it's definitely the lack of sleep.

Tuner's Hardware is one of the few guy hangouts located inside of the town. Friends usually pass by at odd times, even when they don't need any supplies. It's quieter than the bowling alley, doesn't drain as much money as the bar, and wives have no reason to wander in there.

Roger enters to find the usual crowd, Turner, Harris and Phil, standing around the front counter, talking loudly about whatever. Most likely sports. Turner is at the register; an old retired Marine who's stacked on a few pounds, but a good deal of it is in muscle. Harris works down at the mill, so you can always find him dressing the part in plaid shirts and jeans. His wife hates that. Phil works down at the docks. He loves sports to the point he wears a different jersey every day. The challenge is his finding ones in his size all the time.

"Hey, Rog!" Phil says as he sees Roger, in between bites of the chili dog he dribbles on his shirt.

"What's doing, guys?"

"Ah, we're just trying to educate this bum on the difference between *real* players and those overpaid rookies they got on the court," Harris answers.

"Yeah, good luck with that," Roger says with a chuckle. He holds up a nail and shows it to Turner. "I can get a pound of these?"

"Sure thing. Just a sec." Turner heads off to check the nail drawers near the counter, but upon not finding them steps out from behind the counter and heads down the nearby aisle towards the back room.

"So what kind of chance do you see the Bulls having this year?" Phil asks Roger.

"Depends if their passing forward gets a pair of glasses or not."

"I'll say. How many shots were messed up last year because of him?" Harris adds.

"Well I…" Roger stops in mid-sentence as he catches Turner walking into the back room. He sees a few shelves as Turner walks past them, but then the room falls into…nothing. Absolutely nothing.

"Rog? Roger? Hello? Earth to Roger?" Roger hears Harris say finally. He shakes his head and blinks. "You alright?" Harris asks. Roger looks back up as Turner comes back out of the room, and again, from nothingness.

"ROG!" Roger jumps as he comes back to the conversation. "What's wrong with you?" Harris asks. Roger notices the others all looking at him as Tuner approaches with the nails.

"Uh, yeah…I just haven't been sleeping well. Look, I'm gonna go. Thanks, Turner." Roger takes the nails and quickly makes his way out of the store.

That night, Roger shoots up in bed again drenched in sweat. The damn dreams seem to be getting more persistent now. Used to be these kinds of nights would be a few days apart, but that grace period is quickly shrinking as the days go by. And that constant warm sensation, that's a new development that's making itself a frequent nuisance.

Roger quietly slips out of bed and heads down to the kitchen, still sweating. It has been feeling ungodly hot lately, he thinks. He decides to make some coffee to soothe his nerves. As it brews, Roger glances over to the clock on the oven and notices it's closer to morning than he thought. In fact, it's just about the time the paper gets delivered.

Roger quickly turns and runs out of the kitchen to the front door. Sure enough, there comes his paper flying into the bush to his right as the paper boy speeds on past the house. Roger shuts the door behind him and takes off after the kid. The boy turns the corner and Roger swerves into a neighbor's driveway down to their backyard. He vaults himself over the fence into the next yard and proceeds to run out towards the street just as the paper boy passes that house. He grabs the bike's seat and slows his run down so as to get the boy to stop without pitching him off.

"Whoa, slow down, junior!" Roger calls as the boy turns the bike around and comes to a stop. Roger lets go of his seat and walks towards the front of the bike. However, something about it seems strange; almost familiar. Roger shakes it off as the boy looks up at him. "Listen, son, I don't want to tell you how to do your job, but…" Roger's sentence seems to get lost in his throat as he finally notices the boy's face under his baseball hat, or rather, the lack of a face.

Where his face should be, there's absolutely nothing. A flesh-colored totally blank slate. The boy doesn't even have any hair! Roger steps back in horror.

"What's the matter, mister?" the boy asks. Hearing his voice, Roger is able to process through the terror he feels why the boy seemed familiar. The voice belonged to Jimmy, the old paper boy, and so did the bike. That same, green mountain bike with the scratched-up spokes and rain-warped superhero stickers along the frame.

"Mister?"

"What made you decide to do this?" Regina asks as she and Roger head towards Dr. Jensen's office. "I thought I would have to call your old C.O. to issue a order to get you to see a psychiatrist."

Roger stops their walking and takes a deep breath."I've been seeing…things."

"What kinds of things?" Regina asks, puzzled.

"I'm…not sure. Just…things. Strange things."

Regina looks at her husband with concern. "Well, let's see if your doctor can help."

"I don't see why she can't," Roger replied. With that, they continue on towards the office. Roger opens the door and allows his wife to go in first. He follows shortly after, only to find himself standing back outside next to her. Roger looks around, dumbfounded.

"Now see, wasn't that worth the trip?" Regina asks him. He looks at her sideways.

"Wasn't *what* worth the trip?! We're back outside!"

"That *is* usually what happens when the session is over."

Roger looks back at the office, then back at her. Over?! It didn't even start yet!"

"What are you talking about? We've been in there for an hour."

That night, Roger was determined to get some sleep and sought the help of a sleep aid. For the most part, it worked. He slept soundly and the dreams didn't come. But, what he couldn't possibly anticipate was the burning. A horrible, searing, burning sensation that suddenly covered every inch of his skin. It was like he was on fire.

Roger shot up, awake and screaming out. Regina woke with a start and quickly turned on the light on the nightstand.

"Roger?! What's wrong? What—?"

"BURNING! I'M ON FIRE! CAN'T STOP THE BURNING! AAAAAAAGH!"

Regina sits on the exam table with Roger, holding him against her. The pain subsides by the time they reach the hospital, but Roger has the doctor run the full work-up on him anyway. Now they wait for those results, Roger still reeling from the horrible pain he felt, not knowing what's happening to him. First betrayed by his mind, now his body.

The doctor enters the exam room and the couple perks up slightly. He shuts the door behind him and opens the folder he carries.

"Well, Mr. Eames, I'm not quite sure what happened to you, but as far as I can tell all your tests came out normal. The only thing of note are some elevated levels of stress, which can be explained by your lack of sleep and recent mental duress."

"That's impossible," Roger says angrily, sitting up. "How can I be fine? How can nothing be wrong with me when I felt like I was on fire? Does feeling like you're burning sound fine to you?"

"Honey, calm down…" Regina starts.

"No, I will not calm down! Not until the doctor here tells me how I can be here in the goddamn hospital and yet be 'fine.' So, tell me, doctor, how am I fine?"

"I really can't explain it, Mr. Eames. All I can tell you are what the tests say; and they all say you are a perfectly healthy man. Maybe whatever has been causing your recent delusions has more psychological significance. If your mind tells you something is wrong with you strongly enough, your body will believe it."

"Great, so I'm going crazy AND my mind wants to kill me." Regina puts her arms on her husband and tries to soothe him.

"Mrs. Eames, if I may—?" the doctor says, motioning towards the door as he opens it.

"I'll be right back, honey. You just try to calm down." She kisses him on the cheek while she rubs his arms before standing and following the doctor into the hall. Roger watches them talk, unable to hear what they say. The doctor touches Regina's arm as she nods before he disappears down the hall. Regina comes back into the room and walks back over to the table.

"What was that about?" Roger asks as Regina helps him stand up.

"The doctor just gave me some advice on how to help settle your nerves. Now come on, let's get home. It's almost dawn and I'm sure Mrs. Ritoni would like to go home to finish sleeping in her own bed." She gently guides Roger towards the door. He stops and looks at her, a great sadness in his eyes.

"Regina…what's wrong with me?"

"I don't know. I don't know." She gives him a reassuring hug. "But, we'll face it and get through it together. You just focus on getting better."

Roger sits in his favorite chair of the living room, leaning forward and holding his head. He is at his wit's end. The dreams, the room that doesn't exist, the faceless boy…what does it all mean?

Roger leans back and looks at the ceiling and notices something. He curiously looks around the room and realizes something is…off. But, he can't quite place what.

He decides he needs to do something. "Just sitting and wallowing in vague feelings and growing depression is not helping the situation," he thinks. He picks up the paper on the table next to him and opens it up to read. He stops when he notices the date.

"What the hell?" The paper was from a month before he went on his last tour. "Damn faceless paperboy…can't even bring me the right newspaper," Roger coldly jokes to himself, tossing the paper back on the table. He stands up and looks at the bookshelf in the wall for something to read. However, upon realizing he's read all those books, he decides a trip down to the library might be in order.

"A walk might do me good," he says to no one as he grabs his keys off the hook in the hall and heads out the door.

Twenty minutes later, Roger arrives at the library and heads inside. Roger wipes a bit of sweat off his forehead. Though not as bad as during the night, the heat refuses to leave him. Shaking off the warm feeling, he looks around. In a small town like this, the library is a small, fairly modern building with only one floor. One thing Roger always liked about it, though, was despite the visible lack of space, they always managed to somehow cram the shelves with tons of literary goodness.

Roger makes his way down a row of shelves and starts browsing the books. He stops when a title catches his interest and grabs the book. Opening up the book to read a page, he's shocked to find pages full of gobbledygook: letters, numbers and symbols all over the pages instead of actual words. Flipping through the book he finds every page inside is the same.

Putting the book back, he grabs another one. Again, gibberish. And the next four after that, all the same. He finally comes across a book that has actual words inside of it. Flipping the cover closed, he sees it's a book he's read before.

"What the hell is going on here?" Scooping up all the books he pulled, he makes his way to the front desk and puts the books down on it. Mrs. Crabtree, the librarian who had been manning the desk since he could remember, looks up at him.

"Checking those out, young man?"

"No, reporting a problem. Take a look at this." He hands her one of the gibberish books. She flips through the pages and looks up at him.

"What's wrong with it?"

"What's—? Look at it! The book makes no sense!"

"The book looks perfectly fine to…" she stops in mid-sentence. Roger's eyes grow wide as he realizes it's not just her words that froze, but her entire body! There Mrs. Crabtree sits, as if someone had pressed the pause button on the remote control of life.

Roger carefully reaches out to her with a shaking hand, and touches her shoulder. An electronic ripple runs from the spot he touched across her whole body. He pulls back quickly as the woman shimmers back to solid form.

Then, as quickly as she froze, she returned to life again.

"Oh, checking those books out, young man?" Slowly, Roger starts backing away from the desk.

"Young man?" Mrs. Crabtree stands to look at him curiously as Roger turns and takes off out the library door. "Young man!"

Roger runs towards the main shopping thoroughfare in the center of town. He stops on a corner and leans against a building, trying to catch his breath. As he begins to regain his composure, he takes notice of all the people walking around and going to the various stores. Half of the people he sees all have faces he recognizes, be it his fellow soldiers, former classmates he's seen at recent reunions, or people he recalls having passed in the street. The others are all faceless, just like the paperboy.

Everywhere he looks, Roger can't escape the warped version of itself that reality has become. Feeling dizzy, he stumbles towards the nearest store to get off the street and try to collect himself. He opens the door and steps inside, only to find himself back on the sidewalk. He turns back and looks through the open door, seeing nothing through it.

"Are you okay?" someone asks. Roger turns to find himself looking at someone who resembles Declan Rooney, a man he served with that was killed right in front of him during combat. Roger steps back and bumps into someone who looks like Julianna Rodriguez, his college girlfriend. Everywhere Roger looks, faces from his life mixed with no faces, closing in around him, suffocating him. Suddenly his eyes roll up in his head and he passes out.

Roger's eyes open to find Regina sitting above him, looking concerned.

"W-what happened?" Roger asks.

"Oh, honey, the doctor says you had a fever and passed out in the street. You were delirious, babbling." Roger sits up and finds he's in their room at the house.

"I still feel hot..." he mutters. She puts a hand to his forehead.

"You're burning up. Let me get you some water. I'll be right back." Regina quickly gets up and leaves the room as Roger lies back down. He stares up at the ceiling, trying to will himself to cool down while noticing the peeling paint he never got around to fixing.

Suddenly, something clicks. He shoots up in the bed and looks towards the closet. He stumbles out and walks over to it. Opening it and slowly kneeling, he reaches in and pulls out a large box. Removing the lid, he sees his uniform with a batch of letters sitting on top of it. He struggles to focus through the growing pain as he flips through the letters until he finds the one he wants.

In it, Regina talks about how she finally got someone in to the house to paint the living room while he was overseas; a project he never had a chance to do. It was painted a nice, light blue. The problem is, the living room is still the same green it was when he left.

"ARRRRRGH!" Roger cries out as the burning sensation returns full force, covering every inch of his body. Tears come to his eyes as he tries to fight through it long enough to make it to the bedroom door and struggle down the stairs.

"Regina!" he shouts.

"In here," Regina's voice comes from the living room. Roger quickly moves towards the entranceway and looks at his wife and daughters sitting on the couch.

"Regina, what in the hell is going on?"

"What do you…"

"Don't! Don't even! Something is…AAAAAAGH!...going on! Everything is right, and yet it's wrong! Why…why am I on fiiiIIIIIIRE?! Why am I on fire? Why am I… Why is everything so screwy? Why am I going crazy? Why is this room NOT blue?!" He tosses the crumpled letter onto the floor as he leans against the doorway, breathing heavy and trying to fight the pain.

"You're not home," Regina tells him. He looks at her, confused.

"None of this is real," Chantal adds, suddenly sounding a lot more adult than she ever has before. "This is a computer simulation pumped directly into your brain, made up entirely of your memories."

"I don't understand! Why…who…why am I here?!"

"Honey—you were wounded," Regina responds with concern in her voice. "Overseas. You were caught in an incendiary blast and most of your body was badly burned. To save your life, the medics hooked you up to a Virtual Stimulation Unit that puts people into an induced coma to help with the healing process. It keeps the brain occupied so that it, combined with morphine, dulls the pain receptors and allows recovery with a minimum of discomfort."

"Then why do I feel like I'm on fire?!"

"Because the system is failing," Denise states frankly. "You're becoming aware. Waking up."

"The technology is new and limited," Chantal adds. "It can only create based off the memories stored in your subconscious. The mind records everything you experience and retains it, even if you cannot actively recall it. That is why you cannot go where you have not been, read what you have not read, and only see people you have seen in your life. Ordinarily, you would not notice these inconsistencies."

"What happens when I wake up?" Silence. "What happens?!" Regina gets off the couch and moves towards him, putting a hand to his cheek.

"You'll be on your own. I'm sorry." Roger finds it hard to believe, but he can see the sadness behind her eyes. So much like his wife, so real, so lifelike. How can it all be in his head? How can this be fake? This must be a joke. It has to be.

But, it's not. Roger looks past her to see the room begin to become pixilated. It gradually breaks down, square by square, leaving nothing but a heavy darkness in its wake. Roger looks towards Regina's concerned face. The darkness soon envelops everything behind his daughters, and then his daughters themselves.

"I'm sorry," Regina says again. Roger painfully reaches up to hold her close to him as from all around the darkness draws closer to the spot they stand on. He can feel her beginning to lose density in his hands.

"No! No, don't leave me like this! Don't leave me like this! Don't leave me!!!"

The world goes black.

"Don't leave me like this! Don't!" Roger continues to cry out as he struggles to move. But, he is firmly bound in place by his wrists, ankles and torso. He lies where he has always lain; in the VSU, with a helmet over half his face and the rest of him covered in bandages. A cracked plastic bubble covers his body on top of the table he's on, with wires and cables running from it and the helmet into a computer terminal.

"Hello?! Anyone?! Anyone out there!? Hello!" Roger calls. But, with the helmet blocking his vision, he's unable to see there's no one to answer. He can't see all the equipment and pieces of the building that lay strewn about with bodies of the medical staff and some of the patients. He can't see the small fires still burning while the charred remains of others dot the floor and walls. He can't see any of the devastation left after the hospital was hit by enemy fire, disabling the VSU and condemning him to his fate.

"Hello?"

SURVIVOR

By Liam Webb

Based off art by James Rodriguez

In 2147, mankind sent out an unmanned exploration rocket to the Pleiades system.

In 2151, the discovery of planets in the system ushered in a new age of exploration. Because an unbroken journey would be impossible to survive, both private and public interests either invested in cryogenic technology or scoured the spaceways to find more planets or planetoids to use as jumping off points between the Milky Way and Pleiades systems. Finding these jumping off points would make manned missions to the Pleiades a reality.

In 2185, the construction began on the first relay stations to allow man to travel to the Pleiadean system without the use of risky cryogenics.

In 2202, mankind made contact with extraterrestrials. This event was hailed as the most wonderful, enlightening moment of that or any age. This new race, known as sauroids to earthmen, came from the fourth planet from the star-sun Alcyone, and had much to share.

In 2264, mankind began its first war with extraterrestrials. Having seen the wonders of the sauroids' world, certain Earth governments decided to take by force things that the sauroids did not wish to share.

In 2269, mankind's first war with extraterrestrials ended. For all the saber rattling of politicians and propagandists, neither side could claim victory. Both species knew that to continue fighting would be folly, and in a surprising moment of galaxy-wide common sense, hostilities simply ceased. No treaty was signed, no winner or loser officially declared. Human and sauroid forces simply withdrew, slowly and quietly. The governments on both planets consciously unwound their populaces from jingoistic fervor, and beginning after the second year of the pull out, secretly speaking to the other side. Many on both planets said the Earth people had lost; not only were the Earth people unable to conquer the sauroids' planet, but they also simply did not gain anything from the sauroids in technology or achievement in that time.

In 2276, after both sides had recovered and rebuilt, open diplomatic relations began.

From 2285 to 2292, the intergalactic highway was built, to join the two "in friendship and understanding." The highway wasn't a conventional road; rather, it was a series of space stations built at equidistant points in space from the Milky Way to the Pleidean. The highway was necessary because the planets and relay stations of yesteryear were no longer available. At the end of the war, the forethinking military minds of both races destroyed most of the planets the stations were on so that the other race either couldn't follow them home for retribution or advance another attack, whichever the case may be. Rates of travel approaching light speed were still possible, but doing so used an enormous amount of power, depleting fuel cells before the trip could be finished. Using the old relay stations, a ship could refuel and their small crews could rest. The intergalactic highway was an improvement on the planet system because, built at strategic points in space, it was more direct. This allowed for larger cargo and passenger ships, because with the new system they could rest and refuel more easily. In the spirit of friendship and co-existence, each station was to be manned by both species at all times.

On August 3, 2292, in a moment of rest in his office, Tlak, the sauroid station doctor, watched from his window as a new, Western Hemisphere Government-owned ship docked on Station 3X2-4A.

After checking his harness belts twice and firmly gripping the safety bar, the crewman's gloved hand pressed the "open" button. The sound was deafening even through the safety doors and with his helmet on. Guy King shut his eyes against the wind, though he knew he couldn't really feel it. He also knew it wasn't really wind; it was air being sucked out of the docking station into space. There was a slight problem in the seal on the door, which allowed some atmosphere to pass through. It wasn't enough to cause a major problem beside the noise, so Central Control hadn't deemed it necessary to fix quite yet. This was after he had filled out ream upon ream of paperwork that the government agency required.

Years ago, Guy had spoken to his grandfather, an old military man, about the comparative sizes of their paperwork. They had decided that never before in the history of civilized man had someone been required to fill out that many government forms for something so simple. But, his grandfather observed, that was just a natural result of the two planets' governments coming together in joint oversight over the highway stations. His grandfather told him you could even file to pay a punch-your-superior-officer-tax in the New York City tax system while filing a Freedom of Information Act lawsuit and *still* have less forms than Guy had over a few minor repairs.

The sudden lack of noise after the docking bay doors shut jolted him from his memories. Guy opened his eyes to see that it was a new, streamlined government job coming in to the docking bay. He thought it must be the new crewman they just got. He checked the screen to his right, reading the ship's mission display.

"Inventory clerk? Good luck with that," he said to no one. "If she's got to pick up after Fat Judy's mess," he thought, "this new girl has her work cut out for her." Guy knew that Judy had messed up the inventory so badly the new girl would probably spend her first month simply figuring out just what the hell they had. The only wonder left in Guy's mind was why they didn't fire Judy months before they did. "God," he thought, "I hope the new clerk isn't another dumb fat chick."

The ship in the bay, Guy closed the bay doors. Now that the shrieking air stopped, the silence felt physical, like someone stuffed cotton in his ears all at once. After another minute to restore cabin pressure, the ship's door opened.

The new clerk got off the ship. Covered head to toe in the standard space suit, the glass of the helmet was still blacked out to protect against seeing un-atmosphered starlight on the trip over. The new crewman was carrying two bags with her.

"Probably has more on the ship, too," Guy thought. Guy signaled the new arrival over to him as he flipped the switches to operate the forklift. The newbie got to the door of Guy's inner chamber and Guy buzzed her in.

"Welcome to station 3X2-4A, or 'The Triple X Ranch.' I'm Guy and I'll be your cowpoke today," he said.

She took off her sun-screened helmet.

"Thank you, Guy, I'll be your tenderfoot. I'm Mayumi Yefrimova, your new inventory clerk," she said with a slight, undistinguishable accent. "Oh, um, call me May. Sorry," she haltingly added after a pause that was just a bit too long to be natural. Her long black hair peered out from under the ball cap she wore under her helmet, framing a finely featured oval face. Upon meeting her, Guy thought two things immediately: one was that he couldn't tell if she was part Asian, Indonesian, or was Hawaiian, and the other was that he really wished he had remembered to shave that morning. Guy then deliberately turned his attention to guiding the forklift in through its access door, and transferred the control to the remote beacon that he stuck in his pocket.

"Uh, right this way, uh, May," Guy said, turning away from her. She followed him through the docking bay door into a corridor.

At the end they made a left and came to a service elevator. Guy pressed the button and they waited for the elevator car in silence. It wasn't until after they got in and the car was in motion again that Guy broke the silence.

"Just signed on?"

"Does it show?" she asked self-consciously. "This, uh, is my first real job since I graduated college last spring."

"Nah, just keep quiet and observe things for a couple days, and you'll do fine," he said. "What did you get your degree in?"

"Psychology," May responded. "Industrial-organizational psychology, actually," she added, almost as an afterthought.

"So they put you in inventory. Morons," he said. "I've got an applied mathematics degree myself. I'm supposed to be the consultant to any wandering or stationed engineers, but in three years I've yet to come across one engineer, so I spend my time running the dock."

The elevator stopped and they got off, heading straight. Guy pointed down hallways as he talked, trying not to face her directly while also trying to not make it look like that was what he was doing.

"Now, to our left is the common area. Play poker, watch movies, whatever you wanna do when you're off duty. Up there on the left," Guy said, pointing with his entire right arm, conveniently blocking his stubbled chin, "two hallways down is the library and learning center if you feel like improving yourself; not that it'll do much good." Not looking at her, the dockmaster swept his arm to the right, almost brushing her chin. He was embarrassed, but at least it got her to look in the room and away from him. "Oops, sorry, over here on the right will be your living quarters and work area - most of us live near our main job areas as a convenience - and in the center is the command post." They stopped in an intersection of two halls. "You can get to the center just by going down any main hallway. Place is set up like a giant wheel, with a bisecting hallway every other pair, like giant H's." Nodding his head forward for her to follow, they walked down two more short halls. Finally, he had to turn and face her. "So, get settled and I'll be by to pick you up later—I mean, pick you up to get you to meet the rest of the crewmen on duty and process your badges."

He opened the door to her rooms and left as quickly as he could without being noticeable, heading directly to his rooms for a quick shave and shower.

About an hour later, May heard a knock on her door. When she opened it, instead of seeing Guy, whom she had expected, a slim middle-aged brunette woman stood in the doorway. She had a not unpleasant lantern jaw which accented her face well. Her dark brown hair, a bit gray at the temples, was pulled back in a bun. Her well-ironed conservative dark blue suit was meticulously clean and her posture gave the air of unadorned business. At first, May had almost expected to be handed an affidavit, but upon seeing May, the woman gave her a warm, soliciting smile and her whole deportment changed.

"Hi, I'm Sally. You must be the new girl," the middle-aged woman said.

"That's right, my name is May," she replied.

"I came to pick you up and show you around."

"I thought…um…Guy, that was it, was going to do that?" May asked.

"Yeah," Sally said flatly, "I know. That's why I'm here. I spoke to him and convinced him it would be better this way." Sally continued conspiratorially. "If Guy had come, he would have made a pass at you in ten minutes or less, just like every other woman on this station. I think the current record is seven minutes. Flat."

May knew she was going to like Sally.

"I'm the accountant, so you and I will work in tandem. We have to consolidate inventory with costs once a month, so be prepared for that. The tracking of the explosives on site is our highest priority. They are the most expensive things, and of course the most dangerous."

"Explosives? We have explosives here? Why?" May asked.

"We use them to break up very large asteroids that are headed our way," Sally said, now all business. "Space, for all its room, is a rather busy place with all the crap floating around, and it's in our best interest to look out for asteroids floating our way. Some are small, others the size of houses, but on rare occasion we encounter stadium-sized rocks. In that event, we use one-man mini-ships to travel to them while they're still far off and plant explosives to break them up into smaller chunks that we can deal with using our station cannons once they come in range. Also, please remember that the mini-ships' fuel tanks are large enough to get to the next station. They can be comfortably driven by either species, and every crewman here has a designated mini-ship, if it ever comes to that."

"Okay," May replied.

"The explosives are your most important job," Sally repeated. "That's why you're replacing Judy by the way. There was an asteroid on its way and she misplaced the fuses. They were found after a brief search, and she was sent packing." Sally brightened. "But hey, forget about it, you'll have enough time to get used to it all." As they strolled down the hall, Sally began rotating her left arm, her shoulder blade making audible pops the first few times. May winced at the noise. "Sorry, old field hockey injury," Sally explained. "So, Guy said this was your first job off planet. Have you ever met a sauroid in person?"

"Sure I have!" May answered. "Well…actually, no," she admitted.

"Did you take many classes on our 'galactic partners'?"

"One," May replied, "…my first year."

"Alrighty, then," Sally exhaled. "Tell me what you know."

"Um, they're Pleiadean creatures from planet Vulcan, third from their star like us."

"True, though Vulcan isn't the name they have for it. But we can't pronounce their word so Vulcan it is."

"And…um, no human has mastered their language yet."

"Not true," Sally countered. "Their language is fairly basic structurally; it's just that it's unpronounceable growls and hisses. But don't worry dear," the older woman said as an aside, "it sounds like an enraged drunken Russian two year old anyway."

"They've got a younger planet—"

"No, they don't," Sally interrupted. "We believed that their solar system was much younger than it is; their star sun is blue which we thought meant that it was young, but in fact their particular stars are older than ours and are actually dying out. It is rare, but some stars end their life cycle on the blue end. We have galactic youth on our side, but they don't."

"They range from six to ten feet in height, are exoskeletal, and polytheist," May recited from some dim college memory.

"Yes, the best way to think about it is they are what would have happened in evolution on Earth had the dinosaurs not been extinct. But their stomachs are soft so please, for God's sake, don't joke around play-punching any of them; they can be extremely sensitive about that area of their bodies. And their gods correspond to their different races, really. They never really got past tribal thinking in that way."

"They are highly intelligent, on average," May chimed, as her memory came back to her.

"Which can lead to vanity and ego in their species, so be careful what you say around them," Sally warned. "We don't need any temper tantrums here. Some even think they actually beat us in the war, if you can believe it."

"Well, you could say they did, in a way," May replied.

Sally gave her a long, evaluating look.

"You *did* just get out of school, didn't you? It's not your fault they filled your head with that nonsense, but here's a helpful hint; don't repeat that opinion here if you want to get along."

"Okay," May said slowly, now a bit uncomfortable with Sally.

"Forget it, hon; you're new," Sally said, suddenly cheerful again.

As they entered the command post May heard a man bark a short order.

"Everyone up!"

Everyone turned and faced May and Sally. Guy was there as well as a few other people and three sauroids. The sauroids did indeed remind her of Earth dinosaurs. One was tall and light brown almost to the point of being tan. His skin looked the most like light armor, and for some reason she thought he would be faster than the other two. The next was shorter and a dark brown. He could have been just as intelligent as the first, but seemed more sedate. The third sauroid was almost as tall as the first but wider, a dark gray. His skin looked rougher than the other two and he was covered with short horns around his head and along the outside of his arms and tail, with a spiked ball at his tail's end.

"Welcome, Miss Yefrimova, to 3X2-4A," said the blond man at the head of the line of crew. "My name is Captain Benjamin Drake." Drake was a well-built man, of medium height, clean shaven, clear of speech and sure in his bearing. Except for a slightly large nose, he could have been cast as Captain America in a film.

"Going down the line is Guy King, math whiz and dockmaster, whom you've met, of course." A now well-groomed Guy waved May a short hello.

"Just to be formal, Sally there next to you is our accountant and chef."

"This is Albert Owusu, our mechanic." The gentle-looking, overweight, bearded black man nodded, and smiled a little.

"Next to him is Harita Patel, head of hospitality." The short, perky woman waved at May enthusiastically.

"Hey, hon, how you doin'?" Harita bubbled. May could see why Harita was in charge of taking care of the tired jet jockeys that came in overnight.

"Oh, I'm just fine," May replied.

"On the other end is Bhral Ch-tan, operations manager." The short, darker sauroid bowed his head to her.

"This," Drake said, walking over to the largest sauroid, "is Tlak Curr, our station doctor." Tlak was the light brown, sleeker-looking alien; he extended a friendly arm claw to May.

"Do not worry, young one," Tlak said, with a thick, hissing guttural accent. "I am expertly versed in treating humans as well as my own race; you have nothing to fear." His voice was kind and warm, despite his accented tones. May, to her credit, gingerly shook Tlak's hand and was surprised at how comfortable it felt.

"And finally, this is Shrra Chran and Sean Boyle, co-heads of security." Shrra, the horned gray sauroid, gave a short nod of his head instead of shaking her hand as Tlak had done. The sauroid security agent kept his arms folded across his chest. Sean was equally as distant, giving her a short wave with a quick "hello." Sean, at almost six foot five, was also the largest human there, in both height and width. Looking at Sean, May thought that he would be the perfect specimen of 19th century New York cop known as "the Irish Whales."

"I hope your time here is enjoyable, Miss," the captain said. "Don't hesitate to ask anyone questions, and if you have any problems, please see me or Sally. All right, everyone, let's get back to earning our millions." There were chuckles of good humor as the group broke up to go back about their business.

Sean and Shrra took seats across the room while most of the others left, so May went over to personally introduce herself to her first sauroid. Just as she was coming up to them, Shrra spun on her.

"What, you never see a sauroid before, huh?" Shrra growled.

"No, I-I mean, I didn't—" May stammered.

"Didn't what, fresh meat? Didn't know how big and ugly we were? Or what we eat for our meals?" Shrra ran his tongue over his serpentine lips. "Heard that we aren't choosy in the meat department, huh? Maybe even Earthman steaks, when we get desperate...huh?"

May turned to run, but Sean blocked her path. Sean looked down at her, expressionless. She was about to scream for help, hoping she'd be heard by someone, anyone, when both Sean and Shrra broke out in howls of laughter.

"She bought it! She bought it! I can't believe she bought it!" Sean said, in between rolls of uncontrollable laughter.

"Here's your fiver, man," Shrra said, handing Sean the bill. "'Earthman steaks!' Ha hoo hoo hoo!" Sean and Shrra were almost pounding on each other. May just stood there stunned.

"Oh man, kid, you did real good. If this ugly ass did that to me on my first day, I'd've popped him one!" Sean told her.

"Yeah, boy, just try it!" Shrra told Sean.

"Yeah, I'd beat yer ass all over this floor ya dope!"

"Yeah, right, my tail horn, boy!"

Sean and Shrra then got in either a short fight or wrestling match, she wasn't sure which. As he got Sean in a full nelson hold, Shrra told her "Yer all right by us kid! You're now officially welcomed!"

Finally understanding the joke, May was flooded with relief.

"Hey, settle down, morons!" Drake yelled across the room as he walked over to them. Sean and Shrra sat down and got back to work for real this time, and not just to bait new crewmen over. Satisfied that they were working, Drake came up to May.

"Come on this way," Drake told her. They walked out of command toward the common area. "Forgive those two; they never got out of high school. They do it to everybody, so don't feel bad about it." They entered the common area. Drake motioned to her to sit while he went over to a vending machine rigged to take no money. "And if you're wondering, I let them do it because it keeps them happy, and lets us all resent them as a team." Drake picked up the soda from the dispenser. "I've found it's kind of like a bonding experience for the rest of the crew." He walked up to May, extending the can to her. "Soda?" She took the can he offered her. "It can get pretty routine here, so things like that break up the day. But like anything else, it's what you make of it. Have you ever done much inventory work before?"

"No, sir," she said.

"I didn't think so, looking at your file. And don't call me 'sir' unless there's an inspector around. Call me 'Drake' or 'Ben', whichever you prefer."

"O-okay. Ben," she added, again just after exceeding a natural pause.

"Don't worry about it," he said after studying her a moment. "It's your first day." Then confidentially he added, "If you prove you can keep a secret, I'll tell you about Albert's first day. It's still hilarious."

May smiled and was about to thank him, when an alarm went off and his wrist communicator began to flash red. Drake was on his feet in a moment.

"Go ahead," the captain said into the communicator.

"Sir!" the voice said over the speaker, "we got a full crew here damn near dead! They just got here, it's a mess!"

"Where's Tlak?"

"I can't get him, so I called you!"

Drake turned to May. "You don't have a communicator yet. Run, find Tlak, call out for him to go to the docking bay." He turned and was jogging out and called over his shoulder. "Try down this hall, it leads to his lab and quarters. If you find someone else, stick with them to find Tlak." The last words had barely reached her ears as Drake disappeared down the hall.

Drake ran down the corridors, all attention to his communicator.

"How many?" he yelled into the speaker on his wrist, genuine concern creeping into his voice.

"Seven...I think," the voice of Shrra replied.

"No, count again; you must know—not just guess!" he replied as he rounded the corner to the docking bay. Not for the first time, but especially in times like these, he wished there was another real officer on board. He knew that Tlak had potential but he didn't have the detachment needed; the sauroid cared too much.

Drake surveyed the scene as he put on his hazard suit. The bay held an awful sight. The ship that had docked was a CL-N model transport ship, or at least that's what Drake thought it was. It had been badly beaten in an asteroid shower; most of the body was burned with wires hanging from the fuselage, and a third of the left wing was gone. But the greatest sight to see was the sofa-sized jagged asteroid embedded in the starboard side.

"You said there are survivors?" he asked, incredulously.

"Yes, sir," replied Shrra over the room's speaker. "A damn miracle, the rock is an airtight fit in the puncture. There was even some atmosphere left when it got in here."

"Really?" Drake interrupted, pulling on his gloves.

"Not enough to live on, but enough to let the crew suit up in time. Poor bastards."

Drake wondered why Shrra said the last two words, but as he opened the safety door he understood the sauroid's pity. Drake heard their tormented screams even through the dense safety helmet.

All five were pale, their faces shining with orange flecks as if they were dusted with glitter, and all were either hallucinating or totally withdrawn.

As Drake was about to issue orders, he took a firm look at Guy. In all the excitement, Guy had forgotten to secure his helmet, the bottom of which was almost dangling from his chest. Drake exploded with worry and anger. The captain ran over to him and slammed the helmet lock down on Guy's collarbone, causing him intentional pain.

"You're quarantined, moron! Don't move!" he ordered Guy. Drake whirled to the communication station, trying to control his voice. "All sauroid personnel to the bay in hazmat suits. Code Red." Drake turned from the board just in time to see one of the transport's crew running toward him, a homicidal look in the sick man's eyes. Drake readied himself, and, at the last moment, stepped aside and grabbed the sick man. The captain got the infected man down as fast as he could without harm and stunned him unconscious with his pocket stun gun.

"Poor bastard," he murmured.

Drake heard a sharp noise. He turned, on the defensive, but it was just Shrra and Bhral coming through to help. In quick succession they sedated the other three sick transport crewmen. As Drake watched Shrra hold down a convulsing woman, he heard Tlak arrive. As the sauroid opened the door, Drake heard a female voice.

"What can I do?"

Drake's eyes widened when he saw May behind Tlak—without a hazmat suit of any kind.

Drake's last words were still echoing in May's ears as she watched him almost vanish from the common room doorway. Frozen in disbelief, she shook herself out of it and though still nervous, headed down the hall Drake indicated as fast as she could go. She hadn't gone far before she ran bodily into Tlak. Tlak roared and they landed in a flailing pile of arms, legs, and tail.

After a moment on the ground, May heard the sauroid moan. Picking her head up she saw him holding his stomach, his large eyes shut against the pain.

"….oh…gods…why?" Tlak said to no one.

"They need you in docking bay, right now! A whole crew of sick and dying," she told the sauroid. Almost in her defense, the corridor speakers turned on.

"All sauroid personnel to the bay in hazmat suits. Code Red."

With an angry growl Tlak got up to a crouch and, before May knew it, the doctor had picked her up and brushed her to the side of the hall. Surprisingly, the large creature was incredibly fast and gentle. Then he was off. Her fear made her follow him.

May caught up to Tlak in docking bay. As he suited up, Tlak was barking orders to Bhral over a comm-link. He opened the door and she saw Shrra holding down a convulsing woman while Drake was coming towards them. May ran up to Tlak.

"What can I do?"

"Get the Vrgrah back, human!" he yelled. "We are immune from human germs, you're not!" With that, he flung her back. She was thrown with greater force than he intended, so much that she would have skidded halfway down the hall if not for the padded door she fell against, gashing her head on the doorknob on the way down.

As soon as Harita got the word of the new visitors to the station, she called Sally.

"Meet me in sick bay," she said. "Bring what you can." Harita grabbed all she could from the stock for her cart. No one really appreciated how the small comforts go a long way when you're ill like Harita did, which was why she was the best hospitality staff in her whole space sector. With Sally's help, they laid all the supplies out in record time. They had to; they knew that protocol was isolation for any new sick visitors before Tlak could diagnose and/or contain them. Finished, the two women retreated to the common room.

"Thanks a lot, Sally, you're a big help," Harita said.

"No problem. Any word on the visitors?" Sally asked.

"Not that I've heard, except that they're ill and whatever it is, it seems bad." After looking around for a moment to make sure they were alone, Harita went over to her cart and pulled at the underside of the tray. Harita pressed a latch and pulled the handle bar up and off the cart. Sally saw the handles were hollow and that a can of Pleiadean wine cooler was hidden in either end of the bar.

"I was saving these for a rainy day. I think this qualifies," she said, handing Sally a can.

"Ooh, these are nice," Sally said. "Wish I thought of that trick."

When May awoke, the first thing she saw was Captain Drake standing next to her. She was in bed, her head bandaged.

"Good, she's awake," he said to someone. She raised her arm to reach out to him but her hand was stopped by something, and then she noticed the clear plastic tent over her bed.

"Sorry, May, you've been quarantined, just like Guy over there," he told her. She looked over and Guy was in the next bed, similarly curtained.

"Hell of a first day," she said weakly and they all laughed. Looking straight ahead she saw the visiting crew in an adjoining room, separated by thick glass.

"We found a sixth crewman in the ship, still at the controls," Drake explained. "Poor guy's so delirious he thought he was still driving on to safety."

"How are they?" she asked, gesturing to the other patients.

"Too early to tell yet, but they should be fine," he lied. "You and Guy just rest. If you need anything just call us," he pointed to the wrist link someone put on her arm, "and we'll see you get it. You'll need to stay here for seventy-two hours. I'll see you then." With that, the captain left.

After May went back to sleep, Guy watched the goings on across the way, as the sauroids attended to the sick crewmen. He especially watched the young pretty redhead, before drifting off to sleep himself. By morning, the pilot and redhead were dead.

Three days later, Tlak released May and Guy from quarantine with a clean bill of health. Guy had hoped to see more of her after that morning but it was a week before he saw her again, when she finally came down to the docking bay. She had gone to see Guy who, she discovered while in sick bay, had an excellent knowledge of astronomy. He wasn't on shift in the dock. She found Bhral there instead, checking the interfaces.

"So, whatever happened to that ship from last week?" she asked him.

"After Doc took some samples it was jettisoned towards the nearest star," he growled. "Took a couple hours to get it out of here, too. What a pain in my tail. I almost wish I came down here without a suit like you. I could use a rest."

"Oh....I'm sorry, Bhral," she said.

"Ah, don't be. It's just life. No rest for the weary, huh?" he growled as he shut an instrument panel cover. "Good to have you back, kid. Glad you're okay."

He turned and left, and for a moment, just a moment, she thought the squat alien was going to bump her intentionally, but he passed by without so much as disturbing the light on her hair. Looking out of the control room at the docking bay, she saw how large it looked without a ship in it, and beyond the bay how much vaster space looked through the plasteel windows. Suddenly feeling very small, she hurried into the safety of the hallway.

"Eleven o'clock!" Sean shouted. Shrra swung the heavy port cannon about. A ray blasted a stray asteroid to dust.

"Three!" Another blast rang out. "—and, oh shit, nine!" he said as he swung Shrra and the cannon around one hundred and eighty degrees. Shrra and Sean made it a friendly game to see who could rack up more asteroids firing from one of many side cannons used to protect the space station from rogue asteroids, a job made all the more important after seeing what happened to the transport ship the previous week.

"What the hell, man?!" Shrra growled, annoyed at Sean's intervention.

"What? That gun won't swing that fast, you'd have missed it and it would've hit the ship by the time you got around," Sean replied.

"Bullshit," Shrra snapped. "Maybe if I had your reflexes, but I'm a four time all around champ of space crush, This petty game is nothin'!"

"I meant the motor couldn't make it, ass—" Sean interrupted.

"Maybe it's somethin' to you humes," Shrra continued over Sean, using an old war slur, "but not a son of Ghreckt house!"

At that, Sean took hold of the port cannon, snapped its gyro and spun Shrra around two full circles and cruelly laughed at his now helpless crewmate. The cannon hadn't settled before Shrra jumped off, fists flying. They rolled halfway across the floor, punching and kicking, until at once they were both kicked savagely in the head by a captain's dress boot.

"What the hell do you two think you're doing?!" yelled the enraged Drake. "You two were trying to kill each other! Explain yourselves, now!"

They answered at once, talking over each other.

"He insulted humans," Sean said.

"He insulted sauroids," Shrra said.

"That's it?! An insult?! You," Drake said to Sean, "get to the starboard cannon. You," he said to Shrra, "get back to port cannon. K.P. for a week, *each*. Do your jobs in absolute silence. I'm going to review the logs and if either of you says one word that isn't directly related to asteroid alerts, or doesn't say something to warn the other of an asteroid when they should, you'll think you were *born* in the kitchen!"

"Yes, sir!" they replied.

"Get to work," barked the captain as he turned to go. Ben knew now more than ever that without him, the ship would crumble in under a day. Why he ever had to be saddled with such a crew was beyond him.

Making sure he had all his instruments, Tlak put on a breathing mask to protect against infection. Then the intercom lit up, and Tlak took off the mask.

"Hey, Tlak, I'm going to take some parts for some side projects, okay?"

"Sure, Albert, that's fine," Tlak answered into the intercom.

Putting the mask back on, Tlak carefully approached the human cadavers from the cargo ship. He had no concern for himself, since it had been long established that humans and sauroids could not cross-contaminate each other with disease, but he was cautious on Albert's behalf, who was assisting him in his investigation by reconstructing the cargo ship's recording devices in the next room. Tlak turned on his lab's recorder and picked up the microphone.

"Investigation of contamination of human crew of the CL-N freighter 'Blue Sunday' continued. Samples of tissues are free of infection. Blood discovered to be contaminated with the virus; further investigation showed virus is not blood-borne but virus is actually *of* the blood cell itself. This development led me to discover that the virus nests in the spleen to keep diseased cells in the system, and also infects bone marrow to alter the production of blood cells to keep the virus alive. Today I shall continue my investigation with—"

"Hey, Tlak," Albert cut in over the intercom, "ship's recorder is done. There's not much left but by God it's weird. Oh, and I'm going to pick up an older telecom unit to work on too, okay?"

"Sure, that's fine. Patch the recording through," Tlak replied, turning on his viewscreen. At first there was just static and then a man, the now-deceased pilot, appeared. He began to speak.

"Log 713, day two of our current run. Cargo now non-toxic resin in addition to half a load of metal ore. Ore going to Earth and resin to Jupiter. Half of metal ore original load delivered to Plieos. After run—" The pilot was interrupted by a loud noise and the recorder cut out. When it came back, the pilot, now in a space suit, looked haggard and scared.

The pilot spoke. "—got it running? Thank God. This is the Blue Sunday, identification 9-181T. We have been struck and pierced by an asteroid of unknown origin. The metallic rock isn't common to either the terrestrial or Pleidean system. We're testing and so far found no…" There was more but the recording was too degraded and a message flashed before the section ended, saying that Albert cut the end of that tape. Tlak almost thought that was all until the static faded once more. Now, the pilot looked visibly ill, but more than that, he had a new, haunted look and was whispering, in a higher pitched, child-like voice.

"—ecret log. Don't tell the others. This is *my* ship, and I *will* lead it to safety. I've locked up half the men for their own good. They got sick y'see, and aren't well. But I'm fine. My stomach hurts but maybe it's just from hunger. I've missed meals because I must keep flying, I *must*. If I give up a relief shift, they won't give it back. I can tell, I've heard them plotting. But I'm too smart for them!" The pilot turned his head and Tlak could hear muffled sounds of violence behind the pilot. "Oops, I hear someone, I have to go now. Bye-bye. Kisses."

The screen fell black.

Tlak bounded over to the bodies and raced through a cranial scan. Sure enough, he found abnormalities in the brains of all the dead crewmen. A viral locator revealed that the brain was a hotbed of viral activity, most notably in the hypothalamus, amygdala, and frontal lobe region. A quick check of his medical text confirmed his fears; those were the human brain areas that controlled emotion, impulse control, and personality. Focusing on the viruses in the brains, he quickly made slides and compared them to the blood-borne virus. He thought the first slide must've been contaminated, because it had an almost sauroid orange tint, probably somehow diluted with water. He was about to throw it away but paused in shock as he realized the virus in the blood sample was active, larger, and more pointed than before. Fearing the effects of water on the virus, he rechecked his sample source, for fear that any spilled in the lab! He stared at his pipetter in horror, and only wished it was the effect of water.

In his haste he mistakenly used the blood sample he took from Bhral and Albert that morning for their annual physicals.

Tlak bounded out of his lab in a hazard suit. The alien doctor still could not believe it; a virus that could infect both sauroids and men! He was free of infection and initial tests showed that he was immune — maybe his life among disease immunized him somehow, but still he took precaution. He had to find Albert and Bhral! But he found Harita first, walking ahead of him, crossing the hall at a junction of two passageways.

"Harita, my comm-link won't work! You've got to help me find—"

"Noo! Get away!" Harita screamed at him. "I'm starving! These're mine!"

It was then that Tlak came closer and took a good look at her. Her face was shining a glittery orange through its cover of food and dried vomit. Her arms were loaded with half eaten ration packets.

"Get away from me!" she screamed and began to run away from him.

"My God…" Tlak whispered. Then it struck him—he had been in his lab almost two terrestrial days! The virus had spread to the whole crew by now, incubating over the last twelve days. The whole crew could be as symptomatic as Harita. Turning the corner, he heard muffled noises. It was Harita, hiding in an access hall, gorging. Then he heard gagging; she was choking on the food. Tlak ran up to her, giving her the Heimlich maneuver. She vomited and then straightened up and just stood there a moment in a daze. For a brief instant, Tlak hoped and prayed the fever or whatever it was broke in her, but then she got her bearings and began gorging again, this time on some of the food she had just vomited. Heartbroken, Tlak stunned her unconscious for her own good with a sedative pen, picked her up and walked to the infirmary.

As the sauroid was entering the infirmary, Sally appeared. At first she hoped she could help him. One look at her changed his opinion.

"Ooh," Sally cooed child-like, "you're giving out rides! I want one too!"

"What?" Tlak asked.

"Hey, I want a ride too, why can't I have one? A-a longer one?" Sally whined.

Tlak thought quickly.

"Sure, you—you can have a ride, Sally, just one moment while I put Harita down at the, uh, 'ride's' end, okay?"

"Hooray!" she squealed. Tlak put Harita in a sick bed, and began strapping her down, in case she should wake before he returned.

"I want a ride too!" Sally yelled, grabbing and pulling at Tlak's hazard suit. Tlak turned on her, yanking her off of him.

"Just wait one moment more, Sally, just watch for a moment, no one else can see but you."

"Okay," she said, and stared intently at Tlak as he finished securing Harita.

"Ooh, I want a bed too!" Sally cried.

"Of course you can have a bed, Sally," he said. Leaning closer, he confidentially added, "take the one on the right, it's softer and has nicer safety straps."

Squealing with glee, Sally ran to the bed. Tlak strapped her in, taking care not to harm her for fear she'd rebel if she knew what he was really doing.

"What's that?" Sally asked, seeing Tlak's sedative pen.

"Something special, just for you," he said, as he sedated her.

As Sally's shallow breathing calmed and she slept, he only wished they all be this easy. He turned to the cabinets to get more sedative pens, and froze. He saw himself in the mirror over the cabinets, and slowly turned to the side hoping he wouldn't see what he knew was there. Sure enough, the air tubes had ripped right out of the back of the suit when Sally grabbed him, or when he pulled her off. Knowing the suit was useless now, he closed his eyes a moment then began to take it off.

May made her way down the hall with caution. She was terribly afraid of who or what might get her from any of the side halls or accessways, but she couldn't stay where she was either or else they'd all know just where to go to get her. She knew now they were all after her, especially those monstrous sauroids. If only she listened to Sally sooner! They were all monsters, all of them, even the other people! She wasn't sure before, but this morning she saw them—she saw them!—and she just knew. Sean was kicking the vending machine but she *knew* it was just in preparation to get her. Albert was ripping parts out of the wall. He said it was to build something but he didn't tell her what; he didn't have to, she knew it was something to hunt her down with later. If only she could find somewhere she could be safe. Then she thought of the captain! But only, only if he didn't want to get her too…

* * * * * *

Drake turned out of the communications room, satisfied. He had shut down his entire station to any new traffic and diverted all ships on their way to auxiliary ports. This new shutdown wouldn't be questioned by the other captains after the disease outbreak the other day, which was fine by him. He couldn't have anyone coming until he had whipped his ship and men into proper shape. The captain marched down the hallways, incensed, mumbling into his dead comm-link.

"No one knows how to run a good ship but me! Just look at that floor! Scuff marks all over from people's feet! Disgraceful! You'd all die without me! Well, I'll pull you all together if it's the last thing I'll do!" Drake pushed open the doors to the common room with a bang. Sean was on one side of the room, smashing into a badly damaged vending machine with a concrete block, and Guy was on the other side of the room, staring at something in rapt attention.

"Guy!" he yelled, moving into the room. Drake could now see Guy clearly. The dockmaster was on the couch, watching adult films on the massive screen. "Pull your pants up now, mister! You're drafted to protect this ship, and you're coming with me! And get that damn orange glitter off your damn face!"

"Oh yes, sir!" Guy leered, walking over to Drake. "Got to protect the women, don't we? And don't worry; I'll take such wonderful care of them. Then again," he said slowly with an evil grin, "I never thought of it before, but I could even take good care of you. Sir."

"Stand up!" Drake ordered Guy. "Straighter!" Guy stood at attention. "Straighter!" Again Guy tried to comply. "Straighter!" the captain screamed. Then Drake caught sight of Sean. "Sean!" he barked, commanding the other man. But Sean didn't respond, he just kept pounding away at the vending machine. Drake went up to him and caught his bloodied wrists. "Good work, Sean, mission accomplished. Now, where's Shrra?"

Sean's tomato red, glittering face slackened as he tried to remember, the foam settling at the sides of his mouth. Finally he remembered who Shrra was and more, what Shrra had done to him.

"Shrra...? Shrra got me in trouble." His face darkened again into blackest rage. "I'll make him pay. I'll make that monster pay!" Sean shoved Drake aside and ran for the doors to find his intended victim. "Shraaaaa!"

Tlak stole carefully down the air duct. He would move then listen, move and listen, to cover as much ground as he could without being surprised by any of the deranged crewmen. He was trying to focus on the danger so he wouldn't focus on himself. He didn't know what to do. He had never faced a situation like this before. It could take weeks, or even years, to find a cure, and he knew his friends didn't have that time. And if someone got out, if the infection spread—! He couldn't let it, he *wouldn't* let such a monster spread; he'd have to stop it here, he'd have to—

Tlak heard a stifled giggle. He looked down through a grating in the air duct bottom. It was Albert, in his personal quarters, amongst a giant pile of, well, everything. There were all sorts of things crammed into the room, furniture, machines, clothes, food, random mechanical parts, even some wall panels. But the worst was all the plastic wrappers and foil ends, glittering like twisted jewels in a pile of demented toys. Albert was circling it all, sometimes rubbing and rolling against it, in feverish delight.

"Mine, all mine! All my beautiful treasures!" the mechanic exulted. Then Albert laughed a sound that made even a sauroid feel cold. "And no one will take you from me, no one!" Albert looked around suddenly, but thankfully he didn't look up, then his gaze returned to the hoard. "You're mine, all mine, and I love you all! I love you, love you, love you!" The burly mechanic began laughing again. Tlak had seen enough.

Tlak punched through the grating and leaped down, reaching for Albert with arms and tail. Looking up, the man screamed in horror. Albert fought back for a few moments, but the sauroid grabbed hold of him and forced him against a wall, holding the man there mainly with his tail.

"Gratch!" Tlak cursed at himself. The sedative pens were gone. He hadn't secured them before he went through the grate. They had fallen out and could be anywhere in the giant mess.

"It's mine, they're mine, I got them, they're mine!" Albert screamed, "My treasu—" Hating himself, Tlak covered the black man's nose and mouth. After a few moments of struggle, Albert lay still. Tlak checked and made sure Albert was breathing. The doctor knew he had to tie the man up right there, he couldn't afford the time to get him to the sick room; if everyone was this far gone there was no telling what the others might do. He went to look in the pile for something to tie him with and stopped. He looked at the pile in front of him, and saw that it was so…just so big and messy. Tlak stopped, sat on a chair, and began to weep.

May hadn't moved for two minutes. She was afraid to stay there any longer, but nor could she face what was around the curve in the hallway, so she just stood in the recess of the doorframe. Then she heard a voice and the sound of feet rapidly approaching.

"Shrra! Shrra, come out and fight me like a *man!*" Sean whirled around the corner with murder in his eyes and blood in his drool. "Come get me, monster!" As Sean ran towards her, May panicked and fell backward. The door opened and she fell through. The door shut automatically and she was left in darkness, the only light coming from under the door. For a moment, she felt safe. Then she heard the coarse hiss behind her. She spun and backed against the wall, her back triggering the light panel. It was Bhral and he was…sleeping. He gave the coarse hiss again, then started.

"Huh, wha-, who is it?" Bhral asked, groggy. Then he saw May. "Oh, it's you. Go 'way, leave me 'lone. I'm tired." And with that he rolled over to sleep again.

May ran out into the hall. She had to get away from Bhral, no telling when he'd wake up hungry for human steaks! She ran down the corridor, feeling a bit safe now that she knew Sean had run the other way. Catching a glimpse of the captain, she ran into the common room. Any other time, the scene would've been side-splitting. The glittering, feverish captain, wearing a paper hat, was lecturing a very rigid Guy on the finer points of leadership, while Guy was doing his best to look alternately at pornography or the captain's backside from the corners of his eyes.

"Now, I must save the crew, and you must help," Drake was telling Guy. "Ah, May, you're here. See, my brilliant plan is working," he said to her, in all seriousness.

"Captain, thank God I found you," she exclaimed, "they're all out to get me!"

"Fear not, young one," Drake said, "I shall protect you; I will protect you all."

"Young one...?" said Guy, as he realized someone else was in the room. "Baby!" Guy went for May, his hand on his trousers already.

"Halt, crewman!" Drake commanded, grabbing Guy by the shoulder. "You must save everyone with me first." Guy brushed him off, and Drake punched him in the jaw, knocking the dockmaster out. "Insubordination will not be tolerated!" he yelled to the unconscious man.

"Oh, thank you captain, thank you, I knew I'd be safe with you," she said.

"No fear, my lamb," Drake said in a daze. "Where's my real crew? Tell me, that's an order."

"B-Bhral is just down this hall," she squeaked.

"Excellent, crewman!" Drake said. He took her by the wrist and began to pull her after him. "With him, we'll really make this a fine crew!"

Drake opened the door to the room May indicated. Bhral was still asleep.

"Wake up, crewman, wake up!" shouted Drake, poking the dark sauroid with his foot.

"Nngh. Go 'way," Bhral slurred, not looking up or even opening his eyes.

"Get up, get up, no sleeping on the job!" Drake ordered.

"I did my job, I did all my jobs, I can sleep now," came the muffled reply.

"But it's not done. You have to help protect everyone. I'm always the one who does it but I'll show you how if it's the last thing I do!"

"If you want to protect ev'body," said the lethargic alien, "why don' you jus' get some weapons f'm th' armory?"

Drake's feverish face lit up like a child's on Christmas morning.

May was being pulled along a strange hallway by Drake who was holding up a square, dark blue key in his other hand.

"By George, Crewman Yefrimova, I have it!" he told her. "We'll arm ourselves, then we'll be a real crew and I'll be an even better leader." May felt even more scared in this new hall, despite Drake's presence.

"But what if someone else got there first?" she asked.

"Nonsense," he replied, "I was first to think of it. None of the lowly crewmen could think of it on their own. Besides," he added, "I have the only key."

But when they got there they saw that someone else *had* thought of it. Shrra was beating the heavy door, and had almost gotten it open.

"Hggraah! Humans!" the sauroid shouted when he saw them. He reached a claw into the armory, grabbed the nearest weapon and pulled. The gun was too big to fit through the slim opening and after two or three tries, Shrra abandoned it and turned on the captain and May, roaring and spitting, claws extended and tail flickering.

"Shraa!"

In a flash, May was shoved from behind, wrenching her right forearm from the captain's grip. She fell against the wall, a screaming in her ears. Sean screamed savagely as he broke between May and Drake and fairly flew into the body of the waiting sauroid. The two bashed at each other, locking to each other, each desperate to destroy the other, careening down the hall and slamming against walls like a living wrecking ball. Drake lost no time taking advantage of the new space between them and the combatants. Using his key he activated the damaged door and slid it open as far as it could go. Stepping in, he called to May.

"Here, take a weapon, be useful for once."

Regaining his composure, Tlak finally stood up. He knew he had to forget about himself, forget all the horror he'd witnessed, and continue. If this virus, if this…this monster got out of this way station, the days of all life, human and sauroid, would be numbered. With a deep breath and renewed purpose he climbed back into the air ducts. First things first: he had to get more sedative pens, a lot more, because Shrra and Sean were still out there. He was about to exit the vents into the infirmary, when he heard a terrible crashing noise in the distance and felt a bit of a shock run through the whole station. The lights dimmed, then came back spotty and at half strength. After he waited a moment to ensure he was safe, he began to move forward again, but stopped when he heard a long, low whistle.

"My my, lookee what we have here," he heard someone say. Tlak ducked his head down quickly to see through the grate on the duct wall. It was Guy. He had his back to the grate, standing between Sally's and Harita's beds, looking lovingly at them. "Oh, ladies, you shouldn't have…" Guy began reaching for his belt. "…but I'm ever so glad you did. Now, let's really let the Triple X Ranch earn its name."

Tlak exploded from the ducts, surprising Guy. Seeing the knife in Guy's hand, the doctor just reacted. Taking the human's head and shoulder in his claws, Tlak bashed him against a wall. Guy lay there, very still.

"He'd have been dead in a few days no matter what," the alien told himself, "and I had to protect the others." He stared at the body. "It's not the first time I've lost a patient," he thought. "I never liked him anyway," he admitted after a moment. Draping a sheet over the body, Tlak gathered all the sedative pens he could find and vanished into the vents.

Drake chanted as he marched up the corridor and spun. "I don't know but I've been told!" He came back towards May. "Without fur a dog is cold!" He put down his long range disintegrator and stood at ease. "And that's how we patrol to protect everyone," he told her, looking at her with what he was sure was controlled leader-like benevolence. May looked at his glittering face and couldn't help but be a bit afraid of him, but of course she couldn't tell him that.

"We have to protect people, and this ship, from the sauroid monsters. Grandpa Jake told me all about the war when he was young," Drake's eyes bored into May. "And he even showed me how to fire. Watch!" With that he spun, and in rapid succession shot out the ceiling panels all the way down the hall. Half the lights went out, pipes were exposed, one or two pipes hissed steam, and wires began dangling all over. The whole area looked like a puppeteer's abandoned workshop. Drake waited to turn to May again until the last electrical sparks died out from the severed wires.

"See what a good captain I am? See? See?"

May slowly backed away from the panting captain. She turned and ran, afraid for her life, but Drake followed, first at a trot, then at a run.

"We have to keep the unit together!" he called after her. "You're not being a good soldier anymore!" he yelled, suddenly angry. She un-holstered the gun from her leg and wanted to turn to fire but feared falling over, when she felt something cut her arm and heard and awful crash behind her. Tlak had jumped out of the grate on the wall and was on top of Drake. May ran and hid around the corner, holding her gun at the ready.

For half an hour after his violent return to the infirmary, Tlak tried to find the rest of the crew. Move and listen, move and listen. Finally, he heard a noise coming from the repair bay. He crept down to the grate, which hung diagonally on a slanted wall, and looked in. The room was a shambles; blood, both red and orange, covered a good portion of the floor. Equipment was battered, a forklift was on fire, and there was even a half fixed mini-ship on its side like a giant discarded toy. Sean, one leg gone, was beating the body of Shrra with Shrra's own severed tail. Bloody power tools were strewn everywhere. The remains of Shrra's neck ended in a dark orange pool flowing from under an engine block that was cut from its suspending chain. Sean, oblivious to the sauriod's death and his own pain, just kept pounding away. Tlak looked down at his sedative pens.

"If only I found them sooner," he thought. Putting the pens down,

Tlak quietly unscrewed the grate with his claws. He put the grate down without a sound and crept into the room behind Sean.

"You, fuck you, you bastard!" Sean panted, enraged and exhausted at once. Tlak grabbed Sean's head, looked up to the ceiling, and twisted with all his strength.

Tlak made sure there was no pulse or respiration under his hands then backed away, keeping his gaze focused upward until he could turn around without seeing any remnant of violence in front of him. As he was walking back to the ventilation system he saw a large blast mark in the wall that he didn't notice coming in. Noting the generator behind the wall, he realized that must've been the shock he felt before and why the lights were lower. Evidently one of them got into the mini-ship that was facing in, probably the one on its side now, and shot at the other.

"Well. This was certainly one hell of a fight," he thought, picking up his pens and replacing the grate.

Tlak checked each grate as he passed them for May and Drake, and, again not seeing either, was about to move along when he did a double take. Sure enough, the armory was opened and even from across the hallway, the sauroid could see multiple weapons missing.

"That's it, then," he thought. "It's them or me, and it can't be them or that monstrous virus will get out." Tlak stopped just long enough for one earnest prayer asking forgiveness, and went on his way. He had gone some way when all of a sudden the silence was broken by rapid fire three halls down. Tlak raced toward the noise. Reaching the grate, he thanked his gods it was one of the larger vents and one that came out straight onto the floor.

"…good captain I am? See? See?" he heard and looked out. It was Drake. Clearly the captain had the disease, but May had her back to Tlak. May backed away.

"Maybe she doesn't she have the virus," Tlak thought. "Maybe she's immune like me." But one look at her when she turned around, showing him the by-now tell-tale glitter proved he was wrong.

"We have to keep the unit together!" Drake called out, focusing Tlak's attention on him and on his gun. Seeing Drake give chase and knowing him to be the bigger threat, Tlak waited to leap until he knew he could land on the captain. Tlak threw his weight against the captain and the grate that the doctor pushed with him on his way out while also trying to make a grab for May, hoping to take them both down at once. He was only able to scratch her arm with his claw as she passed by, but in reaching for her, was off balance enough for Drake to push against the grate, successfully throwing Tlak off.

"Monster! Monster!" the captain shrieked, and raised his gun. In a flash, Tlak coiled his tail about Drake and spun him around, grabbed him, then threw him to the floor. They landed with an awful impact, but it wasn't enough for Tlak, not with that disintegrator still in the captain's hand. Pinning the man's shoulders with his tail, Tlak took Drake's head in his claws; he lifted and shoved down, once, twice, three times, thinking of nothing but survival and fear as he did so. The captain stared back at him, dead. There was an iron pipe behind his head, one that Tlak neither saw nor felt until that moment. Before that, all he could see was the gun.

"The gun!" he thought. "Where's May?" He got up, looked in both directions of the hall and even down the vent he came from. His breath was hissing in and out, his vision was blurred at the edges and there was a ringing in his head, but he saw clearly enough to know she wasn't anywhere to be seen. Hoping she wasn't too far gone, he tried to reason with her.

"May!" he called. "May, it's Doctor Tlak! It's okay, I'm not infected! Let me help you!"

"Get away from me!" she cried. Tlak could hear the paranoia in her tone but he couldn't tell where her voice was coming from, his head was still ringing too loudly. He had to talk her into revealing herself or he'd never stop the monster disease. He couldn't let the monster get away, he just couldn't

May turned the nearest corner and slammed against the wall behind the open doorway. She could hear the sauroid beating the captain to death.

"Oh God, it's the monster, he's coming for me!" she thought.

She heard him call her name. "Oh God, oh God, oh God, oh God!" She could barely breathe. Then she remembered the gun in her hands. She knew she couldn't let the monster get away. If she did, there was no telling when or where it'd come after her again; she'd have to be on guard the rest of her life.

"I know you're scared," the monster said, "it's part of the disease."

"He's lying," she thought. "Didn't he give me a clean bill of health a week ago?"

"It's all right! I can help you," the monster continued. "Together we can stop this disease; this—this monster right here so it can never hurt anyone again! We can't let this monster get away!" She saw his claw appear on the side of the doorway.

"It will all end, right here."

She knew the monster was lying, knew from his vicious hissing voice. He was almost on top of her. So scared she couldn't think anymore, she whirled into the hallway, screaming.

Tlak struck down with tail, claws, and fangs.

May fired.

The last survivor of way station 3X2-4A lifted a dead arm that was covering both eyes. The crewman turned and just lay there a moment looking at the ceiling to collect their wits. Rising, the last member looked down at the body it was just entangled with. Looking at it, the crewman realized the fight wasn't over yet.

"I have to make sure that the monster doesn't get away," the survivor thought. With an aching head, barely in control of its own body from complete mental and physical exhaustion, the last soul on board saw everything as if in a dream, as if the crewman was watching their body from afar. The surviving crewman watched as feet slowly made their way down to the docking bay, and the hands and feet got the body into a flight suit that almost but didn't quite fit, but the mind was just too tired to care. Finding a mini-ship that was in good repair, the eyes made sure it had enough fuel to get to the next station, and the legs and body got in and taxied it in front of the door.

That done, the arms lifted the canopy and the legs got out, shambling across the bay toward the fuel drums, behind the airtight security shields, nestled in a recess in the floor. The hands opened all the fuel drums in the docking bay, tipping a few over just for good measure, the fuel filling the recess like milk in a bowl. Painfully walking over to the repair bay, the hands did the same with the fuel drums there.

The eyes and arms found a lighter in a toolbox and a small explosive charge in the back of the overturned mini-ship. Then, in a supply room, and after more help from the gloved hands, the eyes found a fifty foot coil of fuse. The feet then stumbled their way back to the docking bay, the hands clinging to the fuse. Attaching the fuse to the explosive, the feet carried the explosive over to the middle of the open fuel drums and the hands placed it firmly down.

"The monster mustn't get away," the survivor thought. Playing out the fuse to its full length around the secure room, but being careful not to have any of it touch the area near the fuel until it was time, the hands set it down, opened the door, and followed the shambling feet back to the ship. Starting the engines in the mini-ship, the legs jumped down and ran back to the fuse. The gloved hands quickly lit the fuse, opened and then slammed the door shut, locking it, and the feet tore back to the ship. Getting in and slamming the hatch down, a right handed digit tapped at the controls and with a loud noise and rush of air, opened the hatch doors. Firmly, almost desperately, the gloved hands pressed the stick forward and flew out.

Now safely away, the hands banked the ship so it could see the way station. After a moment of fear that the fuse was faulty, there was a satisfying bloom of fire, as the station soundlessly disintegrated in space.

"I did it. The monster is gone," the survivor thought. Taking off the helmet, the lone pilot laid it on the empty seat to the right. Now that the fight was over and the survivor was safe, the body began to collapse in the chair. The lone pilot's head began to throb and the vision began to wobble a bit, a result of all the events of the last few days settling themselves into reality, now that the last crew member felt safe enough to come out of survivor mode. As the hands laid the course for the nearest way station, the eyes looked back at the explosion, a beautiful blue and red cloud in the vastness of space.

There was a reflection in the plassteel cockpit dome staring back at the survivor. The left half of the face was obscured by the light of the explosion, but the right half looked back serenely. Backlit by faraway stars that twinkled through the reflection, the face had a beautiful, almost magical luster to it. Looking through exhausted eyes, the survivor couldn't tell just what made the reflected face gleam so alluringly. Was it sweat and exhaustion effecting the eyes, or the stars outside that caused the face in the glass to gleam…to even glitter with a shine?

What was it, really?

MEET THE CREATORS

Tricia Arnold

www.flickr.com/people/babbletrish
babbletrish@gmail.com

M49

Tricia is a freelance illustrator from the suburbs south of Boston who started drawing almost from the moment she could hold a crayon. She was—and still is—influenced by nature and the pop culture of the time period when she grew up. Recently, she has decided to pursue illustration and animation as a career and joined the Comic Artists Guild to network with other artists and talk about the field.

Chris Buchner

www.comicspace.com/AtomicMedia
atomic_comics@hotmail.com

Chris is a freelance writer and editor who has literally been creating comics and stories since he was four years old. His first published comics work was in *CAG Anthonology* #7, followed by CAG's *Iconic* vol. 1. He has done comic reviews or articles for Spiderfan.org, EstellasRevenge.com, and 215ink.com. Currently, Chris is the Editor-in-chief of Guild Works Publications and co-writer on their flagship title *Hell's Blood,* as well as the CAG New York chapter & publication coordinator, and a writer on Marvel's *Official Index to the Marvel Universe.*

Stephen Carr

Stephen Carr is a native Rhode Islander, Sci-Fi fan, stay at home dad by day, Optician by night, and now fledgling writer. His first published writing, an adventure serial "Cloud Breaker" appeared in *Sky Pirates of Valendor: Valendor Chronicles.* His second story *Global Unity* is the product of a complex and confusing collaboration with his old friend and accomplice Everett Soares. Stephen is looking forward to developing new story ideas as well as finishing the restoration of his 1968 Firebird and taking his kids to school.

J.M. DeSantis

www.jmdesantis.com

J. M. DeSantis was born in 1982 in Teaneck, New Jersey. He is a writer and illustrator and holds a BFA from Pratt Institute in Brooklyn, New York. DeSantis's stories and illustrations have appeared in *Planet Lovecraft Magazine,* various *Comicbook Artists Guild* publications, and *Atlas Unleashed.* He was the Featured Artist of *Heavy Metal Magazine's* January 2009 issue and was a contributor to *The Night of the Living Dead: Reanimated* project. *The People from Beyond the Stars* marks his first and long awaited prose fiction publication. For more information about J. M. DeSantis and his work visit his website.

Willie Jimenez

http://westwolfonline.com
westwolf270@yahoo.com

 M33

Willie started his career drawing manga, and doing anime style illustrations for t-shirts and websites. He got into comics when he started freelancing as a colorist. He joined CAG in order to expose himself more to American-style comics. After helping out on a few projects Willie was made part of CAG's leadership and head graphic artist. He's worked for many well-known companies like Antarctic Press, Arcana Studios, Atlantis Studios, Chimera Studios, and Blue Water Productions.

Jacob Ketron

Born on August 11, 1991, Jacob has always lived in Connecticut. He is currently a senior at Valley Regional High School, graduating in June 2010. Aside from being the writer of *Ruthstorm,* Jacob is an aspiring artist. Jacob, though, has been busy using his art for different purposes. For instance, he penciled *Observations,* a one-shot webcomic written by Dwight Baldwin. Expect to see more from this young man since he plans to begin his own pet project for the CAG Webcomics Initiative in the near future.

Lindsay Kraemer

www.LindsayKreamer.com
KraemerLindsay@yahoo.com

Lindsay is a proud CAG member that currently resides in New Mexico after pursuing a musical theater career in NYC. Her passions include dance, art, and creating stories. Independently, she is developing comic books in the Humor and Science Fiction genres and, collaboratively, she is creating a children's book. She has interest in collaborating on future children's book and comic book projects.

Albert Luciano

Albert has been drawing since the age of five. After high school, he took a few drawing and airbrushing classes. He is married with 2 children (Christopher and Erin), and his family fuels his creative energy. He is an avid collector of art books and is proud to have 3 Andrew Loomis original art books. He works and also teaches Photoshop to the kids at the local community center. Albert's first published work was the story *Prometheus* in CAG's *Iconic* vol. 1.

Rigel
Distance: 862.88 ly
Luminosity: 50,600x Sun
Class: B8I-a

Michael Marcus

http://idea-men.us & smacc2010.us
Michael@idea-men.us

Michael Marcus is a man of many talents: he designs games, including *Gamer's Dozen, Sudoku: Tactics, Kechi,* and *GAME;* publishes short stories and comic book scripts; designs book covers for novelists; edits copy for various authors, ghost-writes short stories, and runs most of the business and sales elements for Hamtramck Idea Men.

James Mascia

www.islandofdren.com
jmascia@islandofdren.com

James Mascia has had numerous stories published in *A Thousand Faces*—a journal of superhuman fiction. Based on the stories published in *A Thousand Faces,* James published a novel called *High School Heroes,* due out summer 2010 from L&L Dreamspell Publishing. James works as a teacher in Maryland, where he resides with his loving wife, Shelley.

Matt S. Mundorf

www.comicspace.com/tornadoknight
mattm@trafconinc.com

Matt started his art career in 1989 as a graphic artist designing custom screen printed apparel at Dier's Sportswear, and then at Trafcon Signs producing decals, graphics, banners and signs. He has penciled, inked and lettered comics sporadically over the years and for the last 3 years has been the CAG Midwest Coordinator. Matt enjoys spending his free time with Patricia, his wife of 18 years, and three daughters Christin, Stephanie and Audrey in Lincoln, Nebraska.

Keith J. Murphey

www.gwpbooks.com
Comicartguild@sbcglobal.net

Keith J. Murphey was born and raised in Connecticut. He learned much about the comic book industry through his mentor, Silver Age artist Frank McLaughlin. Keith loves all aspects of the comic book creation process including inking, writing, and coloring. He is an accomplished painter and has several published covers to his credit. Murphey founded the Comicbook Artists Guild in late 2000 and is primarily responsible for production of the first four CAG anthologies. Currently he runs Guild Works Publications with Hector Rodriguez and serves as art director on *Sky Pirates of Valendor.*

Alex Rivera

www.alexriverainker.com

M33

Alex was born in New York and raised in the Bronx. He went to the Music and Art High School and majored in art. After trying his hand at penciling he found he was a better inker and has done so since. He has done work as an inker for the graphic novel *Quantum: Rock of Ages, Sky Pirates of Valendor* and numerous projects for the Comicbook Artists Guild. Recently he has also done work for Guild Works Publication's *Hell's Blood*. He is happily married to a wonderful woman and plans to spend the best years of his life inking comics.

Hector Rodriguez

www.gwpbooks.com
hbdeviant@yahoo.com

An illustrator with an eye for detail, his works include short stories for the *CAG Anthology* and *Psychosis* from Guild Works Productions, now known as Guild Works Publications (GWP), which he is now a partner in. He also pencils for the children's book *Mandie Pandie* from Crazy Comics and his own creator-owned titles *Hell's Blood* and *Battle Arms.* He is also the president and proud member of CAG and is currently working on pin-ups and a zombie short story for GWP's *Best Shots: Bullets & Babes* and *Worst Case Scenario: Outbreak.*

James Rodriguez

www.myspace.com/novastarstudios

Born and raised in New York, James attended the High School of Art and Design and The School of Visual Arts where he studied under Comic legend Walter Simonson. He has done work in advertising, comics, theatre, television and film. James' 1st comic endevour was serving as penciler on Dreamchilde Press' *Quantum: Rock of Ages* He also serves as the co-coordinator for CAG's New York branch. James also produces original content under his studio banner, Novastar Studios. 2010 saw the release of the studios' flagship title *The Chronicles of Sara* which can be read in multiple languages online at www.novastarstudios.webs.com

Joe Sergi

www.joesergi.net
joesergi@cox.net

Joe lives outside of Washington, DC with his wife, Yee, and daughter, Elizabeth. He has written short stories and comics in the science fiction, horror and superhero genres. A list of available titles can be found at www.joesergi.net. When he is not writing, Joe works for an unnamed government agency.

Rigel

Luminosity: 50,600x Sun

Class: B8I-a

Scott Sheaffer

http://phantazine.blogspot.com
KmacAlp@aol.com

Scott Sheaffer's comics work has appeared in *CAG Anthology* #4 and *Psychosis* #1. Another example of his work, a two page story, appears online at http://www.drunkduck.com/THE_VIGIL. He's also had nonfiction published in *Alter Ego* #40 (September 2004), *Robert E. Howard and the Power of the Writing Mind,* and *Two Gun Bob: A Centennial Study of Robert E. Howard.*

Everett Soares

www.skypiratesofvalendor.com

While Everett Soares, the creator of Sky Pirates of Valendor, had been working on this concept for over 2 years, it truly did not come to life until he met Brian Brinlee, current penciler for the project. In December of 2006, the 2 were introduced. They started working on concept sketches and before they knew it, Everett's words came to life on Brian's 11 x 17 art boards. In the process, Everett has also become conversant on all things pirate and steampunk. Besides his work on Sky Pirates, Everett is stretching his writing skills through a variety of pending projects, working with a collection of very talented artists.

Reggie Themistocle

www.sketchodie.deviantart.com
regg502@msn.com

Reggie recently started doing comics, particularly penciling, coloring, and inking, but has been drawing since age 11. Before that, he painted, animated, and did graphic design work in college. His past comic work has been with Severed Head Comics and The Boston Comic Roundtable's Inbound Anthology series.

Liam Webb

Charteris43@hotmail.com

Liam Webb has written prose stories, film and comic scripts, news articles and miscellany. He was executive editor on Iconic, editor on Iconic 2, contributed comic stories to both of those books as well as two prose stories to *Worlds Beyond,* co-writer with Chris Buchner on *Hell's Blood* beginning with issue 2, and has some comic and prose stories in development. He looks forward to the day when he can be a full time writer, and always welcomes new projects. As always, he thanks his wife, Cortney, for her loving support.

Michele Witchipoo

www.witchesbrewpress.net

M33

Michele Witchipoo a self taught naive New Yorker who grew up on both 80s Alternative music and comics. She produces two self-published titles under WitchesBrewPress, *Psycho Bunny* and *Babablon Babes.* In addition she draws for the webcomic *Shitty Mickey* as well as working on other projects. Her website is www.witchesbrewpress.net. You can also check her out on DeviantArt: http://michelewitchipoo.deviantart.com/

Christopher Wrann

http://aquariumdrinking.com
christopherwrann@aquariumdrinking.com

Christopher Wrann was born in New Hampshire in 1979. He is the creator of the Aquarium Drinking web comic which was launched at the end of 2009. He currently lives in the woods in Connecticut with his wife and son.

Rigel
Distance: 862.88 ly
Luminosity: 50,600x Sun
Class: B8I-a

Hector Rodriguez - President
Eric Lopkin - Vice President & New England Coordinator
Chris Buchner - New York & Publication Coordinator
James Rodriguez - New York Coordinator
George Burnett - Boston Coordinator & Webmaster
Matt Mundorf - Nebraska Coordinator
Misty Sullivan - Membership Coordinator
Keith Murphey - Founder & Treasurer
Willie Jimenez - Head Graphic Artist